Thane let Stella go almost as soon as bodies touched. Her mouth came after his a second longer...slower to let go, but he didn't make anything of it. She'd been taken by complete surprise.

"What in the hell was that?" she asked, stepping back several paces.

Not only did he not blame her for doing so, he silently commended her. Heartily.

"I don't know," he told her honestly, running his hand through his hair. "I just had to shut you up and that's the only way that ever worked." He sighed. Then he looked straight at her as he said, "It was inappropriate and I apologize."

She nodded. Pressed her lips together. But held her ground.

Watching her, admiration swelled up inside him. Followed quickly by the frustration that always came with being closely involved with her.

"Maybe I was a bit dramatic there," she told him, "but I meant every word I said. I don't want to do this without you, Thane. I trust you."

Dear Reader,

Welcome to a very special, and different, book. Stella was silenced as a child. She had a secret that she and her older sister were forced to keep. That secret shaped her entire life. She swore to herself that no one would silence her again. And she lost her marriage to the love of her life to keep her vow to herself.

Life shapes all of us. We make choices. And we make mistakes. If we're lucky, we're given second chances. This story is a series of second chance choices. For Stella, for her ex-husband, Thane, for the past and for the future, too.

I didn't know when I was writing this book where it was going to take me. Nor did I know how I was going to get there. I sat down with emotions that had to be given their chance to speak. And I ended up a better person for it. More complete. With new understanding.

I hope you give Stella a chance to take you on her roller-coaster ride! It's more than worth the cost of admission.

If you'd like to know more about my choices, it's all at www.tarataylorquinn.com!

Tara Taylor Quinn

GUARDED PAST

TARA TAYLOR QUINN

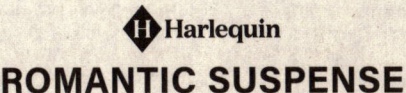

ROMANTIC SUSPENSE

If you purchased this book without a cover you should be aware that this book is stolen property. It was reported as "unsold and destroyed" to the publisher, and neither the author nor the publisher has received any payment for this "stripped book."

MIX
Paper | Supporting responsible forestry
FSC® C021394

Harlequin® ROMANTIC SUSPENSE™

Recycling programs for this product may not exist in your area.

ISBN-13: 978-1-335-47189-5

Guarded Past

Copyright © 2026 by TTQ Books LLC

All rights reserved. No part of this book may be used or reproduced in any manner whatsoever without written permission.

Without limiting the exclusive rights of any author, contributor or the publisher of this publication, any unauthorized use of this publication to train generative artificial intelligence (AI) technologies is expressly prohibited. Harlequin also exercises their rights under Article 4(3) of the Digital Single Market Directive 2019/790 and expressly reserves this publication from the text and data mining exception.

This is a work of fiction. Names, characters, places and incidents are either the product of the author's imagination or are used fictitiously. Any resemblance to actual persons, living or dead, businesses, companies, events or locales is entirely coincidental.

For questions and comments about the quality of this book, please contact us at CustomerService@Harlequin.com.

TM and ® are trademarks of Harlequin Enterprises ULC.

Harlequin Enterprises ULC
22 Adelaide St. West, 41st Floor
Toronto, Ontario M5H 4E3, Canada
www.Harlequin.com

HarperCollins Publishers
Macken House, 39/40 Mayor Street Upper,
Dublin 1, D01 C9W8, Ireland
www.HarperCollins.com

Printed in Lithuania

A *USA TODAY* bestselling author of over one hundred and thirty novels in twenty languages, **Tara Taylor Quinn** has sold more than seven million copies. Known for her intense emotional fiction, Ms. Quinn's novels have received critical acclaim in the UK and most recently from Harvard. She is the recipient of the Readers' Choice Award and has appeared often on local and national TV, including *CBS Sunday Morning*. For TTQ offers, news and contests, visit tarataylorquinn.com!

Books by Tara Taylor Quinn

Harlequin Romantic Suspense

Mitchell Family Secrets

Shadowed Past
Guarded Past

Sierra's Web

A Firefighter's Hidden Truth
Last Chance Investigation
Danger on the River
Deadly Mountain Rescue
A High-Stakes Reunion
Baby in Jeopardy
Her Sister's Murder
Mistaken Identities
Horse Ranch Hideout
Cold Case Obsession

The Coltons of Owl Creek

Colton Threat Unleashed

The Coltons of Alaska

Colton's Secret Weapon

Visit the Author Profile page
at Harlequin.com for more titles.

For Rachel Marie Stoddard—
you have my unconditional love forever.

Chapter 1

"Big, beautiful creatures full of life are dying every day at our hands. Do we care? Do *you* care? Because whether you want to be aware or not, it's happening. And for every day that you choose to ignore the situation, to walk away, more lives are lost. So I'm asking you, right here, right now, *Do You Care?*"

Standing just to the side of the platform, watching his ex-wife do her thing, Thane Wilson shook his head, more in admiration than denial. She was good. The best.

And a pain in his ass. As the hired activist on tour, she was being paid to get people riled up enough to take action. As Save Marine Life's hired legal counsel, his job was to make certain that Stella executed her rights to free speech in a way that did not incriminate the nonprofit organization that had hired her. Stella's passion made her great at raising awareness, compelling people to action. And too much passion could, in some recipients of her words, result in violence. Or rioting.

They were there to peacefully educate.

He couldn't have the activist getting herself, or the company, in trouble for inciting action that got someone hurt.

"Let me hear what *you* have to say," she yelled at the

Tuesday morning crowd gathering around the Florida city park—the site she'd chosen for the first of a monthlong tour of events in the state's richest areas. *"Do you care?"* She held the mic outward, mouth open, leaning forward, making it hard for anyone within her sight to just stand there. A small roar of "Yes" came back at her.

Bracing himself, Thane waited for the next step in her call to action. Prepared to trip on the cord that was providing electricity to the sound system she was using if he had to, to keep her, and Save Marine Life, out of court. She'd take his head off for doing so.

If she'd still had access to it, that was.

He'd jumped that ship. Had lately been experiencing some regrets. Right up until he was standing side-stage, watching her.

When it came to fighting for a cause, Stella had no boundaries.

"Let me ask again," she was saying, strutting her sexy self from one side of the stage to the other, *"Do you care?"*

The roar grew louder. Markedly so. Stella didn't play on her looks, but Thane saw how the sweet beauty in her face, soft cheekbones, the wide blue eyes framed by sassy reddish gold hair, the body that was slender and strong at the same time, gave a vibrancy to every word she spoke.

She owned the stage she was commanding in figure-hugging black pants and the black-and-white-tweed jacket he'd bought her for Christmas one year. She walked with purpose.

"No!" The bone-chilling scream came from the distance, but Thane had barely registered it when a series of deafening cracks lit the air. Firecrackers?

Staring at Stella—he could hardly believe she'd have fireworks for a day rally—he saw in slow motion as her mic fell from her hand. Her right hand. With the left clasping her right bicep. And something red.

Staining...

Thane was running. Hearing nothing. Seeing nothing but his ex-wife standing on stage looking stricken. Looking toward him.

Though quaking inside, he was ready when her gaze found his, automatically holding her steady with messages of strength and reassurance flowing to her for the few seconds it took him to reach her.

Without conscious thought, or plan, he picked her up, turned his back to the crowd, and ran her to the safety of the opened back of the box truck that had brought the rally stage to the park.

"Paramedics!" he yelled at the top of his lungs—the force of the command scraping his throat. And then, softly, "It's okay, Stel, just focus on me. Look at me."

And when her shocked gaze settled on him again, he held on to it. Leaning down he put his face to hers long enough to promise, "You're going to be fine."

Then he looked at her right arm. Saw the jacket covering her flesh flooded with blood, and ripped the sleeve off his own dress shirt to use it to tie a tourniquet around her injured limb up near her armpit. He wasn't a doctor, had no medical training other than CPR, but he knew that blood loss could be critical to even the healthiest body.

"Where does it hurt?" he asked gently, his tone filled with the love consuming him as he glanced into her eyes again.

Shaking her head, Stella moved her mouth. No sound was forthcoming. Licking her lips she said, "Nowhere. I think something touched my arm, but I can't feel it now."

Touched her arm. *Some*thing. Oh God. Panic swirling

inside him, Thane nodded and was telling her, "There's a bit of a nick there…" as a couple of paramedics—one male, one female—rushed up. Both of their gazes were pointing directly toward the blood pool on Stella's jacket. And from there to her torso. He'd wondered, too, how much of her had been damaged.

Had been telling himself the lack of blood anywhere but her arm was a good sign.

He wanted to know if anyone else was hurt. But couldn't ask in front of her. Not while she was thinking she only had a "nick" in her flesh.

"The rally," Stella said then, looking up at him as the paramedics cut off the sleeve of the Christmas present jacket. Her "I have to get back," was proof to his thought process.

She had no idea…

Before he could get a clear picture of how bad it was, Stella's arm was being wrapped with white gauze—a lot of it—just above the elbow.

"I'll bring the bus around," the male paramedic said and had already spun on his heel and was jogging off by the time Stella seemed to catch on to a bit of what was happening.

"What bus? I need to get back out there…"

Sharing a quick glance with Thane, the dark-haired, no-nonsense-looking female medical worker, said, "The rally's been canceled. And you need stitches."

A second glance at Thane seemed to warn that she was speaking best-case scenario. Stella needed stitching up, but there could be a whole lot more.

"I'm not riding in any *bus*," Stella said then, standing up. When she sat right back down again, fear struck Thane's heart. No matter how bad Stella felt, she never exhibited weakness. It was something he'd always had a hard time with, her refusal to reveal any cracks in a seemingly indomitable armor—even to him.

"There's a lot of blood, Stel," he said quietly, close to her ear. No way he could let her risk her life without letting her know what she was up against.

She nodded then. Staring straight ahead. She hadn't even glanced at her arm. Or down at the bloodstained hand that had initially held it. "You coming with me?" she asked.

Not "will you" but "are you." He got the distinction. She wouldn't directly ask for his help. But the fact that she'd asked the question at all told him what he had to know.

She needed him there. And so, "Of course," he told her. Then, for both their sakes added, "There could be financial obligations for the organization."

Stella didn't care why Thane was there. Only that he was. Over the next couple of hours while she lay in an emergency room cubicle, fully clothed other than the sleeve that had been cut from her jacket, Stella found her calm in the legalese with which her ex-husband always spoke to strangers. More particularly when they were educated professionals like himself.

She'd been shot. Somewhere along the way, she'd figured that one out before she actually heard someone mention the fact out loud. Lucky for her, the bullet had been a through-and-through—she'd twinged with irritation when she'd heard that one. *Bullet* and *lucky* did not belong in the same sentence.

No bones had been involved. Nor pertinent veins. Due

to the bullet hitting the outside of her arm, no muscles had been damaged.

She'd lost a lot of blood. Had a crapload of stitches, both inside and out. And was going to have one hell of a scar.

No one else had been hit. And while she cared most about all the people who'd been spared, that one bothered her, too. Not because she wanted anyone hurt. To the contrary, her whole life was about sparing pain from those who were suffering. But...being the only one hit likely meant that she had been the target.

Fear struck anew every single time that fact surfaced. Which was often as she lay there trying to prove that she was strong enough to get up and walk out on her own.

How in the hell did one prove one's ability when one was being forced to remain half supine in a bed?

"What are we waiting for?" she asked Thane when she looked over to see that he was off his phone. Finally. He'd been texting or emailing, or whatever for too many minutes. At least five.

In his suit—the man couldn't seem to relax his style a bit, even in Florida—with his short dark haircut, he looked the part of a man used to commanding answers. Time for him to give some up.

When his gaze lifted, landed on her, Stella had a moment. Everything about Thane was conservative, except those hazel eyes. They seemed to hold all of life's mysteries in round masses of possibility.

There'd been a time when she couldn't wait to find out all the secrets those eyes held. Until she'd discovered that the news hadn't been good where she was concerned. Not that she blamed Thane for the demise of their partnership. She'd never really expected it to succeed to begin with.

"For you to drink that orange juice." Confused for a second, she reconnected with the question she'd asked.

What they were waiting for. "I don't like orange juice and I'm not thirsty. How long is it going to be before the doctor is back with my discharge papers?"

He glanced up from his screen to meet her gaze briefly. "You were just shot, Stel. I'm sure they want to give you some time to make sure there are no aftereffects of shock. Your heart rate was elevated when you came in."

"It's normal now." Had been since they'd shot her arm up with numbing medication. Or maybe since she'd heard that stitches were all she needed. The day's rally had been a bust, but they'd be able to keep the next day's schedule.

When his gaze left hers to return to his phone, she tried not to let any hurt register. She was being a pain in the ass.

And...he was there.

But...she couldn't be expected to just lie around and not get antsy. "Who are you talking to?" she asked as his thumbs flew over the face of his phone.

He didn't look up, or stop typing as he said, "Ben."

Oh.

Ben Latimer. His best friend. A lawyer who was also a private investigator with a lot of influence. And...her brother-in-law.

But...wait... Frowning, she said, "He and Kara are in the Bahamas." A really long second honeymoon of sorts, as they gave her pregnant baby sister, Kara, time to recover emotionally from the trauma of the past months and rekindle the marriage that had been in jeopardy. It all came rolling back to her. More like crashing back. In huge powerful waves that were over her head.

Kara's veterinary clinic had been bombed. She'd been abducted.

But it was all okay. The jerk behind the attacks had been caught. Was locked up tight. Forever. As death would have it. She still couldn't believe Kara had actually shot at the man. It hadn't been her baby sister's bullet that killed him, but her gun had been one of the four that went off in the moment the man had died.

"Ben's putting me in touch with Doug Zellers," Thane said distractedly, without looking up from his screen.

Doug Zellers. North Haven, Georgia, detective extraordinaire. At least to Stella. First, he was from their hometown and anyone from North Haven got an extra notch of trust from her. Not that a notch meant much. On a scale of one to ten, from zero to one wasn't a long way to travel. Doug, though—he'd helped Ben save Kara's life, more than once, and catch the murderer who'd been terrorizing her.

"This doesn't have anything to do with what happened," she said then, with all the authority at her command. Which, while not her best effort, was still a pretty decent showing.

Thane nodded. "We know that," he told her, a touch of irritation in his tone. Because she came across like the expert on everything, he'd said in the past. Her doing so had, at times, made him feel as though she hadn't respected his vast mental capabilities.

Truth was, she'd been intimidated by them. Fearful that she wouldn't be able to keep up. That she'd miss something and end up hurt. Or hurting him.

Turned out, both had happened. Her getting hurt. And hurting him. She pushed too hard. But it was who she was. And being good at it served so many great causes. Easing pain and suffering all over the world. Her work was her life's purpose. Without it... No, she couldn't go there.

Watching Thane—because it took her mind off the invisible bugs that were starting to crawl under her skin—she jumped when he suddenly dropped his phone in the pocket of his suit coat and said, "I'm sorry, Stel. I just needed to get on top of this."

She didn't know what "this" was. Her stitches? His job was to foresee and offset any and all liabilities that might encumber his client. Her current employer. And she'd just been injured while under their employ.

"Doug's working with police here and will keep us apprised of the investigation, every step of the way. The shooter's still at large, but they have a suspect."

Wow. That had happened quickly. Not that she was complaining. Overall, she trusted law enforcement to do their jobs to the best of their abilities. It was just that human beings were so fallible.

And saw the world differently than she did a lot of the time, too.

Thane had more to say. His frown as he continued to hold her gaze told her so. He was waiting for some kind of response from her. She'd rather watch him and think about her feelings regarding police.

She didn't want to know that she'd been the target. After all they'd been through with Kara, she needed a break from the sense of constant threat hanging over them.

"They've got witnesses. An ID. Someone who's invested everything in a new way to produce seismic air guns less expensively and the company set to buy them has suddenly become conscious of marine life and is looking at other ways to find gas and oil deposits."

Stella felt the muscles in her body accept the comfort the bed had been trying to offer her. Actually aware of the draining away of tension from all parts of her, she nodded. Then said, "It's the cause that he was angry at. I was just the messenger."

Nothing like the man who'd targeted Kara because of who their mother had been. Because Kara had broken cardinal rules she hadn't even known about and had done internet research on the woman who'd left them shortly after Kara had been born.

Thane's chin stiffened, but he held his tongue for a long minute. She waited. Preparing herself. She was not going to like whatever he was about to say.

"Both Ben and Doug are strongly advising that you skip the next few rallies, at the very least, Stel. Most certainly until this guy is in custody. Then they can determine whether he was working alone. The threat is currently considered critically high."

No. She would not be threatened into silence. Or frightened into inaction, either. The world had taken much from her, without her having any say in, or control over, the situation. She was not going to lose the one thing that sustained her.

The one good she could count on. And control.

The knowledge that she was making the world a better place, full-time.

He stared hard. For what seemed like minutes, but was probably only a lot of seconds. She barely blinked. Didn't waver from her hold on his gaze. Or in her determination. She was going to be onstage in Dubly, Florida, the next day, as planned. Whether he, or anyone else, liked it or not.

And when he finally nodded, she did, too.

But differently.

He'd relented. With extreme reluctance and disappointment.

She'd accepted his capitulation.

Which served her life's purpose. But reiterated why she was single, too.

She was doing the right thing. Not only for herself, but for the world. And just had to keep hoping that someday, where Thane was concerned, her being who she was wouldn't hurt so much.

Chapter 2

The guy was still out there. Did the woman want to get herself killed? Ha. To the contrary, Stella seemed to think that if she said something, she made it so. If she determined that she would be safe continuing with the tour, then she would be.

Or, more likely, she cared more about her causes than her own life. Or anyone else in her life.

There'd be no reasoning with her. No point in belaboring a point which she'd settled upon. Thane had that one down loud and clear. Hence, their divorce.

Stella had way too much determination to change the world. Which left her with very little to give to anything—or anyone—else. Except for Kara, her baby sister. And probably Melanie, too. If he had any hope of keeping Stella offstage, at least until the known perpetrator was caught, it would be through her sisters.

Which was part of the reason he'd called Ben, Kara's husband. Yeah, the man was on his second honeymoon, with his veterinarian wife he'd almost lost. To a danger none of them had known existed.

Ben and Kara were his best chance to convince Stella to take a break. At least until they had time to process some evidence.

Beyond that, in Thane's analytical mind, the attack against Stella could be the result of a lurking component from the past. He needed his best friend's opinion on the matter. When Tory Mitchell had testified against the powerful mob boss who'd killed the father of her youngest child, she'd thought leaving her precious daughters behind while she entered witness protection would save them from any fallout from her actions. Protect them from all danger.

And it had, until Kara had started searching the internet for information on the mother she'd been raised to believe was dead. Doug Zellers, Ben, the FBI, and Marshal's service were all certain that with Matthew Humbolt Grossman's death, all future danger had been eradicated. Grossman's boss, Torrence Spelling, the head of what was once a powerful family with major criminal ties, was in prison for life for the murder of his younger adopted brother, Chancellor. Chancellor, Tory's very brief lover, had had no prior knowledge of the powerful family's hidden branch of illegal business dealings and had just discovered a discrepancy. He had been about to expose his brother as the criminal he was.

The younger brother had also turned out to be Kara's biological father. And the reason Tory had deserted her family. She hadn't been able to risk Torrence ever finding out that there was a biological heir to the Spelling fortune. Half of which had already passed to Chancellor, Kara's father, and would now be Kara's.

But thirty years had passed. All but Torrence Spelling were gone. Other than Kara, there were no heirs to the legitimately earned fortune still sitting in a series of Florida banking and investment accounts. Money that Grossman had been quietly guarding, overseeing, living off—siphoning—for three decades. Upon Torrence's death, Grossman had been set to inherit it all.

The remaining funds, which were still hugely substantial, would just sit until Torrence Spelling's death, and then would transfer to Kara.

Who didn't want a dime of the money. She'd already said she was going to donate every bit of it. Except for what she'd spend to find their mother. Something that Stella was hugely and vocally against. Which boded for one hell of a rift between the two sisters sometime down the road.

Ben's problem. Not Thane's. Kara's lawyer husband was hoping that the money Kara donated to Stella's causes would ease any tension between them. Thane didn't share his friend's optimism.

None of which was forefront in his mind as he drove Stella back to the hotel where they'd both been guests the night before, compliments of Save Marine Life. Two rooms. Separate floors. He'd made certain of both.

Just as he was going to insist on staying glued to his ex-wife until they knew more. She wouldn't agree to any kind of formal protection, but she wasn't arguing Thane's presence. Nor his mandate that she wasn't to be out of his sight except to close the bathroom door in her room long enough to take care of business.

Not that he hadn't seen her pee before, but whatever.

By the time she came out, he had her things packed. Having traveled with her so much during their marriage, he knew how she liked things just so. And she knew he knew. With a nod at her closed suitcase, and the smaller open one on the bed, waiting for the bathroom bag in her hand, she placed the toiletries in their spot, closed the bag and zipped it. Then, without argument, or even question, followed him down a couple of floors to his room.

As she stood inside while he laid his suit coats and pants carefully in his suitcase, he reminded himself that she was only doing so because he was her insurance with Save Marine Life. If he, as their lawyer, told them that keeping Stella on the payroll put them at an undue risk of lawsuit, they'd let her go.

Then hire another professional activist, with a smaller following than Stella, and potentially be at the same exact risk they were currently facing. Putting on rallies, staging population information gatherings and protests, was part of their mission statement. Their documented means to the end they had in mind. As their lawyer, he had to minimize risk, while making it possible for them to most successfully fulfill their mission.

Which meant Stella. He passed within a couple of inches of her as he headed to the adjoining bath. Noticing that the color in her cheeks was good, even as her limp right arm seemed to glare at him. Feeling too much like what they'd just come through with Kara.

His personal feelings couldn't come into play. Except that they were. Which meant he had to find a way to do his job and keep Stella safe, too.

Right. To that end, "Doug sent a car for our use. It's got bulletproof glass, and cameras implanted on all sides so that everything around us can be monitored at all times. It'll be downstairs, with the fob at the front desk. Our vehicles will be here overnight, and then Doug's having someone drive them back to North Haven. We're to leave the fobs in a box of chocolates at the front desk for a Sara Huckabee." Likely huge overkill. He wasn't taking any chances.

Zipping up his shaving gear, he passed by her one more time.

He dropped the kit into his bag, grabbed his satchel with his computer and the electronic cords and devices that went everywhere with him, and threw it over his shoulder. He was so set on his need to get their things downstairs on his own that it took him a second to realize that Stella wasn't arguing.

Stopping with the handle of his big roller bag in one palm, he reached for the handle of hers, and stared at her. "You feeling okay?"

"I'm fine," she told him. Her tone lacking any hint of her usual take-charge attitude.

Checking her color again, finding it within the realm the nurse had told him was normal, he nodded and headed out the door. Made it to the elevator with her. Then, inside, the two of them alone, with nothing to do but watch floor numbers light up as they passed by, he said, "You're okay with me driving you around for the next few days?"

She shrugged. Her messy red-gold hair framing her face seemed to be the only light emanating from her at the moment, and his heart skipped a beat. "Stella, you don't have to do this. You lost a lot of blood. No one is going to fault you if you want to head home."

He knew the second the words were out of his mouth they were the wrong ones. The steely glint that shone from her eyes was a familiar one. And while his system tightened in response, readying him for acerbic proclamations of inarguable intent, he was also a bit relieved to see those pinpoints.

"I'm a little tired," she said. "And hungry. But no way I'm going to let a few stitches slow me down. I'm not a quitter."

He did know that about her. Unless, of course, the game was, say, marriage. And to be fair, which he always tried to be, she wasn't the one who'd ended their union. She'd never even obtained a lawyer. Had just signed the papers his lawyer had drawn up.

"Doug left a pistol for me under the seat of the car," he said then.

At which she huffed, and said, "You? A gun? You don't know how to shoot."

"Actually, I do." They were almost at the lobby level. Two more blinks of the lights. "I started training with Ben a few years ago. Seeing you on the circuit, the inciteful words you used, I figured one of us had to be able to protect our home. Just in case."

Thane almost wished they hadn't reached their destination, that the doors weren't sliding open, when he saw Stella's jaw drop.

That anomaly was one he'd have liked to sit with for a second or two.

Given other circumstances, in a place and time that didn't have danger written all over it.

He was thinking about it later, though, as she settled into the room he'd reserved for her, adjoining his, in a more upscale hotel than Save Marine Life had allotted to them near Dubly. At his own expense. Not something Stella needed to know.

He was the one who required security cameras in every hall, on every elevator, and in the lobby, along with plainclothes security there to protect the anonymity of guests who didn't want to be accosted by fans. Or, more likely, paparazzi.

"This is some place," Stella said, walking around the spacious room with its king-size bed, full sitting area with plush sofa and chairs, and kitchen nook with its small marble counter and wet bar. "You expect me to believe Save Marine Life is paying for this?"

"No."

She stared at him. Hard. Thane stared back. She could give him her best shot. It wasn't going to hit him anyplace that counted. It was either his way or the highway. If she didn't go along with the parameters he was setting, he was going to tell Save Marine Life that she was too much of a liability to have on the tour.

He hadn't yet spelled it out to Stella. But she knew how it all worked. He waited, feeling a bit of an adrenaline rush as he anticipated her attack. Whatever she came up with would carry validity. And power. She was good. At the moment, he'd be better. Her life could depend on him being so.

Holding his gaze, she opened her mouth, and he poised to pounce right back on whatever she spit out.

"Thank you." With the two innocuous words, she turned to the heavy case he'd lifted onto the luggage counter, and reaching with her left arm, started unzipping.

That was it? The unusual docility, while…nice…making his job easier, kind of alarmed him.

And before he left her to her one-handed unpacking, with a command to leave the adjoining door opened between them, he checked her color one more time.

Just to be sure she still looked okay.

Stella couldn't meet her own gaze in the mirror. She just wasn't going there. She'd learned young how to tune in and tune out. To choose a course of action and focus on it. Period. Giving in to emotion made her weak and vulnerable.

And hurt like hell, too.

A pain with no killer. Nothing she could take to ease the suffering. Unlike her arm, which was throbbing as she unpacked the bathroom supplies she'd need over the next twenty-four hours.

She had a pill she could take for that particular discomfort.

Thane had insisted on stopping at the hospital pharmacy before he'd led her out to the local cop Doug had arranged to take them back to the hotel. They'd ridden the few blocks to the rally with Amelia Lockhart, the promotions director of Save Marine Life, who'd stayed behind at the scene to give statements and oversee the packing up of the stage and sound equipment.

Stella had already spoken with Amelia twice, assuring the ten-years-older woman that she was fine and would be onstage at her appointed time the next day.

And she would be. Stella didn't doubt that. Or even have qualms about her current ability to do her job. No, the doubts were... *No.*

"You ready for some dinner?" Thane's voice reached her from the doorway between their rooms, and Stella almost met her gaze in the mirror. The idea of sitting alone with Thane in a restaurant appealed not at all. And if she demurred?

He'd see it as a sign of weakness. Which would not strengthen her.

"Sure," she called out. Finding the fight in her when she needed it. As always.

"I've got the room service menu here," he called back. "They've got Asian chopped salad with cabbage and tofu."

A blip of anticipation hit her. The first she'd experienced since she'd heard the loud pop onstage. "Sounds good," she said, meaning the words. "I'm actually feeling a little hungry," she added with complete truth, coming out of the bathroom.

Room service meant she could eat on her own at the desk in her room. And knock off a day's worth of emails, too.

Thane was still standing in the doorway. "You haven't changed," he pointed out, as though she'd somehow shocked him by the lack.

"It's too early for pajamas..." Plus no way was she walking around in the sleep shirt she'd been wearing to bed since their divorce. "And I don't want to waste another day's outfit." Packing for the road, being on tour, was an art. One she'd mastered years before.

He nodded, glanced toward her exposed arm, and turned back into his own room.

Taking some of her already depleted energy with him.

There were bloodstains on her jacket. The Stella he knew would never be okay with walking around in such a state. Garnering alarmed looks from the strangers she encountered. Her whole life was about easing the suffering of others—generic others—not creating harsh moments for them.

And while the new bandage on her stitched wound was much less big and bold than the huge band of gauze the paramedics had first applied, it still covered a significant portion of her upper arm. And...she was sleeveless. With a ragged cut marking the spot where the arm of her jacket had been removed.

Uneasy, he called in the dinner order. Used his food delivery account to pay for it and pulled the table for two over so that she'd have a view of the beach while she ate.

Then stopped himself before he started acting like a husband, or friend, rather than business associate. Yeah, he'd taken one look at the hotel's room service menu and had made the executive decision to order Stella's service from an outside restaurant. Chopped Asian salad was her go-to. He'd searched until he'd found a place that offered it exactly as she'd want it.

He'd have done the same for any client who was in her situation. If he'd had cause to know their comfort foods.

She'd had a rough day and deserved a bit of consideration. Most particularly since Stella never seemed to provide any for herself.

As hard as their marriage had been on him, she'd been so much tougher on herself. He'd never met a less selfish person. Nor one more single-minded.

To the point of getting herself killed?

The thought was still taunting him when the knock on his door indicated that dinner had arrived. Carrying it inside, he set the table, complete with the couple of single-serving bottles of wine he'd had sent up to his minibar when he'd made their reservation. Stella wasn't much of a drinker. But he knew her well enough to know that she wasn't going to take the pain pills he'd insisted that they stop and get.

And she needed some rest. If she was going to insist on being onstage, he had to know that she'd had enough sleep to be fully alert. Not only to the message she had to impart, but to her surroundings as well.

A chat they were going to have, with explicit details via Doug, on their way to the next day's event.

Walking to the opened door between their rooms, he peered in enough to see her sitting at the desk, her right arm hanging limply, her left on the mouse, gaze appearing to be focused on the screen. Except that her eyes weren't moving as though she was reading.

Noting that there was no blood seepage showing on her bandage, he said, "Dinner's here," and then turned his back and left the room.

She was his client's appendage.

Not his own.

Chapter 3

While a part of Stella was a bit put out that she had to get up, moving her damned arm, to collect her food, she was also grateful that Thane was treating her as though everything was normal. Other than the connected rooms, which just made good sense given that her shooter was still on the loose. Most particularly since she now knew Thane was licensed to carry, trained to shoot, and had a gun.

Shaking her head at that, struggling to wrap her mind around it, she winced at the impact on her arm as she took a couple of steps toward the door. And then, with a mental gritting of teeth, she completed the journey to the door of his room. Reaching out with her left arm to grab the salad from wherever he'd left the tray.

And saw, instead, that his room was larger than hers. He not only had a sitting area similar to hers, but a table and chairs, too. Set in front of a window with a view of the ocean. And closer in, the beach.

A view her room would share. She hadn't even opened the curtains.

Nor did she have a table the exact height of the window. Still, she'd have grabbed her bowl, silver, and napkin off the table and headed back to her desk, except that she couldn't take all three in her one nondominant hand. And…he had wine.

Her favorite.

Stella hardly missed a step on her way to the chair he'd left pulled out for her. Smiling politely as he glanced up from the meal he'd already started. Sushi, to begin with. She'd never understood how he could stand the stuff. Plus, the sea creatures that gave up their lives so he could eat them raw…

Stopping the comment before it could escape her mouth, Stella acknowledged that she used products that were made with animal fat, and had eaten meat for the majority of her life. Just…while you were on tour to save marine life…

Sitting down, she started to reach for the wine that had been made from live grapevines, and drew in a quick breath. She was right-handed. The arm had moved naturally, without thought.

She saw Thane's head rise, turn in her direction. Saw the bite midway to his mouth stop in midair. And reached for her wine with her left hand, keeping her focus on it all the way up to her lips, then closed her eyes as she took her first, longer-than-usual, sip.

And praised the man silently when he went back to eating.

Thane was no fool. He'd learned Stella's boundaries the hard way—by trying to break through them. But it turned out that he'd gleaned a whole lot more about his taciturn ex-wife during their time together. Like when she was hurting.

Or upset.

And that at those times, he had to let her deal on her

own. He'd have thought, as a business associate and no longer a husband, he'd have had an easier time doing that.

Not so much. His need to reach out to her, to help, drove him to his own wineglass. And a healthy sip. While he silently sent up hope that she ate quickly and disappeared to the other side of the wall between their rooms.

Where he couldn't see her suffering.

Both arm, and soul. He'd talked to Ben again, to let his friend and ex-brother-in-law know their plans, as requested. Even the no-nonsense detective had been out of sorts about another attack against their family in such a short period of time.

Didn't matter that the source and motive were already known and that, with all the various law enforcement details on the case, the suspect would soon be in custody.

Being under attack at all was not normal life. For any of them.

"This is why I called you when Kara was attacked." Stella's words broke into his intense train of thought. Giving himself a mental shake, he determined first that she was not a mind reader, and more particularly, not reading him.

And then realized that his prickly ex-wife was reaching out to him.

"For Asian chopped salad?" He'd brought her an order of the comfort food then, too.

"No, because you sit with me without picking at the scabs." Their marital ones? Or the current incident.

There was no point in going backward. The divorce had been the closure to those wounds. At least in theory. He was all over giving theory the chance to work.

And opened his container of chicken fried rice.

"I talked to Kara and Melanie." Her next words stopped

his fork mid-skew. Glancing over at her, he saw her gaze pointing toward his rice. And automatically finished collecting the bite he'd been after. Made himself fill his mouth and chew.

"They both begged me to go home." His shrug was nonchalant. And natural, too. Her sisters' reaction to the shooting had been a given.

More so, in light of the number of times Kara had recently almost lost her life at the hands of the man protecting her father's killer.

"Thing is..." Stella paused so long he had to look over at her. To check her color, and the bandage on her arm for any sign of seepage. "I'm a bit rattled by being under attack," she said, and he almost dropped his fork. "I mean, I lived vicariously through each of my little sister's attacks, and now I'm feeling it for myself? For real? How off is that?"

He held her gaze, even as he nodded. "I know, Stel. You'd have to be inhuman not to be uncomfortable with it all." He'd tempered the words as best he could with no warning. In reality, the woman should be shaking in her inexpensive shoes. But that wasn't Stella. Not on the surface, for sure. And after all his years with her, he couldn't guarantee that she didn't have some kind of special steel at her core, too, that allowed her to deflect much of what unhinged others.

"And those hours when we thought she was dead..." Stella's voice dropped off. She sipped from her wine, but had hardly eaten a bite.

"They're both thinking that I'm going to end up like that," she said then. And, as though she'd read his awareness of her lack, stabbed a healthy bite of salad and ate it.

He waited for her to continue whatever conversational

journey she'd started. Mostly because he really wanted to know where she was heading, and also because he didn't want to end up as the roadblock he'd been so often in the past.

"I can't live in a world where I have to let evil win. *That* would kill me."

The conviction in her words grabbed at him. Not all negatively, as they would have in the past. She wasn't complaining about his not being like her. Wasn't upset with him, or needing something from him that he couldn't give. She was…sharing.

It felt like it was the first time she'd ever done so, but that couldn't be right. They'd dated for over a year before they'd gotten engaged. And they'd *been* married. For years.

But it felt new. And as he sat there scrambling, Thane couldn't remember any other time when he'd had the sensation that Stella was giving him a peek at her soul.

Could that be right? He'd married a woman without ever knowing her deepest self?

She'd gone back to eating. A period on the end of their moment? He wasn't ready for it to be done. Couldn't just let the occasion pass as though it was any other that had occurred between them over the years.

She was fighting against the bad because she couldn't live in a world where she had no power to do so. Why the distinction mattered, he wasn't sure. But something was telling him it did.

And so he said quietly, "Then we'll do our best to keep you safe while you do it." She glanced over then, her gaze clearly searching. For what, he didn't know.

Nor did he have any idea who he'd meant by the "we"

in his statement. Him and Save Marine Life? Him and her? Working together? A pair?

He wanted to shake his head at that one. But was too busy watching her. And then, gaining some sense of himself, of his business-only relationship with the woman sitting across from him, he said, "I just need you to continue to abide by my guidelines, which are coming from Doug, not me, and we should get through this just fine." He felt like a fraud as he spoke the words.

He wasn't at all sure they'd be fine. There was a zealous shooter on the loose with a total lack of societal boundaries, aiming his panic in Stella's direction.

And…business only? He couldn't lie to himself. Business mostly, was the best he could do. And at the moment, sitting there alone in a well decked-out hotel room with her, he wasn't even sure the *mostly* sufficed.

She'd been shot right before his eyes. He'd loved her once…

Was it even possible for him to maintain a purely professional distance from that?

She'd looked up at him again. Caught him watching her. Before he could find words to make light of the seriousness of the expression she'd seen, she said, "How certain is Doug that Torrence Spelling is locked up tight with no outward reach?"

The question hit him in the gut. She was afraid. With fair reason. Her mother had been in witness protection for thirty years, remained there still, because Spelling had been just that powerful. And dangerous.

But, for the first time in a very long while, Thane didn't feel lacking in his ability to help his ex-wife. With a warmth he hadn't felt in years, he said, "As you already know, he'd been in isolation for over a month before Grossman's first attack on Kara. Had had no communication with anyone. And as soon as Grossman was identified, Spelling was shipped to a federal prison in Montana. Where he's had no access to phones, television, email, or internet."

"Wouldn't the move alone have alerted him to something going on?"

He'd thought so, too. Had already asked the question. "Not necessarily. All it would take was a hint that someone on the inside, a guard or other inmate, had gotten too close to Spelling to initiate the move. Or, if he had any unauthorized dealings at all, even disallowed conversation, on the inside, he would assume he'd been caught. According to Doug, Spelling had several such infractions. This isn't the first time he's been transferred to different federal facilities."

Stella's shoulders relaxed visibly, and, after a sip of wine, she started to eat in earnest.

And Thane was suddenly content to sit with her for as long as she chose to be there.

There would always be facts she lacked. Circumstances she'd never understand. Stella hated the not knowing.

Which made it difficult to live with herself sometimes.

A lot of the time.

With her right arm painfully out of commission, Stella's lack of comfort in her own skin had reached new heights.

How in the hell was she going to defend herself if the situation arose? For that matter, how was she going to take a damned shower?

Not with Thane's help that was for sure. She needed him to chill a bit, not ramp up his opposition to the choices she made. With her salad almost gone, along with half her glass of wine, she was starting to feel more like herself. "I think we're both more uptight than we might have been, due to what happened with Kara," she told him. "Doug and Ben and my sisters, too."

She saw the shutter come down over his expression, which spurred her to push on with more force. Glad to feel the surge of determination where weakness had been creeping in, she continued with, "This guy today. Clearly, he acted out of desperation, but he isn't some fiend looking to create mass destruction. He shot what, three bullets? And only at the stage, not the crowd, and not at me in particular or I'd be dead. For all we know, he didn't mean to hit me at all. As quickly as I move onstage, my arm wound could just be a fluke."

All viable statements. Yet to be proven true or false, but, given what they *did* know, valid scenarios just the same. "You never said whether or not he has any kind of criminal record."

Thane's gaze was sharp and distant as he said, "He does not."

Relief fluttered through her. "There you go, then. We're just all extra sensitive right now." Feeling much better, she finished her salad.

She put the fork aside and the empty bowl in the bag from which it had come. "I need to get out on my socials and let everyone know I'm okay," she said then, fully energized to get back to work. "And that I'll be at the rally tomorrow as planned." Over the years she'd amassed a group who followed her from rally to rally. Activists who spent their own hard-earned money out on the circuit—physical bodies and voices to encourage others to join in, to listen and learn—instead of just donating and moving on with their lives.

Those dedicated individuals were part of what made Stella such a draw to organizations like Save Marine Life.

She'd started out as one of the loyalists who traveled to rallies on her own dime while still in high school. By the time she'd graduated college with a bachelor's degree in communication, and an emphasis on public speaking, she'd already had companies wanting to pay her to promote their causes. She'd formed a limited liability company of her own so that she could choose the messages she was paid to impart.

While she had to make a living, she wasn't in the work for the money. But to change the world, one bout of awareness at a time.

Thane was on his phone again as she stood, right arm hanging at her side, bag of trash in her left hand. Staring at his bent head for a second, she figured he was contacting Doug, or Ben, to make sure someone was monitoring her socials, and with a "Thanks for dinner, and the wine," she shoved the bag under her left arm, bent awkwardly to grab the wineglass in her freed left hand, and then walked with a bit of a lilt to keep the trash from falling to the ground as she headed back to the doorway that would take her to her own space.

Where she let the bag drop. Set down the glass. Then bent to pick up the dinner remains and throw them out.

Where there was a will, there was a way. And Stella could not give up her will.

It was the only thing that enabled her to live a productive life.

The woman was obstinate. Infuriating. Anger inducing. And somewhat admirable, too. Over the next couple of days Thane remained on high alert, as tense as he'd ever been, while he watched his ex-wife shine onstage and off.

Donations for Save Marine Life were flowing in far beyond expectation. In part due to the shooting. Stella used her maimed right arm for all it was worth, riling up the crowds to fight against silencing by violence, by donating to good causes.

She was a powerhouse to be sure. One who called to him deeply even while she raised intense defenses within him.

Duane Riker, her shooter, had been arrested and was remaining in custody until a court appearance later in the week. The man swore he hadn't meant to hurt Stella. Only to stop the rally as he'd had an appointment later that day in town with another company who was interested in his cheaper seismic air guns.

Local detectives believed him. Doug wasn't so sure. But Thane had to acknowledge, if only to himself, that Stella could be right in her assertion that they were all reacting, in part, to Kara's being hunted by a man who'd murdered many people during his lifetime.

A fact no one, including Ben and Doug, had realized at the time. They'd been after the partner of a serial killer whose wife had threatened Ben, and evidence of whom had been found at one of the crime scenes. It made sense that they were a bit overly cautious. And doubtful of the evidence at face value.

Most human beings, and certainly any good cop, would learn from such a frightening and near fatal incident.

As would the ex-brother-in-law, Thane, who'd been called by his ex-wife while she'd been in the throes of her deepest terror. And had been consulted by his best friend when his wife had been kidnapped, and was then in hiding.

All of which Thane logically understood as he stood, all senses on high alert, tense and armed side-stage on Friday, three days after the shooting, in yet another Florida beach town. With one of the largest crowds she'd drawn on her current tour.

None of which he discussed with Stella. He didn't want to reinforce her sense of safety and end up making her any less diligent in her own self-care.

He was pleased with her seeming awareness of the dangers that could be in her path. And had been tending diligently to the care of her right arm. Having him help her dress it when necessary, as he'd heard the hospital instructions with a clearer mind than she'd had at the time. Thankfully, typical Stella, the arm was healing well with amazing speed and not a single hint of possible infection.

Standing center stage, facing the crowd, she suddenly stopped. Talking. Moving. She just stood there. Her gaze perusing the crowd. Thane would have been alarmed, hunting the hordes of people himself for whatever evil had attracted her attention, except that he knew the moment was part of her gig. A quiet moment before she geared up for the ending segment.

"So let me ask you," she said quietly, still holding the microphone in her left hand. "Can you turn your back on that?" Using the mic, she waved toward the ocean in the distance. "On them? The glorious creatures who live there? Can you sleep at night knowing that whales are losing their abilities to communicate due to the noise pollution created by us, the people?"

"Families can't call out to families. Children lose their way. Mothers can't source food…" He was already hearing the words before she actually said them. And felt a lurch in his gut when, instead of continuing the emotional, yet quiet and peaceful call to action, her voice was silent. He saw her look his way, briefly, before there was a loud splinter and she disappeared from sight.

Chapter 4

It was just a rotted stage board. She was in the midst of a slew of bad luck. Had somehow pissed off karma?

Unless you looked at the bright side. While bruised on her left thigh and buttocks, Stella came away from small-town Lompte, Florida, with no serious injuries, no damage to her injured right arm, no bumps on the head, and a donation pool that surpassed all projections.

Save Marine Life had opted to use a permanent stage in the park they'd chosen for the rally, rather than paying to have one set up for the event. Per Thane, the stage had been inspected the night before, but someone hadn't done a thorough enough job. That individual's head was going to roll.

Stella's was in good shape.

Worried that members of her following were going to start to feel unsafe, she put a notice on her socials for anyone who'd like to meet up that evening in the ballroom at the hotel where she was staying. She'd rented the space and would be providing nonalcoholic beverages and snacks.

The only thing left to do was tell Thane. He was still insisting that they stay in adjoining rooms—a choice she allowed because it made dressing her wound easier—and would know when she vacated for a couple of hours before dinner. Which he'd also just assumed they'd be sharing during their time of connected rooms.

She could have argued that one. Wasn't sure why she hadn't. Except that she was on a mission to do everything she could to keep him content enough to not pull the plug on the tour.

And as a business associate, she was kind of enjoying eating with him again. He knew exactly what she liked, how she liked it, and managed to find places that she'd probably have chosen for herself. Didn't mean anything. It wasn't like he was pandering or anything. They'd lived together for years and had always shared a lot of the same tastes.

She was just pulling on the loose sweater she was planning to wear to the informal gathering downstairs, instead of the black-and-white-tweed business jacket, minus a sleeve, that she'd worn onstage, when Thane tapped on the mostly closed internal door between their rooms. "You decent?"

"Of course," she answered, with a bit of sardonic humor. Like she'd be anything but, with him next door. All her personal ablutions were taking place behind the very locked bathroom door.

Pushing the wooden entry open beyond the crack of space she'd left, he said, "I was thinking about ordering in for dinner tonight."

Of course. He would be on higher alert. And because she personally didn't care one way or the other, she said, "Fine."

He mentioned a Mexican restaurant that delivered. Feeling overly amenable, she nodded. And then used his interruption to say, "Can we make it a little later? Say around seven?"

Eyes narrowed, he eyed her sweater, then met her gaze. "You going somewhere?"

"No," she said. She'd agreed not to leave the hotel without his knowledge and under whatever conditions he and Doug determined were safest. But added, "Just downstairs. I rented the small ballroom an hour ago. Just set with some stacked chairs people can pull down to use if they want or need them. And a table of prepackaged drinks and snacks."

She watched his chest rise and fall with the deep breath he took. Doing so was preferable to continuing to let his gaze bore into hers. She didn't want to fight with him. "I'm just doing the job I'm being paid to do, Thane. Giving opportunities to the roadies who follow along wherever I go."

His chin jutted. Hers lifted. And she met the narrowed look in his eyes head-on.

With a short, succinct nod, he asked, "Were you going to tell me about this event?"

She wouldn't go so far as to call it an actual event. She'd just reserved private space so that she and her activists didn't get too loud in the lobby.

And so they'd be...safer. Maybe.

"Of course," she answered after a second. "I was on my way in to do so when you knocked." The frown on his brow bothered her more than it should have done. Thane had never been a possessive man. Or one who tried to rein her in.

He was just doing his job. With Doug at his ear getting reports and advising him every day. And...in his defense, a stage had given way beneath her just a couple of hours before. "You can come with me, if you'd like. And invite security in, too. It's just that... I'm paying for this one, so, technically, as Save Marine Life's lawyer, you have no professional cause to be there."

She heard the couched challenge in her words as she said them. The speech hadn't been planned. Hadn't even occurred to her until right then. But the words were spot-on. He couldn't claim that he was protecting Save Marine Life's interests when she was on her own free time and conducting her business separate and apart from them.

When he bowed his head, she knew he'd received the message. "I accept your invitation," he told her, turning his back as he added, "Let me get my coat."

Because he was still one who would never go anywhere professional in just a shirt and tie?

Or because he was keeping his gun in the inside pockets of the jackets that matched his pants?

Probably both, and his choice of apparel really had nothing to do with her. Had no place on her radar.

A fact she reminded herself of when he headed out the door before her and she watched him turn to face her, his shoulders straight and broad in his dark blue tailored coat that fell mid-hip, drawing her attention to the way the man's thighs and...other things...filled out the pants that had been fit to him.

"You forget something?" he asked her as she stood there a second too long, suffering from a mini attack of dry mouth.

"No, we're good," she told him, charging in front of him to push the button to call the elevator to get them.

Before she did something very dangerous, like remember how incredibly good the sex had always been between them.

Even when they'd been fighting.

Business associates dissented, they didn't fight. And they most definitely did not have sex.

Period.

Thane stood by the door, drinking water. If Stella's fans and compatriots took him for hotel staff, that was fine with him.

He recognized some of the women clamoring around her. Had seen them at previous rallies over the years. And at the current ones as well. Of the couple of hundred people in the room, he figured he might know a couple of dozen of them.

Meaning there were almost nine times that many who were completely unfamiliar to him. Doug had told him what kind of behavior to watch for, ways a suspicious character might appear, things they'd do, like stay on the edge of the crowd, insinuating themselves in the moment, yet not drawing attention to themselves.

In a room filled with activists, he wasn't seeing any of that.

He didn't see any excessive perspiration, but with the hotel's air-conditioning blasting, he wouldn't expect to do so. Nervousness...maybe a few people were exhibiting some. But they were meeting an icon. No oversize clothing—something he'd been told to watch for at the rallies themselves, but could fit a ballroom setting, too.

He wasn't noticing any unusual body language. Nothing that stood out to him. And, having spent as many hours in court as he had, that was a language he was proficient in.

And asking a lot of questions...that's where he was faltering. Everyone who got close to where Stella sat on the edge of a long table against the wall, had questions. They were calling them out, yelling over each other, every time Stella finished with the answer to the previous one.

His ex-wife was compelling. Honest. She knew her topics well. Spoke from the heart. And Thane had a few minutes of finding himself drawn in without realizing what was happening.

He even took a step forward, which knocked renewed sense into him. He wasn't there to be a Stella Mitchell follower. A groupie. He'd already fallen under her spell. And had fought his way out, too.

He wasn't there to admire the woman. To, in any way, fall for his ex-wife's charms. He was there to protect his client's assets. And, at the moment, Stella happened to be one of them.

Their bank account that could be damaged if anything was to happen to her under their employ, could be another. She'd signed a contract. A lot of the liabilities she took were hers, not Save Marine Life's. But the stage that day…that was on them.

If Stella had been hurt again…

He shook his head when a resurgence of the dread he'd felt earlier in the week hit again. There'd been a random act of desperation at a rally. Stella had been inadvertently injured and was well on the road to healing. A point brought home to him, along with a wave of relief, as he watched her lift her right arm to get a piece of wayward hair out of her eyes.

As long as she healed completely as the doctor had expected she would, there'd be no undue financial burden to Save Marine Life for the incident. He wanted the thought to have been first and foremost on his mind in those seconds after he'd witnessed the sign of returning health.

It hadn't been. And he had to admit, at least to himself, that he wanted Stella to be fine because he cared about her well-being. He'd been worried as hell when she'd been shot. Denying the facts would only get him into trouble later.

It didn't mean that he was still in love with her. Or in danger of falling again. It just meant that he was human. Knew her well. Admired her commitment to her life's work. Her success. Her authenticity in everything she said and did. He just couldn't have his life joined with hers. He cared from afar.

The thought landed. Took hold. He accepted it without grief. Drew in a long, genuinely easy breath—maybe the first since they'd started the tour.

And tuned in to hear a male voice ask, "What about the shooting the other day? Do you think us being out here, speaking out, is more dangerous now than it used to be?"

Since the question was one Thane would have asked if he'd thought Stella would hear him with an open mind, he tuned in to his ex-wife's focused expression, her mostly natural shrug as she said, "No more dangerous than anything else we do as we go about our lives. Every time you get in a car, your life is more at risk than if you stayed home and sat on the couch. Except that too much couch sitting puts you at risk of physical malfunctions, too. Life is a risk. The shooting was an anomaly. Desperation on overload. I wasn't specifically targeted. No one in the crowd was injured. It was the lashing out of one person who was looking more to stop the moment, than to hurt anyone."

She spoke the truth. Made good sense. Thane admired her calm. Wondered how deep it went. Was she really already at peace with what had happened? Because he wasn't.

"So you don't think you're in danger? I mean, look what happened today, with the stage…"

Moving a few feet to the right so he could get a full look at the speaker, Thane didn't recognize the rather skinny younger man who stood right in the middle of the crowd, closer to the front than the back. Somewhere between eighteen and twenty-four, he'd guess. The almost white hair, long nose, freckles… Thane didn't remember having seen the kid that day or at any of the previous rallies on that tour. Which didn't mean a damned thing. He watched the crowd—he didn't take in specific faces. And there were new people at every rally. Locals. Which was why they were traveling around the state.

"The stage was the result of a rotted board," Stella was saying, not appearing to be rocked in the least by the turn the questioning had taken. Instead of specific, more in-depth questions about how the wildlife was suffering or asking for suggestions to help ramp up crowd participation from on the ground, the young man appeared to be bringing out what a lot of the attendees had been silently thinking. Based on their rapt attention and utter silence as they stared at Stella.

"Save Marine Life is trying to save more money for the cause by using existing staging wherever we can. We learned from today's event that we can't trust that every venue tends to their public facilities as well as we'd like to think they do. Save Marine Life has already made the decision to use their staging for the rest of the twenty-three events on this tour."

"And you weren't hurt today?" a female voice called out. Thane couldn't see the woman.

Stella's attention turned to the edge of the crowd farthest from him as she said, "Aside from a small bruise where I landed on the edge of the board, not at all."

"What about your arm?" another female voice asked.

Stella raised her right arm in response. All the way up. Hand to the sky. It had to hurt. No way it hadn't hurt. But her smile didn't falter. She didn't seem to be sweating at all.

Because she was in charge. Of the room. Of her life.

He got that loud and clear. Just as surely as he understood that she wasn't infallible. Somewhere inside of her, she had to know that, too.

"Still, aren't you at least a little bit afraid?" The same young man again, long bony nose, freckles. Even from more than thirty yards away, Thane thought he could see the rapt attention the guy was giving Stella.

He'd seen the hero worship being bestowed upon her many times over the course of their time together. Hell, he'd probably exhibited a bit of it himself when he'd first seen her on their college campus, getting support for a proposal to have filtered water in all the kitchens in the university's dormitories. He'd been drinking filtered water or carrying a water bottle from home ever since.

"I'm more afraid of losing my voice," Stella's comment came with a hint of humor, and was followed by collective laughing from the crowd.

Standing on the table then, Stella raised her right arm again and called out, "To always having a voice!"

Nodding, Thane had to hand her another win as he watched every arm in the room go up, and heard the rallying cry, "To always having a voice!"

Stella hadn't been the greatest wife. But she'd known that. Had expressed her doubts in that area before they'd ever gotten married. She recognized her shortcomings and her strengths.

On tour with her full-time, for the first time ever, Thane was finally gaining his own more complete understanding of the tremendous power behind Stella's ability to touch people's hearts to bring change for the good.

And he knew that he was going to do everything he could to make sure that evil didn't steal Stella's voice away again.

Ever.

Chapter 5

Stella couldn't get to her room fast enough. And was extremely thankful that Thane immediately occupied himself with placing their order for dinner. Leaving her to drop her key and cross-body phone purse to the bed on her way to locking herself in her bathroom.

Avoiding a glance at her upper arm, not wanting to see if there was staining happening there, she pulled gently, slowly on the bottom of the sleeve to her sweater and was pleased when it moved easily, without sticking to the smaller bandage underneath it.

Her arm was throbbing like hell, but she could endure that just fine. If she'd reinjured herself, ripped stiches and opened her wound, Thane would never let her live it down.

Anytime she moved forward when he thought she shouldn't, he would remind her of the time she'd pushed too far.

Not that she minded his warnings. They were good for her. Kept her in balance. But when her mind was made up, she had to follow its dictates. A lesson she'd learned at ten. And the key to her survival.

Holding her breath as she carefully peeled down the shoulder of the cardigan sweater, to get it off her right arm, she let out a gust of air at the sight of the pristinely clean beige bandage covering her stitches. They were all dissolvable, inside and out. She'd yet to see the wound. She couldn't tend to it herself—at least not easily with her left hand—and not at all with Thane there hovering and insisting on monitoring her progress as a requisite to not pulling the plug on her presence on the tour. And so saw no reason to add the sight of the gash to the internal memory bank that tried its best to haunt her in her weakest moments.

Carefully fingering the outside of the bandage, she noted no slippage, no softness or gel-like reaction to the touch, and nodded. She'd created some surface pain for herself in an adrenaline-fueled moment but had caused no damage to the wound site.

All was good.

Getting her arm back in the sweater hurt some, but she persevered. No way she wanted Thane wondering why she'd taken the damned thing off in the first place. It was just the sort of thing he'd ask. And she couldn't lie to him.

Nor did she think it was a good idea that they continue to dine together. But because she wanted to hear his take on the downstairs gathering, she was ready, water bottle in hand, when he gave a tap on their adjoining door and told her dinner had arrived.

Instead of a table by the window, his current room had a couch with coffee table where he'd set up their meal. He'd removed his suit jacket and rolled up the sleeves of his dress shirt a couple of cuff lengths. As she sat, she caught a glimpse of his hands taking the cardboard lid off from the large platter of fajitas and remembered how those strong fingers had once moved over her.

Their combined strength and tenderness had always been a mystery to her. One that had never stopped grabbing her attention. That was, until he'd stopped touching her.

And what was with her? She hadn't noticed Thane's hands since Kara's wedding to his best friend over a year before. That last time she and Thane had slept together. They'd already split by then, but no one had known. They'd waited until after the wedding to finalize the divorce.

"Something wrong?" he asked, as she stood there, staring at the table.

Afraid he'd somehow figure out what was on her mind—he'd certainly been able to do so an uncomfortable number of times in the past—she shook her head and sat. Next to him. Close enough to reach the food they were sharing. But as far away as she could feasibly be to do so.

And immediately started in on her personally allowed reason for being there. "What did you think of the group downstairs?" she asked him. And then, without waiting for a response, she let him know what she thought should be his takeaway. "Everyone seemed as eager as always to help. And thank goodness for the guy who dealt with the elephant on the table. I wasn't sure how to bring it all up without shining undue light on the topic."

When he added a healthy dollop of guacamole to the wrap he'd made for himself, and took a bite, Stella's stomach tensed a bit. Was he stalling? Or just that hungry?

Holding off on her own first bite, minus any hint of avocado, but with extra sour cream, she grabbed a chip instead. Bit off a small corner. She wished she had a margarita to take the edge off the discomfort in the arm she was forcing herself to continue to use—and off whatever was coming as well.

Thane swallowed, and said, "I agree, the questions

helped ease any potential fears or doubts that might have been developing," he said.

Her mouth dropped open, and she couldn't help staring at him for a second. Had Thane just added positive reinforcement to her choice to remain on tour?

He took another bite, so she did, too. Pondering the impromptu meeting downstairs. And the man sitting next to her.

Over the past while it seemed as though her entire world had reinvented itself. And, with Thane's unexpected support still holding her softly, she said, "It's important for me to be able to speak out." The words were nothing new. The thoughts behind them completely so. And before he could travel backward to the many times he'd tried to talk to her and her response had been just those words, she continued with "Do you know why?"

No point in telling him something he'd figured out on his own. Or baring herself to him, either. No good could come of it. Unless she could help clean up some of the mess she'd made of their marriage. Free him to move on to a healthier relationship.

While a bout of darkness dropped within her at the thought, she'd always known that someday she'd have to see him happy with another woman.

"It's okay, Stel. You are who you are. And the world needs you. My mistake was in trying to change that."

It was a testimony to the toll the recent past—amalgamated with her having been shot—had taken on her that tears sprang to Stella's eyes at his words of acceptance. Quickly blinking them away she said, "True, but going through the whole thing with Kara, I realized something else."

She took a bite of food. Not sure she had to say any

more than that. Or should. Hoping he would just let the matter drop, she swallowed. Took a second bite. Wanting to reach for the tequila that wasn't there.

"You planning to tell me what you realized?" Thane's tone held a touch of courtroom, and she glanced up to see him staring at her. Hard.

He hated games. She hadn't been playing one. More like starting something and chickening out. Something he'd never believe of her in a million years.

"I was forced, from the time I was ten years old, to live a lie," she said, finding the words simple, easy, as she spoke them aloud for the first time. "I adored Kara from day one and there I was lying to her her whole life. Each time I talked to Dad or Mel or Aunt Lila about coming clean with Kara, I was shot down so emphatically I felt like I'd be disowned from the family or something if I did what I felt was right."

She'd been looking at Thane, as though his gaze wouldn't let hers go, the whole time she'd been talking. And continued to stare into those hazel eyes as she fell silent, too.

Something was happening. She had no idea what. Nothing drastic. Not life-changing.

But more than anything else in that moment, she wanted to find out what it was.

Thane didn't move. Hardly breathed. Almost twenty years of knowing Stella Mitchell and she'd suddenly sprouted wings?

She'd never, ever given him an insight like the words she'd just uttered. They were drips in the sink and he waited for more. Trickles. Gushing wasn't her way.

The thought gave birth to another. Silence was her way. She was attempting to do something there.

How could he help?

"Because you had to perpetuate the lie that your mother, her mother, was dead," he said. He knew the facts, had heard them after Kara's attacker had been shot dead. Mostly from Ben. A little from Doug. Nothing from Stella, though he'd been there with her when she'd thought her baby sister had been killed. She'd called. He'd come running.

He was who he was and where Stella was concerned, he'd never been able to turn his back if she needed him. Divorce her, yes. For his own emotional and mental health. Keep his distance, of course. But on that one rare occasion when she'd called…

She nodded. Then said, "I had to live that lie every minute of my life, Thane. Not just in front of Kara, but with everyone in the world. The only way to keep us all safe was for Mom to be dead. And Dad and Susan were adamant that in order for me not to make any mistakes, I wasn't to talk about anything different even in our home. Kara's life depended on it. That was the message I took to bed every night. That I took most to heart. My truth would kill my baby sister."

Refusing to allow his bleeding heart to drown out the logic Stella counted on from him, Thane heard a bong go off in his head. The dawning of a different day. One that had just healed some of the broken understanding inside him. Which could maybe help her, too.

He had a vision of a smile. Stella, at ten. A happy kid with a mom and dad and big sister doting on her.

Like Kara and Ben, Thane hadn't had even an inkling that Stella's mother was alive until Kara's near death at the hands of the danger the entire family had been avoiding since Tory Mitchell had testified at the trial of a mob boss and had gone into witness protection. But his ex-wife had known. From the moment he'd met her, she'd been keeping a major, life-altering secret from him. To protect the lives of her family members. Her own life. His, too, by association.

He didn't blame her. At all. But he was beginning to boil a bit against the fates that had changed the course of so many lives.

He ached to have known that ten-year-old before her world had been blown apart.

"Tell me about her," he said. Wanting her to be who she'd been before her father had confessed his yearlong affair to her mother and a devastated Tory had responded with a week in Florida and a love of her own. One that resulted in Kara. And her father's murder, too.

"My mom?"

Stella's firm and unfriendly tone had him quickly setting her straight. "No, the young Stella before she'd been forced to live a lie. Were you happy?"

She'd taken another bite of fajita-filled tortilla. Put the flour wrap down and wiped her mouth with her napkin. Shaking her head. "I'm not sure I even remember her," she said. "For so long I was forced to forget…" Shrugging, she shook her head again. "What I do remember is a fear I'd never known was possible. And the knowledge that it was up to me to save myself from whatever demon had entered me."

God on earth. "Demon? In you?" Had no one seen the child splintering into pieces? Had her in counseling?

Where someone would be told the truth that became more dangerous to all of them with every person who knew.

The only way witness protection worked was if no one mentioned the situation or reached out in any way to what had been. Period. In his earliest lawyering days Thane had interned at a criminal law firm that had had a client testifying and going into the program.

"Of course I thought I'd done something wrong," Stella said slowly. "What young kid wouldn't?" The question was rhetorical. Thane searched for an answer anyway. Needing to give her something.

He was still coming up blank when she said, "Mel and Dad did their best. Keeping me talking. About me. My future. How much I was loved. Keeping me focused on things I liked, activities I was good at." She sounded different to him, softer somehow, but so distant it was almost as though he was watching her on-screen.

Thane was in over his head. Was well aware that he wasn't the therapist Stella should probably be having the breakthrough with. But he couldn't risk her feeling any kind of rejection. Not when she'd finally found a very different voice. "What activities?" he asked. Focused fully on her. Twenty-nine years before, and in that moment, at thirty-nine, too.

She smiled then, though her eyes were too cloudy to reveal any glow. "I liked to dance." With a tilt of her head and a bit of a twisted smile, she said, "Not much of a stretch, huh? When you consider how I move around onstage?"

Had she always put that together? The past her, mingling with who she'd been forced to become? Or was she just seeing it now?

Before he could figure out whether or not he was going to ask the question, Stella blinked, and, looking straight at him with clear eyes, said, "Speaking out truths against bad…it's what I have to do, Thane."

She was done. The message was clear. But in those few minutes she'd given him more than she had in all the years he'd known her. He hoped that talking had helped. That she was better for having finally been able to speak a small bit of her most important truth.

And while Thane needed to hear so much more, he didn't push. He nodded and went back to eating.

But he did so a changed man.

Stella couldn't take another bite. Cleaning up her portion of the dinner, she stood, thanked Thane for the meal, and left him sitting there without looking back, dumping her trash in the can in her room, not his.

As though she could somehow recall and contain the garbage she'd spilled moments before. What had been had been. She couldn't change a second of the past.

And the last thing she wanted was anyone—Thane—feeling sorry for her. She wasn't the one in need of pity. Or attention, either. The victims of the many causes on whose behalf she spoke out had to be the beneficiaries of Stella's life. Her work.

Feeling sorry for herself, or getting lost in the past, weakened her. Stole her very hard-won strength.

So that was what she'd take from the fall from grace that she'd just experienced in there with her ex-husband. Circling around to where she'd come, from where she'd been.

Her mother's leaving had taught her how to find, and rely on, her own strength. To never allow her well-being to be tied to the choices made by another.

The realization allowed her to relax. Sitting at her

computer, getting ready for the evening's work of conversing with concerned citizens on her social platforms, she started an instant replay of the last five minutes in Thane's room.

Heard his somewhat odd, kind yet personal tone of voice. A less guarded look in his eyes. And knew that her childish confession had done more than reaffirm the strong woman she'd grown into. For so long she'd been focused on not screwing up by letting a single word slip out of her mouth. A single inner thought escape. Never drinking more than a single alcoholic drink around others, even in college, for fear that the substance would loosen her tongue.

And she'd failed to see how her forced choices had affected Thane. He'd met the Stella she'd become. Had wanted to marry that woman. It never occurred to her that he'd wanted more than that. He'd never once asked or expressed a need to know her more deeply.

Only to have her stop focusing so hard on the fights she took on for others. To quit trying so hard to right the wrongs she could help fix in the world. He'd wanted her to compromise who she was to fit him better.

But what if...

She shook her head. Booted her computer. Clicked to the first social platform. Checked her notifications, but wasn't taking them in.

What if Thane's dissatisfaction came as much from not knowing what he didn't know, as it had from his displeasure with what was?

The look in his eye in there...after her few seconds of looking backward...

No. There was no going back. And no matter who knew what about her, their knowing didn't change who she was.

What she'd grown out of the ashes with which she'd been left. Focusing on her screen, she looked at the numbers of notifications. The private messages. And the numbers of new followers, just since the night before.

Millions of followers on every one of her platforms. People who counted on her to guide them in helping to educate society to right wrongs.

But only for the causes in which Stella believed with her whole heart. Her integrity, her following couldn't be bought. She took payment for the honest work she did. Most of the time after hearing of an issue, or researching and finding it, and then seeking out those she could help. Not the other way around.

Her email inbox—and in a lot of her social messages, too—she'd find those who wanted to pay her to use her following, her skills, to help them get what they wanted. Most of them were deleted before the end of the first sentence. She had to make a living, but she wasn't working for the money. She spoke out because she could. Because speaking the truth to right wrongs kept her mentally and emotionally healthy.

Without that, she was nothing.

Still, it was…good…thinking that maybe Thane had gained some new insight over dinner that freed him up some. Helped him put his past with her to rest.

She badly wanted that for him. How could she not? She cared about him.

Love didn't stop flowing just because he hadn't been able to live with her as she was, and she couldn't change for him…

"No, hear me clearly…" The man's voice intruded on her thoughts and Stella jumped. Realizing he was walking closer to the door between their rooms. His voice faded some as she saw the door close to within a crack between them.

She should have tuned the seconds out. Returned her attention to her own responsibilities on the screen in front of her. Instead, a premonition—or concern—that Thane's conversation had something to do with her, prompted her to stand. She moved to that slight opening between their rooms, pressed her ear up to it and heard him state, "I have already prepared a lawsuit to file on behalf of my client. It would behoove you to get that wood into a forensic lab immediately and have it tested to prove your claim that you'd had it inspected at the beginning of the week in preparation for our expected event. Assuming you tell me you're willing to have the tests conducted immediately, and get me the certified results, I'm willing to hold off on advising my client to proceed with legal action."

Brows raised, Stella stood there long enough to hear him say, "Twenty-four hours? I'll expect the report by this time tomorrow evening, then. Thank you." And then she did what she should have done from the beginning, and gave her attention back to her own responsibilities.

She opened the first direct message. Read. Then, when no immediate response came to her, picked up her phone and typed. I listened in on your conversation. I'm sorry. She reread, hit Send on the text, and hadn't yet focused on her first social media posts when her phone vibrated a response back.

Thank you for advising.

The formal—completely lacking in any hint of Thane's feelings—response brought a sardonic smile to Stella's lips. He gave as good as he got. As little as he got.

An adversary worthy of her. One who knew how to temper her determination. For better or worse.

Her business associate. Nothing more.

With a roll of her eyes and shake of her head, Stella got to work.

Chapter 6

Thane advised Amelia Lockhart, Save Marine Life's promotions director and head of the current tour, to hire extra security for Saturday's rally. Two instances in a week were not good odds—regardless of the full confession law enforcement had gained from the first incident, and the rotting wood to explain the second.

He introduced himself to the local off-duty police officers who'd been retained at his request, and kept his vigilant watch the entire time Stella was on stage as well.

Two potentially serious incidents were two more than Stella had had in all of her years of being an activist. Both volunteer and professionally.

And for both to have taken place while she was onstage—as though she was the only person who spoke at any rally—did not sit well with him. Or Doug and Ben.

Though all three acknowledged that where the Mitchell sisters were concerned, they were all still a bit reactionary.

Thane was of a mind that overreaction was far preferable to anyone else getting hurt. And was acting accordingly. Out of his own pocket where necessary.

Which was why he'd rented a cottage on a small stretch of private beach halfway between that day's rally and the next one on Tuesday, planning to get Stella there, and keep her out of sight, during the two days she had off. She'd been planning to drive home.

Doug was planning to let her know that she couldn't take the car they were using out of state, if Thane needed any extra support for his plan.

But such a move wouldn't stop Stella. She'd rent a car. Or a plane. Or hop on a commercial jet, if she decided to go home.

Because the woman had a damaged heart that drove her to follow its dictates. Most particularly in the face of someone else trying to tell her she couldn't.

He'd always known that about her. And as of the night before, he knew why. Didn't make a difference to her obstinance. But it made his dealing with it completely different.

Listening to his ex-wife finish her final call to action, he cringed as he thought of the number of times he'd unknowingly pushed her up against a wall she'd had to walk through in order to survive.

If only he'd known…

Wouldn't have changed his inability to have a happy marriage with her, but they'd have fought a lot less. Hurt each other a lot less.

Thane smiled widely, without thinking, as the object of his thoughts came toward him from center stage, catching his eyes, a huge happy smile on her face. And then, out of the corner of his eye, he saw movement.

Darting forward instinctively, as though thinking he was somehow going to deflect a bullet aimed at Stella, he was up the stage stairs, blocking her from the view of the crowd, and half guiding, half lifting her, down to the ground.

Only once she was safely behind the stage did it hit

him that there'd been no blast. No shooting. Which made his actions a bit harder to explain to her. But he wasn't sorry for them.

"Thane?" She was frowning, a light of fear in her eyes as she gazed at him. And a hint of anger in her voice as she said, "What the…"

Her words were interrupted by one of the off-duty officers—a woman with short dark hair and plain clothes—who came hurrying over to them. "You both okay?" the head of the detail asked.

Having met her earlier, Thane nodded. "Yeah, I caught movement out of the corner of my eye and just reacted." He would explain. He wasn't going to apologize for something he'd do again and again anytime the same circumstances arose.

"It's a damned good thing you did," the woman said. "A smoking device flew out of nowhere onto the stage just behind her." She glanced at Stella.

Registering the instant fear in Stella's horrified gaze, Thane heard her say, "A bomb?" Even as he was reminding himself that there'd been no blast.

"Of the harmless, fireworks variety," the woman—she'd been introduced to Thane as Rosemary—said. "But it could have been the real thing and, had it been, those few seconds would likely have been the difference between life and death."

Holy hell. Another incident? Harmless, and yet…not so much when he considered the emotional toll the events were taking. On him, certainly. But he could only imagine the psychological damage they were creating inside Stella. Who'd been taught that keeping her silence, dealing alone, was a matter of life and death, too.

"I don't get it," Stella said, looking between Thane and the officer. "What's going on with this tour?"

Rosemary's gaze was serious, her tone informed, as she said, "Sounds to me as though Save Marine Life has someone who doesn't want your message to leave positive impressions." Turning to look between the two of them, she asked, "Do you know if the organization has looked internally, maybe to an employee on the tour, for any signs of disgruntlement? Or sudden unexplained wealth?"

Even as Rosemary was finishing that last sentence—and Stella took a step closer to Thane—Amelia Lockhart walked up to the small group. "What in the hell is going on here?" she asked quietly. "Tell me what kind of questions I need to be asking of my crew. What might we have seen? Or need to be on the lookout for?"

Rosemary turned to the promotions director. "My guys think the bomb was dropped from a tree off to the left of the stage. They've got the whole area covered under guise of being members of the dispersing crowd. Let's see what they find out and go from there. But from what I'm seeing, you might want to consider canceling the rest of the tour."

"No." Stella's tone was first to be heard. Firmest. And loudest. With Amelia's coming right behind it.

But she looked to Amelia to speak first beyond the initial reaction. The director held Stella's gaze for a couple of seconds and then nodded, before saying, "It's just this type of bullying and scare tactics that allow oppression and greed to win out over right."

Thane's gut clenched at the words, recognizing them straight from one of Stella's speeches. And yet, he had no good argument against them, either. If all people backed down when the enemy came for them, there'd be no good left in the world.

As Rosemary and Amelia made arrangements for the off-duty officers to speak to SML's crew, Thane was hit by a sudden memory of a long-ago case. A woman who'd been a victim of domestic violence. The fiend had gotten away with abusing his wife for years until she was a shadow of herself, because he'd bullied her into silence, using fear to keep her quiet.

His gaze went to Stella then, and when she looked at him, with that familiar glare of obstinance in her gaze, he nodded.

He wasn't going to try to force the tour to shut down due to potential financial liabilities that could be accrued by his client were violence to ensue. His job was to help his client do the work they'd been organized to do, in a manner that lessened legal liabilities as much as possible.

And he'd just stumbled upon the winning argument he'd been hunting since he'd arbitrarily rented the cottage that morning. Dodging another potential, painful head-to-head confrontation with his ex-wife.

A victory, to be sure. A tainted one. He'd take it gladly.

Because he'd be a fool to hope that someday he and Stella might stumble upon an entire day where they could live peacefully on the same page of the same book.

Thane was planning something she wasn't going to like. Stella had known the second she'd met him at the door between their rooms to head to the rally that morning. But, focused on the rally, she hadn't bothered to ask what it might be. Didn't matter. She had the right to refuse whatever it was and had proven time and again over their years together that she had no problem exercising that right.

Didn't mean she liked doing so, though.

After the week they'd just come through, she didn't barge ahead into whatever the fight was going to be as they left Amelia and the officer talking and walked together the few feet to the vehicle parked behind the stage. The one Doug had lent them. Thane's issue from the morning could jump on board with whatever new ones he was conjuring up after the most recent count of vandalism.

A smoke bomb. Juvenile at best. Local police would deal with it, get details to Amelia and Thane, and they'd figure out security going forward. Clearly there were Floridians who cared more about their business in ocean waters than they did the creatures they were killing. She—Amelia—had known that going in.

In the car with Thane, she watched as he turned in the direction of the hotel they'd stayed in the past couple of nights. Laying her head back against the headrest, she figured that whatever he had on his mind where she was concerned could wait until she returned to the tour Monday afternoon. In time for Tuesday's rally.

A few more hours and she'd be home. In her own space where she got along just fine with everyone in residence. She, herself, and me.

Due to her car having been driven back to Georgia after the shooting, she'd already booked the flight. Just had to get Thane—or a hired driver—to get her to the airport. Her bag was packed. And she'd never been more ready to go.

What he was doing, staying in Florida, or driving home in Doug's rented vehicle, was his business. Oh. The issue he'd had on his mind that morning...the one she wasn't going to like...was he thinking he'd drive her home? Just as he'd been driving her around all week?

It wasn't a horrible suggestion. One she'd have agreed to if he'd bothered to mention the plan before she'd made her plane reservations. Which would have to have been at dinner—where she'd dribbled her sorry her-as-a-ten-year-old sob story all over the fajitas. Jeesh. Twenty-nine years of keeping her tongue, plus a month of having been silent after the need to be so had been permanently erased, and she loses control of her mouth when it should have remained silent.

Thane had glanced at her twice. Assessing. She knew the look. And preempted his demand with, "I've booked a flight home, return flight arriving in Fort Desmond Monday afternoon. If you'd rather not take me and pick me up, I'll get a rideshare." She stared straight ahead as she said the words.

Telling herself that she was just tired. Not the least bit uncomfortable with traveling alone to the airport, through the terminals, on the plane, at baggage claim, and the ride to North Haven. She'd been doing it since she was in college. Just because someone had been upset with Save Marine Life and her arm had been caught in the fray didn't mean she wasn't safe.

Kara's would-be killer had lost his life. And he'd been the last man standing. The only one left to benefit from the money amassed by the mob family's dealings that her mother's testimony had stopped.

Being jittery after the terrifying days she'd had while her baby sister had been in danger and then presumed dead, was understandable. Allowing fear to stop her life after the fact was not. Not understandable. And not acceptable, either.

"Someone is out to make a point with SML." Thane's first sentence didn't bode well. But instead of cutting him off at the quick, as she'd normally have done, Stella just sat there. Figuring that letting him talk would buy her a few minutes of rest before she had to go into battle again.

"We'll go with the fact, for now, that you aren't a target," he continued, leaving her to wonder if his "for now" had been a deliberate tactic to light a brief spark of fear in her chest, or just his normal legalese way of communicating. Needing to qualify every statement so that it didn't come back to bite him in the ass. She chose the latter. Because she'd lived with the man for years. Knew him well.

She actually, in a general sense, liked his legalese characteristics. Made him easier to trust. And to predict, too.

"But until we hear back on the forensic report from the rotted stage board, which is due early this evening, and get the police report from today's incident, I need you to stay close. If you choose to travel on your own, I'd have to recommend that SML end your contract as of now. And, if they so choose, and you want to continue, you could sign a new agreement when you return on Monday."

The words took a second to digest. Wow. He'd come quickly with that one. Clearly due to forethought. "How about if I agree to hiring protection for the travel and the whole damned weekend, at my own expense?" she threw back at him.

"You got time to hire a bodyguard before you need to catch a ride to the airport to catch your flight?"

I may have, was her first thought. *Not likely, though*, followed closely behind.

"I rented a cottage on a private stretch of beach halfway between here and Fort Desmond for tonight and tomorrow night," Thane said quietly. "It's part of a small neighborhood, with security cameras along the street and the beach, and outside every house as well. Doug's the one who told me about it. A friend of a friend of his lives two doors down from the cottage."

A secure cottage on a beach. With Thane, yeah, but a cottage on the beach. As opposed to holing up afraid to go out at home.

No, as opposed to *forcing* herself to go out at home. And...seeing Melanie. Who hadn't been herself, either since before the trouble had started with Kara. Something was going on with her older sister. Stella hoped to God it wasn't marriage problems, or Mel's teenage son into drugs or drinking. But wouldn't be surprised by either. Life tended to head that way far more often than it should.

"Are there two bedrooms?" she asked.

He said, "Of course," in that exasperated tone of his that made her question seem incredibly childish. Stella crossed her arms, stared straight ahead and silently thanked herself for having the forethought to purchase flight insurance the night before when she'd made her reservation.

The cottage rivaled any of the nicer hotel rooms Thane had stayed in. Definitely more upscale than he'd been expecting. The detective who lived two doors down pleased him more. The man had been waiting for them when they'd arrived late Saturday afternoon. Had let them in. Given them the key. And assured Thane that the entire beach had been well checked out.

Overkill, he knew. But he wasn't a cop or a bodyguard, so had to take the extra measures. And unlike Stella, he reached out for help when he needed it. The thought brought a wave of compassion for the woman, instead of the usual irritation.

She'd learned as a child that she had to handle her agonies on her own. One didn't go through what Stella had and come out unchanged. Or without lifelong repercussions.

She'd retreated to her room the second they'd arrived. One of the two large suites. He'd told her to choose the one she wanted and hadn't been surprised that she'd taken the smaller of the two. She fought for what she needed, but when it came to material things, she'd never needed much.

Figuring it was best to leave her alone, Thane set up shop at a breakfast bar with four stools separating the large living area—complete with fireplace—from the equally large eating and small kitchen-like area. He liked the idea of sitting up tall on the barstool, as though he could see more. And the ocean view was pleasant.

The refrigerator and cupboards had been stocked as per the form he'd filled out when he'd rented the place. So other than food prep, he had two full days to focus on work. Planned to get caught up on business for other clients. And maybe do some reading. All solitary endeavors. His presence was required only as a safeguard, not a companion.

And while the ocean beckoned, he reminded himself he was on a business trip, not a vacation.

As if his ex-wife had read his mind and was purposely taunting him, her attention-grabbing body suddenly appeared, in shorts and a tank top, on the sand outside the wall of windows he faced. She walked alone. With purpose, even when she didn't have any place in particular to be. Head high. Shoulders back.

For a second, Thane physically ached, watching her. Not just the male part of him that instantly recognized her particular body, with muscle memory that knew exactly the kind of pleasures Stella had always been able to arouse within him.

His entire being tightened with an emotional pain he hardly recognized—and couldn't define. She'd been robbed of her most trusted support at one of the most critical times in a woman's life. Just before puberty, when she'd be at her most vulnerable. Not just because she'd lost her mother, but because her entire existence had become an unending lie with the loss.

He hurt for her. And for himself, too. All those years of loving her, always seeking and never finding the way to reach her...came crashing around him. She'd given him everything she could. And he'd given her grief for things she hadn't been able to impart.

Focusing on his screen, he told himself to do what he'd always done when thoughts of Stella brought him to a dead end. Bury himself in his second love. Work. He succeeded for a bit. With regular checks on Stella walking in the distance, he got through his emails. Wrote a brief in response to ongoing litigation regarding a city water lawsuit in Georgia. Half of it. Until the forensic report came from the stage board.

He read. Shot off emails. Continued to keep track of Stella on the beach. And completed the brief. He had a call from Doug, who was in touch with all local police departments where he and Stella had been and were going to be, regarding the smoke bomb. And he was just finishing up tabulating his billable hours when Stella came in the back door of the cottage. She'd taken her key with her. And locked the door behind her.

Taking his need to know she was safe seriously. Not that that surprised him. Stella always did what she said she'd do.

It had just been getting her to agree to the doing that had been the problem between them. Or, more accurately, to agree to the not doing.

"Did you get the forensic report?" she asked before he had a chance to take the breath he always needed when she walked in a room.

"I did." And was forced to say, "I'd appreciate it if you'd put something on over your beach attire." Her choice. She could refuse.

He wouldn't mention the situation again.

And knew he wouldn't need to as she immediately left the room.

Leaving him to deal with an unwelcome hard-on.

Chapter 7

The man was going to be the death of her. Not the tour. Or any wrath aimed at Save Marine Life. Thane Wilson had always been able to reach her in places no one else had. Sexually first and foremost. It was like he had an invisible hot wire attached to her crotch. One sentence and she was warm there.

Because there was only one reason he'd have said what he did.

With a shrug, she changed out of the clothes she'd packed in case she had a chance to make it to the fitness center in any of the places she'd be staying over the next month. Other than advocating for others, and looking out for her family, Stella's only other real focus was on bike riding. As a ten-year-old, she'd spent hours on her bike every day the summer she'd shattered.

And still found freedom and hope in the feel of the wind against her face, lifting her hair, playing with it. As a close second, the ocean breeze had helped some.

Calming her.

Right until Thane had opened his mouth and let her know the sight of her body was turning him on.

Jeesh. Like either of them needed that complication.

She understood, though. And, once desire quit thrumming through her, she'd be thankful, too. After the mishap at Kara's wedding—the hot sex she and Thane had wordlessly shared even though they'd split up—both of them were on high alert. Intent on avoiding disaster a second time.

Which was why she stepped back into the black pants she'd had on at the rally that morning. And slid her arms into the cropped matching jacket over her white tank top. Her right arm would have preferred to be left unfettered by material over the growing-smaller-every-day bandage that covered it. But it took one for the team.

Slipping on her matching black pumps, she was back out in the kitchen within a minute and a half. "What did the report say?" she asked, standing on the far side of the breakfast bar, exposing only the top half of herself, as she stared at him over the counterspace between them.

"The two wide boards that gave way were positive for high levels of nitrogen and potassium nitrate."

Eyes narrowing, Stella watched as he looked at his screen. Pretty sure he was avoiding her gaze more than looking over detail specifics.

"Those are both damaging chemicals," she said, her heart rate speeding up a bit. She'd done some campaigning on behalf of a neighborhood that had been believed to be exposed to a plant that produced one of them. "You trying to tell me someone poisoned the stage in an attempt to poison me, but that I got lucky and the old stage gave way instead?"

The shake of his head calmed her, until he looked up and met her gaze head-on. "No. I'm telling you that someone purposely doused only those two boards," he said, leaving her confused, until he finished with, "Together they cause boards to rot quickly."

That last hit her as a physical blow beneath her ribs. "To hurt me and make it seem like an accident," she said. Forcing strength into her words. Because it was what she did. All she knew how to do to survive.

"We don't know that."

Eyes narrowing at Thane's response, Stella tilted her head slightly, staring him down. Not in contest, but in need to understand. "What *do* we know?"

"That SML was likely targeted. There was no way of knowing who'd be on the stage when it gave way. But based on decomposition, dousing was likely started the day after the tour stop was announced."

She nodded. Feeling slightly better. While she'd never been at a rally where anyone onstage was targeted, she'd been present when violence broke out briefly in the crowd. And most certainly, many times when naysayers were there protesting the protest. Standing up, speaking out came with a price. For Stella, not doing so cost her so much more.

When Thane's hazel eyes took on a softer glint, she tensed again. For different reasons. No way did she want the man's pity. Ever. That would be the worst. She'd suffocated on the stuff growing up. Poor, little, sweet, beautiful Stella who'd lost her loving mom to death while she'd been lying about the fact because she really hadn't.

She'd lost her mother because Tory Mitchell chose to leave them. Period. End of that story. Kara was fine. Bad guy dead. *Stop. Thinking. About. It.*

"It's also possible that someone is after the city." She heard his words like a pity escape, until he said, "There's records of citizens, members of local associations who use the stage, including for an annual Fourth of July celebration, who've been petitioning for a new stage, claiming the current one isn't up to current standard. That it doesn't provide the connectivity required by most of today's showstopping electronics. There are those who believe that the stage was sabotaged by one or more locals during rental to an outside source to prove to the city that it's a liability."

Taking a deep breath, Stella nodded. Almost grinning at the man who'd made her smile more than anyone else in her life. "Thank you," she told him. Hoping she meant the gratitude as a result of him telling her the complete truth, which lessened motivation for his intensely protective choices where she was concerned.

"And the smoke bomb?" she asked, having spent the past couple of hours trying to relax, rather than thinking about the possible dangers that could drop from the sky to do her in.

"Dropped by a local young woman who is believed to have gang ties. And is a suspected drug dealer. They ID'd her from cameras in the area, but she's on the run. We won't know motive until they bring her in, but they suspect it had something to do with ships going in and out of the harbor."

Which was on the list of SML's targeted activity. And the reason Amelia had chosen the port town.

With her mind back in full gear, Stella looked at Thane professional to professional. "I'm beginning to wonder if maybe we're dealing with an opposing organization," she said. "Someone doing exactly what we're doing, but for the other side."

Without breaking eye contact, he nodded. "A group of activists hired by a shipping conglomerate, or shipping companies who've banded together, or maybe some organization that represents oil companies? Your cause is unlikely to bring forth angry protesters across the general population, but among those affected…"

Filled with renewed energy, Stella nodded. And Thane started typing.

Fast.

Turned out that maybe, postdivorce, they'd found a way to do good work together again.

Stella was actually smiling a little as she looked through the cupboards for something to make for dinner.

Thane wasn't so sure Stella was not being targeted. He got that the evidence was pointing to more clearly delineated sources, but he wasn't ready to loosen up his strict guidelines where she was concerned. Acknowledging to Doug, and himself, that his concerns were likely more due to residual feelings from Kara's recent, last-minute harrowing escape from death, than any current goings-on.

But Kara had been harassed, too, leading up to the almost successful attempt on her life.

Which didn't mean that growing antiprotest movements on tour were at all the same thing.

He'd seen the young man with the long nose and freckles at the rally that day. Couldn't help wondering what he'd thought of the smoke bomb. And hoped it didn't scare him off from supporting good causes for fear of retribution.

Which was exactly what any antiprotest movement would be hoping to have happen. And Thane had just talked himself around in a circle that brought him right back to what he'd told Stella. Law enforcement, with Doug as his overseer, suspected that big money could be behind the recent string of mishaps Stella was facing on tour.

And maybe that was what was bothering him—scaring him—most of all. Big money meant the potential for someone to just disappear, never to be seen or heard from again, when the puppeteer determined it was time.

Chances of that happening to Stella shouldn't be too great. She wasn't the only professional activist around. If she was no longer available, SML would just hire another to continue speaking out for their cause.

But what if Big Money was just out to influence smaller crowds at a time? People like the man with the long nose.

He worked it all through in his mind, and with various searches on the internet while Stella made her homemade spaghetti. He saw her pull out a bottle of zinfandel to substitute the small bit of cooking wine she normally used in the recipe. The one ingredient he'd failed to order.

And was quite pleased with himself when the heavenly scent of simmering sauce started to fill the cottage.

With a break in her duties, she leaned her elbows on the counter, her chin in her uplifted right hand, and said, "You filled out a grocery list, didn't you?"

Did the woman have to figure out his every move? Or so damned many of them?

Since she was so sure of herself he didn't bother to answer.

"It was a good call," she told him. "I haven't made spaghetti since…" Her voice dropped off and she turned her back, heading to the stove to stir sauce that he knew for a fact she generally let simmer for half an hour without touching it. Something about things melding and softening together naturally.

And since he was already on her bad side, he figured he might as well push forward.

"Going forward we need to be prepared for more vandalism," he said, pleased with his professional courtroom tone. "If this is, as suspected, an opposing force trying to sabotage SML's work, then we can count on continued instances of damaging interruptions to rallies."

Turning from the stove, Stella was licking sauce off a finger she'd ducked into a spoonful of liquid she'd pulled from the pot. While he struggled with the tongue devouring that finger with pleasure, she said, "This is good. I'm glad you made the choice. Thank you."

She was glad he'd purposely chosen groceries so she'd make him a dinner he liked? Glad he'd made a choice that brought them into personal territory?

Or she was just distracting him from the conversation they had to have. One she wouldn't want to hear.

Going with the latter, he said, "No matter what's behind the string of mishaps..." He paused, glancing at her right arm. Her being shot was far more than a mere accident. Inches more to the left and she could have been killed. One quarter spin of her body just as the bullet was fired and...

"I know," she said, standing there holding the spoon of sauce she'd stuck her finger in. "We've got a pattern, right? Believe it or not, I listened to you over the years, learned a lot. We need to be on high alert. And on Tuesday morning, before we leave here, I would like to have a business meeting to discuss the new protocols. But for now, tonight, tomorrow, and Monday, can I just have some peace? You did a good thing, getting this place, a hideout where I can be safe. It's a bit dramatic, but, since we're here, can't you just let me benefit from the restrictions placed on my travel plans?"

Thane opened his mouth. Closed it again. And nodded.

The woman was never going to stop going up against him. Putting wrenches in his logical and valid plans.

"You want a taste of this?" Her spoon appeared in his vision as he stared at his computer screen.

And as he lifted his head to tell her no thank you, he caught a whiff of the sauce and said, "Give me that."

Taking the spoon, he put the whole thing in his mouth. Sucking up every drop of the sauce she'd meant to share with him.

And then, with a pointed look, handed the cleaned-off spoon back to her.

They were sharing a cottage. Meals. And a professional road tour.

They were not going to lick spoons—or anything else—together.

Ever again.

Period.

Sunday was just what Stella needed. Quiet time to sit by the ocean. To breathe. And answer to no one. She called her sisters, though she hated to interrupt Kara's time away. Mel had insisted that Kara needed to hear her voice. And, as usual, their older sister was right.

Mel also insisted that, other than her small family still recovering from the shock of Kara's abduction and near death, they were all doing fine.

And she asked Stella to please give up the tour and return home. But gave in without much of a fight when Stella said Melanie knew she couldn't do that.

Other than at dinner, Thane stayed completely out of her way. He worked, she assumed, as he was at the breakfast bar on his computer most of the time she was in the cottage. After their dinner of leftover spaghetti, she'd immediately excused herself to her room. Where she read a book on her phone. Not her usual mode of accessing fiction, but because she'd left her paperbacks at home, she settled for the only way at her disposal that she could get lost in a story.

Other than a brief visit to a medical clinic to be told that her arm wound had healed nicely, and to give her some basic exercises to help her get her upper arm completely limber again, Monday progressed the same as Sunday. Discovering that there was a small laundry closet at the end of the hall, she did some laundry. And then Stella actually fell asleep, dressed in her shorts and tank top with a long blouse over them, on a blanket on the beach just outside their cottage.

And woke up to see Thane, in shorts and a polo shirt, sitting beside her.

"What?" she asked him, feeling far too vulnerable as she scrambled to sit up. "You got more mandates to hand out? No sleeping on the beach? I was reading. Didn't mean to doze off." She glanced down at the phone that was lying face down on the blanket not far from where her shoulder had been.

"No. I came out to tell you that they caught the young woman who dropped the smoke bomb. But when I saw you were sleeping, I didn't want to wake you up."

Thane knew how restlessly she slept. How hard it was for her to just relax enough to drop peacefully off. And looking over at him, she had to say, "You were right to rent this place. And thank you for allowing me to just sit alone and relax."

Glancing over at her he nodded, and then turned his gaze back to the ocean. "You could allow yourself this kind of time at home," he pointed out. And for once, his words didn't get her dander up.

They were true, but most of what he brought up to her about herself was. Maybe even all of it, as seen through his perspective. But he didn't have any vision inside her. And so often hadn't known what he was talking about when he tried to point out the effects of her own behaviors on herself.

Not his fault. Not hers, either. Just the facts of their misguided choice to marry.

"The smoke bomber is a nineteen-year-old known member of one of Florida's largest gangs. She's been on a watch list, but authorities believed that they could gain more with her on the streets than in jail. They were following her in the hopes of finding out who she reported to and where she was getting the drugs she was selling to kids at the high school in town."

Peace flew off without her. Stella felt sick to her stomach. So much evil. No matter how hard she fought, it would always be there. Didn't mean she'd stop fighting. Ever. She wouldn't let the bad guys rob her of her voice. Not again. Nor would she ever be able to stop helping others live better lives in any way she could. Not everyone had to know the lethal stab of pain she'd felt at ten. Many would never know. And the harder she worked, the more of them there'd be.

"Authorities found a large wad of cash on her. She swears it wasn't from drugs, or from any of her usual sources. Said some guy came up to her a few days ago and told her a thousand dollars would be waiting in a coffee can in a particular sewer if she dropped the bomb at the rally." Thane's voice was professional and he continued to gaze forward as he spoke.

"The opposition, just like you thought," Stella told him,

watching him. Enjoying the chance to take in a side view of him without being on point. Or at the end of any of his points. The man's chiseled cheeks spoke of the strength that kept him honest in a world with blurred lines. Where both sides were right, and wrong, too. Where personal rights deserved to be protected, but at what cost? To how many?

Where her challenges were clear-cut, his were often not so at all, as he tried to find compromise and wins for as many as possible.

He turned to look at her, and Stella almost believed he'd read her mind. Or that, as he held her gaze, he figured her out, when he said, "He paid a thousand dollars, Stel. To drop a smoke bomb."

Her intake of breath was so harsh she almost coughed over it. And then noticed that he was still pinning her with his stare. After all that time ocean gazing. Dread started to seep up inside her. "What else is there?" she asked.

"He specifically told her to drop the bomb at the end of your speech. She says he told her your exact words."

Wow. Damn. "The opposition's determined. And good," she finally said, looking outward herself at that point. There was only so much Thane-induced intensity she could take at a time.

Two days on the beach, and she'd never seen another person out. Or even lights on inside the other few cottages, except one two doors down. Doug's friend, she'd figured. But hadn't asked.

"He's studied us, me. He knows my rhetoric for this tour. And since I just wrote it before we came, that means he's been around us the whole time."

"Or had someone recording your speeches."

Yeah. There was that possibility. Didn't change the outcome, but she liked the sound of it better than knowing that she was constantly being watched by some powerful bad guy with enough money that paying a thousand bucks for a smoke bomb didn't seem to faze him.

She stood up then. Stepping off the blanket, prepared to leave it for Thane's use for as long as he wanted to sit there. He stood almost immediately. "Where you going?" he asked, for the first time that weekend.

"Inside, I have a hell of a lot of work to do tonight, since I'm out with the old and will be expected to have new by the time I step onstage in the morning. Thankfully I've already got the most time-consuming part down pat—the research. The rest will come. It always does."

She'd go onstage without a scripted speech if she had to. Wasn't like she hadn't done so hundreds of times in the past.

And if Thane thought that his news was going to stop her, she needed him to know right then and there that he was wrong. She wasn't up for any mental hedging that night. And didn't want to wake up to it in the morning, either.

To that end, she said, "It's clear that he's out to taint my message, Thane. Not to hurt me." Although rotting two of the main boards in the middle of the stage...

Overzealous worker, not intent. And there was still a chance that the rotted stage board was the result of disgruntled citizens who'd used SML's outside rally to prove a point at home.

"I was just going to ask what you wanted for dinner. Since you cooked the other two nights."

She didn't feel much like eating. "I only reheated last night," she told him, and then, in a rare moment of letting down her guard said, "Whatever you want to make is fine," and walked inside ahead of him, continuing to her room without a pause or even a backward glance.

Giving him total control of a situation that directly affected her.

And being at peace, too.

Chapter 8

Thane made meatloaf. Then he chopped up a plethora of fresh vegetables, including a couple kinds of lettuce, mixed it all with chopped meatloaf in a bowl, added his mixture of barbecue sauce and ranch dressing, tossed it well, and put a healthy amount of the mixture in a single serving bowl, with wheat crackers lining the entire thing. With silverware rolled into a napkin under his arm, and a glass of wine in his free hand, he carried everything back to Stella's room. Tapping on her door with his elbow, he stood there with his load when she answered the knock.

"What you like is a working dinner," he said. Saw her look at the food in the bowl, watched as her eyes grew wide, and then just waited for her to unload him.

No way he was walking into her room. Not in a cottage on the beach with no one else around to hear them.

Seeming to understand, and agree with his assessment, she very quickly took his offerings, thanked him, and without meeting his gaze, shut her door.

Five minutes later, just after he sat down at the breakfast bar to eat his meatloaf, baked potato and tossed salad, his phone vibrated against the counter. Picking it up, he read

It's way better than anything I'd have come up with. You remembered. Thank you so much.

The text was probably the longest he'd ever received from her.

Welcome. He texted back and got to work with a hint of warmth hanging around with him. Telling himself that everything was going to be just fine.

But as they left the cottage Tuesday morning and headed to Fort Desmond, and the staging area set up a block from the beach, Thane wasn't comfortable in his skin. It was his job to think of every possible way things go wrong and bring financial disaster or a lawsuit down on his client. Which included keeping their star of the show safe while she was going about their business.

He just hadn't ever walked around with a permanent tightness in his gut while on the job. Not even when he'd been married to SML's star.

"I need to know you're taking the threats seriously, Stel," he said as he pulled into Fort Desmond. She'd had her nose in her laptop the entire drive in. Finalizing her new speech, he presumed.

"I'll keep my eye on the crowd, not just to assess I'm reaching them, and which facts or phrases seem to affect them more, but also for any hint of anyone watching me, but not listening. Someone who's intent not rapt. I'll pay close attention to the outskirts of the crowd, and the second I hear you say my name, I'm down on the ground," she repeated, verbatim, the list he'd sent to her, via email, the night before.

Settling his gut some.

"Extra security has been hired, at least for these next couple of stops. We're expecting larger crowds, and, if we're right, and if Big Money is behind the shooting and other potentially harmful pranks, we have to expect more to come."

He glanced over to see her watching him. And as he turned his attention quickly back to the road, was thankful to hear her, "I read that, too, and I truly appreciate all of the effort you're putting into making me feel safe while I do my job."

Okay. It wasn't about making her feel safe. But about her *being* safe. Thane didn't bother to make the distinction.

He knew there was no reason to waste his breath. Stella had worked things out in her mind in a way that suited her and nothing he had to say was going to change that.

Their years of living in a failing marriage had made that fact abundantly clear.

The new stage had sidewalls and a ceiling. No more bombs, smoke or otherwise, dropping from the sky. Stage occupants entered from steps up and through a door alcove built into the left side wall. Thane would remain in the alcove—with eyes on a monitor mounted to the wall showing him the crowd and front of the stage—while Stella was performing.

She felt good about the arrangements as they were shown to her. Took in all instructions. Found a huge positive in the fact that the newly purchased staging that was going to be traveling with them for the rest of the tour included ventilation, due to the closed in top and sides. Not only was she going to be out of direct sunlight, she could move around the stage in her pants and jacket without sweating up a storm.

Thane and the law enforcement strategists he had

working with him—including Doug—had suggested a complete change-up in the format of the rallies. Something that would vary, with each rally from there on out. And into the future, too, based on a conversation Amelia and Thane had had while Stella had been standing right there.

She listened. Paid attention to everything that involved her. And spent the rest of the time gearing her mind up for her newly vamped presentation—to be given in three parts, instead of one. And in a different order in every city in which she appeared going forward.

Smart moves, actually. Not just for security purposes, but for the success of her content delivery. While she was a firm believer in keeping the messaging consistent from appearance to appearance to help solidify the points she was there to impart, it occurred to her that freshness would perhaps bring more followers to the tour. Who then were on their own socials. Which would then spread the word farther, wider.

Her job wasn't so much one of reiterating the message with energy every single time, as it was to use her energy to accrue those who'd jump on board with her and grow her content with completely new and different kinds of audiences every day.

Eager to get to work, she stood in the small alcove with Thane, feeling his heat, and bobbing her foot. "You nervous?" he asked as they watched Amelia open the event.

"No." Not about the rally, at any rate. Standing so close to him every day from there on out, smelling his cologne, was a challenge she didn't need.

The opening responsibilities had always fallen on Stella. With the new regime, instead of opening the event with her energy to get things started, she was going on second, briefly. Then again in the middle, and she was last up, too. The final call for people to reach into their bank accounts and also head out to their socials to save marine life.

Amelia and a couple of other SML employees would do their usual stints explaining the organization and sharing recent statistics and successes, as well as ways others could get involved.

She was antsy to get out there, to pump up the atmosphere before those already gathered wandered off. And to bring in all the passersby, too. Raising and maintaining crowd levels was one of her most sought-after skills.

Standing so close to her ex-husband that she could practically feel every breath he took was not something she excelled at. She wasn't the one who'd wanted the divorce.

Would still be married to the man if he hadn't left.

Not that she blamed him. She didn't. At all. To the contrary, the second he'd mentioned divorce, she'd done everything she could to make his way easy for him. After all the fights that her being herself had brought on, she'd figured she'd owed him every bit of help he could get to be free of her.

Less than thirty seconds after Amelia picked up the mic and went on, the woman looked toward Thane and Stella, her gaze wide and unsettled, and, figuring the woman had forgotten the lines she'd been repeating for the past week, on cue, Stella grabbed the backup mic and skipped onto the stage, nudging Amelia out of the way playfully, as though rehearsed, and ramped up the crowd.

She was ad-libbing. Following very little of the script she'd written for herself. But she knew her stuff and went naturally into what she did best. Speaking out against something that hurt her heart. Glorious and innocent creatures being tortured alive by people who were unaware of the suffering caused by their striving for advancement and riches.

The one message she took to many of her rallies was forefront in her mind. There were better ways...

To do so many things.

She worked like an automaton. Scanning the crowd as Thane had instructed. Happily recognizing many of her followers in the rapidly growing audience.

And she fought distraction, too. A couple of glances side-stage had shown her Amelia's back as Thane escorted the woman offstage.

He returned almost immediately, but with one of Amelia's employees at his side, not the woman who'd been meant to take the stage just a couple of minutes after Stella's first appearance.

When he caught Stella's eye as she crossed the stage as part of her performance, to lean into the crowd on the other side, he nodded. Telling her, she assumed, to continue as planned.

She finished her spiel. Left the stage with a crowd chanting "We care" over and over, and as soon as she was within hearing of Thane asked, "What happened? Where's Amelia?"

"You feel okay?" he answered with a question of his own.

"Of course. Where's Amelia?" She heard the SML facts being spouted on stage, with half her attention. Had to listen for her cue to reenter the crowd's view. But needed to know what danger she might be facing, too.

"The hospital," Thane told her, and Stella's heart started to thud. "It's okay," he said then. "She's fine. Just had a skin reaction on her hand."

One last factoid from the woman onstage and Stella would be up again. "Reaction to what?"

Thane shook his head. "Don't know yet." With a last glance at him, Stella nodded, took her long purposeful strides to center stage, and, determined not to let fear win, spent the next hour fighting hard for the whales. And her own mental and emotional health, too.

She would not be silenced.

On edge, Thane ushered Stella out the side-stage door and down the stairs the second her last bit was done. While she sometimes mingled with members of the crowd, with her own devout followers, and was introduced to new ones, he now put an arm around her waist and hurried her to their car with the bulletproof glass.

There'd been no sign of anyone carrying in the crowd. No indication that a shooter lurked nearby. He just wanted her out of there.

"Something happened to Amelia, didn't it?" she asked, but didn't demur even half a step as she hurried with him to the vehicle. Once inside, he started the engine and had them off the block where the rally had been held. With no one following them, that he could tell.

Overkill. He got it. Didn't give a damn.

To her credit, Stella kept an eye out around them, and let him concentrate on the road. Until they were heading out of Fort Desmond to the hotel an hour away, in Brightwater, where they'd be staying for the night. She had to be onstage there at ten in the morning.

"What happened back there?" she asked once he'd put on cruise control and relaxed a muscle or two.

He kept his eyes on the road, his words succinct, as he said, "Amelia's mic had a substance on it that made her skin burn on contact. By the time she made it to the hospital her entire palm was covered in hives."

Stella didn't outwardly react. But then, he hadn't expected her to. She'd barely blinked when he'd told her he wanted a divorce. The woman had learned young how to hide every hint of real feeling. Something for which he had a new appreciation, and a boatload of compassion, too.

Something that still pissed the hell out of him, but his anger was no longer leveled at her. Not even a little bit.

"Do they know what it is?"

"Not yet, but the local FBI forensic team was called in, and they have a suspicion based on the odor and symptoms."

"And?"

"Phosgene oxime. It's a manmade chemical that was developed in 1929 to be used exclusively for warfare, but was never put into service."

Stella's gaze shot toward him then. "Amelia's going to die?" she asked with obvious difficulty. Her horrified tone, and lack of air helped calm him a bit. She had to understand the extreme seriousness of the opposition they were facing.

"No," he told her then. "She's going to be fine. Her clothes have already been destroyed, and she's been thoroughly cleaned with soap and water. There was only a small trace of whatever it was on the mic she was holding, which has also been destroyed. When she came offstage, we thought she was having an allergic reaction to something, or we'd have stopped the rally immediately," he added. "I just heard, as you were finishing up what we were likely facing."

She nodded then. Turned her gaze back toward the windshield. And something drove him to keep going with the day's event. To cram every detail into her so that she had to face what she was taking on. If she was going to choose to continue on the tour.

"Within the next day or so it's expected that all her skin that came in contact with the chemical will die. It could take weeks, or even months for her hand to be back to normal…"

She nodded. Nothing more.

And he pushed further. "Had she inhaled the stuff, which could easily have happened based on how close the mic was to her mouth, she could be facing lifelong respiratory issues."

"But they're sure that she didn't," Stella said, more statement than question. Not moving at all. Not even to run fingers through the mass of sexy red-gold hair on her head. Yet she effervesced energy, strength, determination. By doing nothing at all.

Like she was some kind of wizard.

It was no wonder he couldn't get her out from under his skin. As though he'd inhaled her, and she was his lifelong affliction…

"They're sure that there wasn't enough of the stuff on the mic to have made it that far," he told her. And knew before she even opened her mouth that she'd put two and two together.

"It was another warning," she said.

He nodded. There was no point in trying to temper denial with potential dangers ahead. But added, "One with much more serious impact."

Stella bit her bottom lip briefly. Such a small move he wasn't even sure he'd seen it. And then she just sat. A picture of calm.

Leaving Thane frustrated, filled with concern about

going forward with the tour, and somewhat amazed and impressed by the formidable woman a ten-year-old girl had produced all on her own.

The chemical warfare had been meant for her. Stella didn't need the words spelled out or spoken aloud for her to know what Thane wasn't bothering to point out to her.

All their previous rallies—pretty much all the rallies she'd done in the past few years—always started out with her onstage briefly at the beginning, igniting energy in the crowd for what was to come.

Amelia had picked up the mic that Stella would have been using had the day gone as the others before them.

So she'd buy a pair of thin, black leather gloves and wear them onstage from that point forward. The opposition, Big Money, as she was thinking of them at that point, was too smart to resort to actual physical harm.

"That first day, the bullet that wasn't meant to have hit me, it was still a bullet," she said aloud, voicing a train of thought she'd had the night before. "With immediate potential to kill. But we know now who shot the gun, and we know his motive. These other mishaps, they're designed to disrupt, not to maim. Different MO. Different source. Possibly spurred on by the initial incident, but otherwise unrelated."

Thane gave a short nod of acknowledgment. Not looking at all pleased that she'd drawn the obvious conclusion. Even though he had to have known she would.

"Big Money is paying people large amounts to risk being arrested for misdemeanors, targeting me, because without me, this tour of rallies will slowly dwindle and suffocate."

"Use of phosgene oxime is not a misdemeanor crime,"

Thane told her, with a quick glance in her direction. She met that gaze, briefly, because she'd been watching him. And ended up paying for her weakness with a jab to her midsection at the conflicted look in those hazel eyes.

"Fort Desmond is a military town formed around large army and navy bases. Places where war crimes are discussed, researched, and they're the sites of experimental development, too. I'm guessing Big Money chose an overzealous lowlife with some form of access to dangerous chemicals for today's perp."

She could tell by the set of Thane's jaw that he couldn't argue her point.

And folding her hands in her lap, Stella figured her work was done for the moment. They were under advisement. Were taking precautions. Their opponent was out to sabotage rallies, to stop their message, not to splinter lives apart.

It wasn't personal.

They wanted to silence her message, not kill *her*.

And unfortunately for them, SML had hired the one person in the world who couldn't be silenced.

Chapter 9

The woman was smart, beautiful, admirable in her dedication and determination. And about as infuriating, maddening, and worrisome as anyone Thane had ever met.

Over the next couple of days, the next couple of hotel rooms with adjoining rooms, the next couple of tour stops, he waited tensely for the next attack.

He needed the tour done and Stella out of his daily life. He needed her safe, more. The light she offered the world was priceless. And in his universe, it had a tendency to blindside him.

Somehow, over the upcoming couple of weeks, if he had to stay awake 24/7, he had to find a way to see everything that was coming before it was too late to protect Stella from it.

He'd had downloads of camera feed sent to him from every stop on the tour and was slowly scanning every face in every crowd. Much of what had made him a successful attorney was the time he spent scouring every detail of every case to find the one tiny piece that tipped the scale in the favor of his client.

This time, instead of going for the win in court, he was out to save his ex-wife's life. And secure her ability to do her life's work, too. Because the more time he spent with her, observing more than interacting, the more he understood just how vital her ability—not only to speak out, but to effect positive change by doing so—was to her very existence.

Didn't make her any easier to live with, but, other than those weeks on tour, he didn't have to live with her anymore.

They'd had confirmation that the substance that had created such immediate excruciating pain in Amelia's right hand had been phosgene oxime. The PR director was fine, still on tour, with her right hand wrapped. Federal investigators had taken over the case, gravely concerned as to how anyone had sourced the potentially deadly chemical that had never been put into service. Thane hoped their investigation gave a break in the rally cases. Leading all the local law enforcement agencies to what he believed was one source.

And in the meantime, every day Stella got up and did great work. With the highest energy. And in the hours afterward, time allowing, she visited the hotel's fitness rooms—with Thane right there trying not to notice her body as he kept a close watch on her. After the night of giving him that very brief insight to the woman who lived completely alone inside her, she'd opted for dinner in her room. Saying she was working. And over those next few days, when he heard completely different deliveries with new facts and anecdotes pointing to the same message, he understood that she wasn't just trying to avoid him. The new regime was taking a lot more out of her than she'd signed on for.

The greatest part of Wednesday and Thursday's rallies was that, other than a couple of avid hecklers—both of whom appeared both days in both cities—there'd been no sign of any foul play at all. And Stella had taken on the loudmouthed and rude naysayers like the professional she was. Engaging with them when it fit her delivery. Calmly, and factually putting them in their places, and then ignoring them, upping the volume of her microphone so that she could be heard over them, and continuing as if they weren't there.

In those two days, she'd managed to raise more money for SML than the last four rallies combined.

As he stood in what he'd started to think of as "his" small alcove side-stage on Friday afternoon, watching Stella, in lightweight brown pants and matching long-sleeved short jacket over a silky tank kind of thing, he couldn't help a bit of a smile. It went along with the pride swelling within him. The woman was one of a kind. A dynamo. It was no wonder she'd hooked him at such a young age.

And too bad that neither of them had been mature enough, or in possession of enough foresight, to realize that they were meant to be friends, not spouses.

She'd just reentered the stage for her main gig, was walking with her entire body into every movement, keeping beat to each syllable with her steps, drawing emphasis to the words she was calling out, "Is everybody readyyy?" And he found himself nodding like a groupie from the sidelines.

Until everything stopped. A split second of nothing. Stella's voice, her movement, frozen in place onstage. Thane's breathing, his heart, frozen inside him. The second passed, and as he heard her mic drop to the floor, he was already rushing forward. Noted, somewhere in an alternate consciousness, that she was still standing.

Déjà vu and alarm choked him as she looked toward

her right arm. Above the hand that had once again been able to hold her microphone. And then glanced in his direction.

When he saw the tears in her eyes, he pulled his gun out of the holster he'd started wearing. Had it in his hand as he wrapped that arm around her and led her offstage.

"I think I'm okay," she said, her voice only slightly shaky as Amelia came into the alcove from outside. Looking at the PR director, she said, "Cover me, I think I can get back out there."

That's when Thane caught a glimpse of her right arm. And knew a rage he'd never felt before. The sleeve of her jacket was stained once again. Bright red. He shook his head at Amelia, bent to lift Stella to run her to the ambulance that, after recent events, had become part of the protocol behind the stage for every rally.

"No," Stella said, her tone firm. A break from the previous event. Enough that she got both his and Amelia's attention. "It hurt like hell. I thought I was going to throw up for a second there, but I'm fine. It's not numb, by any means. It still hurts. But look." She nodded her head toward the stained jacket. "No bullet hole." And pulled her jacket down, showed them both the lack of red coloring on the inside of her sleeve.

Noticing then that the red stain wasn't seeping, or growing, Thane took a whiff of the soiled jacket arm. "It's paint," he said.

With a nod toward Thane, Amelia went out to pick up the dropped mic, and as Stella righted her jacket on her arm, Thane heard the PR director say, "And that right there, folks, is why we need your support. Our girl is fine and will be back out shortly. The paintball prank was uncalled for, an insult, and proof that our message is a powerful one, too."

Glancing at Thane, Stella said, "I trained her well."

"Stel…" Thane's voice held warning. She had to stop. To realize that she was only inviting more wrath to come down on her head, her person, causing escalation, if she didn't let go of just the one cause.

"We'll talk afterward," she said to him, as, with her first step back out onto the stage, the roar of the crowd, the cheering, drowned out anything else he might have said.

Stella was sweating as she came offstage. Not all that unusual, especially with an afternoon rally in Florida. But she had a feeling it wasn't just the heat and exertion causing her body to heat up. Her arm was throbbing worse than it had the first day she'd been shot.

Her fault, she was sure. To prove that the prank early in the rally hadn't mattered at all, she'd forced herself to use her right hand to hold the mic for her entire performance. Walking down the steps from the stage with Thane glued beside her, she wanted nothing more than to bear the weight of her injured limb with her left hand. Just to give the muscles a break.

She didn't, of course. No way she could show such a weakness to Thane. Her ex needed no more fodder to use against her determination not to be cut from the tour. And she would rather be in pain than have to find more strength to fight against the man she'd fallen in love with the first time she'd seen him watching her at a protest on their college campus her freshman year.

Beyond that, in the larger scheme of things, a sore arm was a very small price to pay for the money they were raking in, and, even more valuable, the awareness being built, which was the main goal. Money just gave them means to reach that end. Educating the masses to save the lives of innocent creatures that were unable to fight for themselves against the degradations being thrust upon them.

Amelia, at Stella's behest, was contacting local news sources in every city they were in that involved a mishap, which was giving them more airtime, reaching the most affected audiences—and therefore the most powerful—in addition to the social buzz her hashtags were building.

The off-duty officer guarding the area behind the stage, most critically their car, stepped aside as she and Thane approached, splitting up as he went for his door and she hers.

The officer was really overkill. A money waste. But she didn't say so aloud. She already knew the response she'd get. It was either spend the money on security or Thane would advise his client to end SML's contract with Stella due to safety concerns.

One of the disclaimers in the agreement that Stella had signed. Which Thane knew better than anyone since he'd written the damned thing.

Good for his client. And actually for her, too, were she to decide that her life was in too much danger, and SML didn't want to let her off the tour.

Neither of which was going to happen. But then Thane's job was to prevent fallout from the unseen, most of which never materialized.

Watching his stoic facial expressions as he drove them off-site and away from the venue, Stella didn't envy him his job. She had enough trouble keeping real-life terrors at bay and hadn't ever really stopped to think about having to not only live with, but conjure up, the ones that didn't happen. It would be like walking into a horror movie every minute of every day.

Or what she imagined a horror movie to be. She'd never actually seen one. Real-life terror attacks, and all...

"I'm driving to Charmaine but will not be giving the go-ahead on tomorrow's rally until after I've seen the full report on today's incident." Thane spoke with his focal attention right where it had been since they'd climbed in the car. In front of them, with frequent glances at all mirrors, too.

Poor, sweet, hugely successful man. Having to live like that. Never just being able to let go and relax.

Something she hadn't really noticed during the years that they were married. She'd always felt as though her schedule, her need to put work first, had been the reason they'd never had time for vacations. Or even two days of peace on a stretch of private beach.

Pushing the train of thought away, she switched back to what he'd just said. "I assumed as much." She offered what she hoped was a little moment of peace for him. She didn't fight for the sake of fighting.

And she could see sense, too.

Glancing over at him, wishing she could run a hand down the tense muscles of his face, maybe massage the shoulders for a second, she saw the stern set of his chin when he said, "I don't think it's a mistake that that pellet, or whatever it was, hit you in the exact spot you were shot."

Yeah, she'd already been there. "Way too much of a coincidence, huh?" she noted with a nod. Then added, "But still, a paint ball? Other than momentary distress, and probably a hoped-for cancellation due to fear, it's just more vandalism. Misdemeanor, not criminal activity. Fits the pattern."

He turned onto the highway that would lead them the twenty miles to Charmaine. Then, still without glancing her way, said, "We might not be able to prove malice, but there's no doubt in my mind it was there, Stel."

She nodded. "I'm pissing them off." She told him what she'd already concluded. "Which means I'm doing my job. I just have to stay my course."

"And hope that they don't get desperate enough to up their game? To make last week's shooting a planned event in the future?"

Fear rent a jagged tear inside her and cemented the vulnerable injury to her emotional cortex. "That guy's going to jail all on his own," Stella said, putting out her take on what would happen, silently cussing out fear and reminding it that it would not defeat her. Reminding herself. "Big Money is just out to play dirty pool in protesting, not to wipe me off the earth. What would be the point? There are plenty of other me's out there. And more being born and bred every single day." Her socials were full of them.

When Thane took a deep breath and just continued to drive, she knew she'd won the round. But didn't feel victorious for having disappointed him once again.

Thane didn't ask for a beach view room. It was more expensive, and the hotel stay was on SML's dime. But when he was told it was either that or he and Stella wouldn't have adjoining rooms, he'd immediately taken the only available, albeit more expensive option.

And was glad he had when Stella called to him through the mostly closed doors between them shortly after check-in. "Open your curtains, Thane. The view is lovely. A little bit like being back at the cottage."

She'd been maliciously targeted onstage that afternoon—only pure evil would deliberately aim for a vulnerable wound—and she was focusing on a view?

But then, that was Stella. Pressing forward. Always pressing forward.

"Seriously, open your curtains," she said, sounding closer, and he looked up to see her head peeking around the door.

He did as he was asked. He'd always tried to please her when he could. Probably because there were so many times when he couldn't. And stopped for a second to take in the picturesque scene before him. The beach that stretched for miles, the ocean that went on forever. And a sunset that was shining a halo across the water and creating a glistening diamond effect on the beach.

He heard Stella's footsteps fall lightly on the carpet just before she said, "Wow, your view is twice as spectacular as mine. We're at the corner of the building and my view is half blocked by a brick wall."

Glancing at her automatically, he nearly lost his thought processes when he saw the lightness in her features, the smile on her face, the wide eyes, as she gazed outward. But caught himself just in time, taking a step away from her to open the curtains wider. And maintaining the new distance between them afterward.

He couldn't help another glance at her face, though, as her gaze moved slightly, seeming to take in every inch of the scene below. In that moment, she almost looked… happy. Reminding him of their wedding night. For that brief time after their wedding, Stella had seemed to shed the weight she carried so faithfully on her shoulders.

She'd been more peaceful at the cottage over the weekend, too.

And he heard himself say, "Why don't we have dinner in here, then?" before he'd thought through the ramifications of such an offer.

For a second that day, when she'd frozen onstage, looking so ill, he'd thought he'd lost her. That she was about to collapse down to her death.

And the past few days, watching her work out in those damned revealing clothes...

There was only so much a man could take without making a mistake. Or a fool of himself. One and the same, really.

Stella's gaze turned slowly toward him. He waited for her to rescue them from the situation he'd unthinkingly created. And heard her say, "Okay."

He nodded. "I'll get it ordered, then. What sounds good?"

"Pizza."

She wanted pizza. A pie they'd have to share. Which meant sitting closely...

"Can you give me an hour or so?" she asked, moving back toward the door leading into her room. "I need to get out on my socials, before rumors about the rally get out of control. As long as I'm out there as usual, folks will relax. And will point others in my direction if they come upon false rumors."

She was thinking about work. As he should be. As he would be. "Of course," he told her, hauling out his computer before she'd even had a chance to make it out of sight.

And dinner together? The perfect time to go over whatever incident reports he had by then regarding the day's violence. And to tell her that it had been one too many attacks and he was shutting down her participation in the event.

He didn't need to see the reports. He'd already made up his mind on the drive to Charmaine. No matter how angry she was with him for quieting her voice just this once, he was not going to be a part of her risking her life one more time.

Period and the end.

Chapter 10

Thane's short rap on her door signaled the arrival of their pizza. Stella knew the second she saw him putting the pizza box down on the small table between two chairs in front of the window that she was about to lose her appetite.

The ham and onion scents wafting through the room smelled delicious, but one glance at Thane's terse expression and her stomach tightened. Leaving no room for food.

She sat because her knees felt suddenly weak. He knew something more than he'd known when she'd left the hour before. And she wasn't going to like it.

He'd poured a couple of glasses of wine.

She was going to not like what was coming a whole lot.

The logical first move was to take a sip of the wine. To savor it. Focusing on nectar on her tongue made more sense than panicking over the unknown.

Or whatever Thane had imagined could be.

He offered her the first piece of pizza. She forced herself to take a bite. To chew. And swallow. The food landed like lead in her stomach, muscles clenching around it. Wine was better. Went down easier. Soothed her.

Thane ate a full piece. Talked about how pristine the beach looked. And a few of the people on it. She saw the water beyond. A big ship in the distance. And hurt some more as she considered the marine life that was disrupted by just that one vessel. Was she fighting a lost cause? For every convert, there'd be a million more to educate. Shipping was big business. They'd never win.

But it wasn't just the shipping. That wasn't even the worst of it. The seismic air guns, used to find oil and other minerals...there were other ways. They weren't going to be able to save everyone, but even if they saved some...

She took another bite of pizza. She couldn't let them rob her of her hope. Steal her faith that she was using her talent to make the world a better place. That speaking truth helped people. She swallowed, bit, chewed, and swallowed some more.

They were trying to silence her again. To force her to let bad win. She couldn't let anyone coerce her into silence. To hiding the truth like it was some dirty secret. She would not pretend she didn't know what she knew and let evil rule the world.

She was not going to turn her back on vulnerable lives who couldn't fight for themselves...

"The paint ball was shot from a rudimentary contraption that resembled a mortar." Thane's changed tone got her full attention. In one breath he'd gone from talking about the length of the leash on a dog bounding up the beach, to the death knell.

"A homemade device?" she homed in on the piece that fell right in line with the theories they'd been working on. Amateurs out to protest a protest by dirty means. Without lethal intent.

"Clearly." Thane didn't try to embellish the point, and she relaxed some. Her read on him of doom and gloom on the way had been off? She was fully on board with being wrong and picked up a second piece of pizza. Looking out at the beach and enjoying the view.

Finding peace. And strength, too. As though the powerful body of water before her was telling her it was on her side. That fighting was the right thing for her to do. That it needed her. And appreciated her efforts on its behalf.

"It was shot from an ordinary plumbing pipe that could have been purchased from pretty much any hardware store in the US, or ordered online. They believe, based on the gases determined to be on the fuse, that the fuse was lit by a flame from an even more common over-the-counter lighter. The kind that are for sale at the checkouts of most convenience stores, and at big-box stores as well. There'd have been a 'pfft' sound, but with the noise eruption you'd just elicited from the crowd, it's unlikely that anyone heard it."

So an amateur with impeccable timing. And, she conceded silently, most likely a well-planned exact point of execution.

"Thing is, mortars don't generally give exact aim," Thane continued. "Tells me this guy is no amateur when it comes to shooting. More likely he's got sniper training."

Fear clutched her with one word. Invading her entire being, the emotion slid through her like a snake, spewing its venom everywhere. She stilled. Recognizing the onset. Her mind blanked, and then hardened. She would not become the victim of an emotion that had been trying to derail her life since she was ten years old.

And she fought back. With realism. "It could also be that he really did just get lucky," she said first. Almost cringing at the weakness of her response. Believing that fate had allowed someone up to no good to hit an exact target by accident made very little sense.

"The pipe was left on a bench not far from the rally site, but not within aim of the stage. It was wiped clean. And with it being so ordinary, there's no real way to trace it. They're looking at camera footage to try to find a face in the crowd within line of fire of your location on the stage, and compare it to local shops, but so far have no luck with any kind of proof of anything."

"They've talked to everyone on camera at the rally who was within line of fire?" The question was more on top of things, but still elementary.

His "Of course" solidified the judgment she'd just placed on herself.

If she was going to win, she had to be better. Faster. Which meant blocking fear so she could think rationally.

She knew how. Had been implementing the practice since she was too young to even realize what she was doing.

Thane had turned, his gaze—and she was sure, his full attention—was all on her. Stella felt as though her face was getting warm under that look. But refused to turn to block the sensation with a steely gaze. Not yet trusting herself to succeed, she continued to stare at the ocean. Thane's choice of room. His invitation to have dinner in front of the very mass, the beings within it, for which she was fighting.

A sign?

A sign.

Given to her by Thane's own hand. Knowingly or not. Didn't matter.

Her cause was critical. Her voice was needed.

"Today's prank, such as it was, upped the game, Stel. The act was cruel, the message direct. You aren't taking their 'advice' and quitting. And they're letting you know they're going to continue to come at you, harder, until you do."

"Or until someone slips up, as people do, they get caught, and the millions of various species of marine life gain more attention. And hopefully, by human action and reaction, find some relief."

"Today's point-blank message has Doug and others looking back at the shooting that first day. Hitting you in the exact same spot a second time… It's looking more like you taking that bullet was purposeful from the beginning."

She had the last word. Encased in her walls, she figured it was time to use it. Shaking her head, she said, "Killing me doesn't do anything but bring sympathy to SML," she said. "They'll just hire another activist to take up where I left off." She paused, then said, "The message I've received from them is that I have to be stronger than the fear they're trying to instill in me. They don't want me gone. They want me off my game. Ineffective. And they aren't going to win, Thane. They aren't going to do that to me."

She looked over then. Saw him bow his head. Reached for the second piece of pizza she'd dropped back into the box at some point.

And heard him say, "Then you leave me no choice but to tell SML that having you on tour is a liability that could bankrupt them."

Stella dropped the ham, cheese, and onion-slathered cooked dough, face down on the floor.

Thane's evening was not going well. In fact, it had stopped going at all. Staring at the door Stella had just closed firmly between their two rooms, he got her silent message loud and clear. If he was taking her off the tour, there was no longer any need for her to kowtow to his wishes.

He wouldn't be surprised to find her changing rooms, or even hotels. And felt worse about that than he had about telling her that she was heading home. Part of him had actually hoped that she'd be at least a little bit relieved.

He'd seen her face when she'd come offstage that afternoon—had been reliving the sight over and over ever since—and he knew for a fact that she'd been in debilitating pain, at least at first. And that she'd been severely frightened, too.

He'd wanted her to continue under his protection details until she was home. Where Doug was set to take over until they knew more about the attacks against her.

Knowing that she was doing exactly the opposite, that she'd walked out on him and any plans he had in place to keep her safe, had him pacing back and forth from bathroom to window as he stopped now and then to check the private, secure messaging he had going on with Doug and others from local Florida precincts who had opted to join in the investigation of a serial vandalizing movement, with possible deadly future plans in the works.

The idea was to shut down what Stella was calling Big Money, before she, or anyone else representing Save Marine Life, ended up hurt far worse than a bullet in the arm or painful hives on the hand. Maybe even dead. Every member of the makeshift team agreed that the day's escalation marked a serious turn for the perpetrators. One that could not be ignored.

And yet, with all the top-rated investigators and state-of-the-art forensic help, no one had a clue as to the identity of Stella's Big Money. Which told them that whoever was behind the attacks was no amateur.

Discounting such a force would not be wise. And could be catastrophic.

And there he stood, over a week after the initial shooting, and not even a small step closer to shutting the perp down before he wreaked havoc from which they'd never recover.

Logic, built on facts, had brought every professional on their unofficial team to the same singular conclusion. A fact that had come to the fore on the messaging board just before the pizza had arrived.

He'd been given one stern suggestion, coated with a heavy dose of warning. His one goal had to be to keep Stella close, with all security measures in place until she was back in North Haven and under Doug's watch.

There'd be no reason to go after her there. Not if it became known on her socials that she was done with SML. Which had been the other thing he'd had on his agenda to tell her over dinner.

Instead, he'd bet the small fortune he'd amassed over the years on her being online right then, spouting rhetoric that would bring more people than ever to the SML cause. Something about being forced off the tour. With a call to action to follow her home and continue to fight with SML to save marine life.

The thought drove him immediately to the phone. Pushing speed dial, he waited for the Save Marine Life's executive director to pick up. Lifted his polished shoe to the edge of the windowsill, tapping his foot. Hard. Two rings. Then three.

He was their attorney. James Morrison always picked up on the first ring.

The guy did have personal moments. He took showers. Could be...

His phone vibrated a text while he waited, and glancing at his smart watch, he saw James's name come up.

Then read the text. On with Amelia. Standby.

Stella's call with Amelia hadn't gone as expected. There'd been no planning for next steps that Stella would do from home. No strategizing the ways they were going to use current circumstances to raise not only more awareness, but a much larger sense of outrage for their cause.

The woman had not known anything about Stella leaving the tour. Beyond that, she'd told Stella to hang tight before she disseminated any information herself.

Holding tight was not one of Stella's strong points. She paced. Looking out at her small piece of ocean view. Figuring that it mirrored her present circumstances. They could take away her broad access, but they couldn't stop her from proselytizing through her own channels.

And Thane?

Tears sprang to her eyes as images of his face flooded her mind's eye. Not just her most recent view of him, but flashes from over the years. The night he'd shocked her by asking her to marry him. His hungry look when he was lying over her. A smile. Fear in his eyes when he'd reached her the week before. She didn't remember a lot about the seconds after the shooting, except his face…

Blinking, shaking her head, she grabbed herself by the arms, and winced when her left hand clasped around her right upper arm.

She'd known it was a mistake to have him on tour. The SML board had outvoted her.

Throwing her phone to the bed, she stripped off her jacket. Glanced as best she could at the harm. Dissatisfied with herself, she went to the bathroom, turning on the light and putting a hip on the counter so she could get a close look at the scar she'd be carrying, in some form, for the rest of her life.

One of the few that were visible. But joining so many more. The wound was still closed. She'd known that from any lack of bleeding.

But the entire area around it had an almost baseball-sized bruise forming.

No wonder she was…

A hard rap sounded on the door between her room and Thane's, interrupting Stella's self-assessment. Hurrying back to the jacket in her room, she was struggling to get her right hand back into the sleeve—made more difficult by the sense of panic Thane's interruption had instilled in her—when she heard, "Stella, open up."

He did not sound pleased. Or even a little bit polite.

She could count on one hand the number of times Thane had all out lost his temper with her. And had a feeling another one of those rare moments was coming right at her.

Which calmed her. Slowed her down enough to get both arms into her jacket and walk to the door. Unlocking it, she pulled it open and met his steely gaze with one of her own.

Then…nothing.

He didn't say a word, just stood there so angry he seemed to be shaking with it.

At her? Or…

Eyes suddenly wide with fear, she asked, "What? Something happened. Or you found out…what? Tell me, Thane don't just stand there. It's rude. And, frankly, unkind as well as bordering on torturous."

Her words spewed forth as quickly as they came to her.

He had the upper hand. Had already taken away her right to be onstage in the morning to help save marine life. But if he thought she was going to shut up then he didn't know her nearly as well as she'd thought...

He'd opened his mouth. Closed it. His expression changing as he watched her. And then, holding up the opened text app on his phone, shoved it close enough to her face for her to read. *If it comes to you or her, we have to go with her. Work this out.*

Her glance jumped quickly to the number from which the text had come.

Eyes widening, in shock without fear, for once, she stared at him open-mouthed. Until she felt the effects of his steely glare penetrating her again.

Shaking her head, she backed up. "Wait a minute, you think I had something to do with that? Well, I mean, of course I did, in that they apparently really value the job I'm doing, but going to them? Over your head? No way, Thane."

She was about to say that it wasn't her way, but, of course, it was. Given the right circumstances. Taking another step back, she shook her head again. "Not this time, Thane. All I did was call Amelia to strategize my work from home. I don't care that I won't get paid or be an official spokesperson. I can still use my socials and..."

A sharp shake of his head, his sudden frown, cut off whatever had been about to come next. "You didn't tell them you wanted to stay?" he asked her, his gaze intent.

As though drilling into her the seriousness of any attempt she'd make to lie to him. "I most certainly did not. I actually thought it was already a done deal. I figured you had exit paperwork for me to sign, except I stomped out. I don't ever lie to you, Thane."

He had to at least agree with that point.

When he nodded, the world started to right itself a bit again. Her ex-husband might not still be in love with her, but he knew her better than anyone else did. Even her sisters. There'd been too many lies living between her and Kara and Melanie for too many years. Lies bred lies. Or, in her case, hiding her truths from them...

"You didn't tell them that you'd work for free? Or agree to sign a disclaimer that they wouldn't be financially liable if anything happened to you?"

Both things she'd done in the past, but for very different reasons. And different clients.

"I did not. I merely told Amelia that we needed to figure out next steps with me off the tour, ways to use the situation to our benefit..."

He nodded then. "I have to make a call," he told her, turning his back on her and pushing the door closed but for a crack.

Because...apparently, she was still under the jurisdiction of his orders.

"Thane?" She pushed open the door enough to stick her head through. "I'll sign that disclaimer, if you want to draw it up," she told him.

And when he frowned and rolled his eyes, she quickly pulled back into her own room.

And did a bit of a happy dance.

She had no idea what was going on. But she wasn't out. That was what mattered most to her.

That and...stopping mid-twirl...she gazed with stricken eyes toward her door again. Debating whether or not to butt in one more time. No matter how much it pissed off her ex.

Because...with all they'd been through over the past

couple of weeks, since even before she was shot, working together again…she didn't want it to come down to a choice between him and her.

The text had said to work this out. And that was what they had to do.

The order presented as surely, as definitively, as the ones that prevented her from not speaking out. She wasn't going to stop. But she didn't see herself going forward, either. Not in the current climate.

Unless Thane was right there with her.

Chapter 11

Count me out.

Thane typed the text. Hovered his thumb over the send icon. Then set his phone on the table that had held the pizza box not long ago. Sitting, he picked up the half-filled wineglass he'd left there, and, looking out at the softly lit beach, he sipped. Pricks of light bobbed in the distance, on the ocean.

He'd known working with Stella again was not a good idea. Had known it would come to a standoff. It hadn't taken a psychic to predict their future. Anyone with first-hand knowledge of the inner workings of their relationship would have immediately seen the foregone conclusion. Anyone...who was neither him nor Stella. Which was why he'd almost turned down the job when it had first been offered to him. He'd known she wouldn't.

Then everything had happened with Kara. And Stella had called him. No one else. Just him. She'd been devastated, having been told her baby sister had been murdered with the killer still on the loose, and she'd reached out to Thane.

He'd already known the gist of what was happening. Kara was his best friend's wife. And when Stella had asked him to come sit with her, he'd put the rest of his life on hold—his business—and been there within the hour.

Those two days together…he'd seen that the good between them was still there. And able to flourish because there was nothing else getting in the way. No expectations. No marriage. No house and life to share.

He'd been able to comfort her. She ate at his behest. Slept for a bit when he promised to stay in the room. They'd talked for hours, working through what they knew, coming to shared conclusions that had turned out to be frighteningly accurate.

And when she'd found out Kara was alive, she'd thrown her arms around him, held on, and sobbed.

He'd allowed extreme circumstances to convince him that he and Stella had turned a corner of some kind. That as long as there was nothing but friendship between them, they could do good work together, as they had back in college.

And there he sat, two weeks into the gig, right back where he'd been when he'd had to file for divorce. At the end of his tether.

Pushed away by Stella's determination. Didn't matter what he knew, or if he was right. Next to the passion and wholehearted belief she put into her work, his contribution faded. Was dispensable. Ultimately, his voice was silenced.

In the end, he'd seen that Stella's need to speak out on behalf of others drove her harder, meant more to her, than anything else.

Including him.

He didn't blame her. He never had. She was a very necessary and positive force in the world.

He just couldn't spend his life beating his head against a solid steel wall.

So what could he do? What did *he* need to do?

Reaching for his phone, Thane read the message he'd typed. Nodded.

And hit the delete key.

Stella was sitting at her computer. Ready to get back on her socials. She'd already been out before dinner to assure everyone that she was fine. To talk about the paintball incident. And the determination to not be silenced, or those in need would never survive. She'd rid herself of her jacket so the damned fabric quit rubbing against her arm. Reminding her how sore it was.

She was filled with verbiage to type and send.

She just needed to know where she stood before she sent it. Had to know what the next day was going to look like on tour.

Without Thane, she wasn't sure how she needed it to look to enable her to give her best work. Couldn't picture anything that felt right.

Make it work. The text had read. Speaking to Thane. Their boss had put the onus on him to make it work. But what did that mean?

And how in the hell was Thane expected to accomplish the feat?

They'd reached another impasse. Their last one had ended in divorce. That was how Thane made it work. He stepped away when her drive led her in directions counterproductive to his own. She didn't blame him. The man was a guru in his own field. Had won so many major cases he could pretty much write his own ticket. He didn't need SML's business.

And when he'd no longer needed their marriage, she'd let him go. He was no pushover, and no way was he supposed to be run down by the woman who loved him.

Funny how life had a way of coming full circle.

Over and over again.

So did she leave the tour? Everything inside her recoiled at the thought. If those who could fight for the underdogs backed down every time a bully tried to silence them, society would be a wasteland of greed and intimidation. She couldn't live with herself if she didn't stand up and speak out.

Yada, yada, yada. Her life. Instant replay.

Unless she found a way to play it differently. She was out of her chair so fast that it tipped backward against the bed. Pulling open the door between her room and Thane's she didn't think to announce herself, didn't even cross her mind that he might be indisposed in some way, she just barged in.

And then, her gaze on his back as he stood at the window, she marched right up and said, "I'll sign the waiver, and any others you think are necessary." It was the first concession that came to mind. One that spoke strictly to his interests as SML's lawyer. To his career.

Hands in his pockets, he didn't react. Taking his lack of flinching as a problem, she opened her mouth and started spewing forth thoughts as they came to her. "I'll follow every dictate you set forth. If your senses tell you that a venue is a particular death threat, I'll skip it. If you need me to wear bulletproof clothing, and to have a SWAT-style escort, even onstage, I'll comply."

He still hadn't moved. If he hadn't been standing, she'd have been checking to see if he was conscious.

"And...and... I'll sleep in an underground bunker,

spend every minute between appearances there…" She stopped, hearing the ridiculousness of how far she was reaching. Then added, "As long as it has internet connectivity." Because she could do everything she'd so randomly spit out. But had to be able to continue to do her life's calling. That was her only bottom line.

Thane spun around so quickly she jumped, her gaze zeroing in on the shimmering glow glaring from his hazel eyes. Saw an intensity she didn't recognize.

And then one she did as, with her heart hammering, he pulled her to him, his arm at her lower back, pressing her hips to his as his lips came down and covered her mouth.

Thane let Stella go almost as soon as their bodies touched. Her mouth came after his a second longer… slower to back away, but he didn't make anything of it. She'd been taken by complete surprise.

"What in the hell was that?" she asked, stepping back several paces.

Not only did he not blame her for doing so, he silently commended her. Heartily.

"I don't know," he told her honestly, running his hand through his hair. "I just had to shut you up and that's the only way that ever worked." He sighed. Then looked straight at her as he said, "It was inappropriate, and I apologize."

She nodded. Pressed her lips together. But held her ground.

Watching her, admiration swelled up inside him. Followed quickly by the frustration that always came with being closely involved with her.

"Maybe I was a bit dramatic there," she told him, "But I meant every word I said. I don't want to do this without you, Thane. I trust you. You're the best at what you do. And this kind of team thing you've managed to bring together with Doug and other local law enforcement here in Florida, it's the way to make this work. To speak out, and be able to let those who want to play dirty know that not only are they not going to win, they're going to pay for their actions."

With anyone else, he might have considered the idea that he was being played. Not with Stella. The upside to living with her stark, "blunt to the point of painful" honesty was that he could always trust her to tell him the truth.

And she deserved the same from him. "I want you home and safe. After what happened to Kara... I don't want the world to lose you, Stella."

He didn't want to know her voice had been snuffed out.

She nodded, her eyes glistening, and opened her mouth, but he held up a hand and shook his head. "I also realized that I let my own feelings as someone who's known you for so many years, whose best friend is your family, get in the way of my professional duties. It wasn't my place to say you were done. Nor was it the right call. SML's mission is to educate, to spread the word, and my job is to see that they be able to do that with as little fallout as possible. One of their main means of doing so is to hold in-person rallies. If you aren't out there, someone else will be."

All things that had already been brought forth. He'd just lost sight of what had to be a priority.

Her serious focus on him didn't change. There was no smile, no hint of gloating, or even of victory, as she asked, "Have you been in touch with James and Amelia?"

He nodded. And was a bit startled when he saw the relaxing of her muscles, the softening of her expression, and heard the relief in her voice as she said, "Thank God."

But not when, blinking, as though realizing how far she'd just let down her guard, she turned toward the door. She said, "Okay, I've lost a couple of hours here, and I need to get to work if we're going to have the biggest crowd possible in the morning."

That was when he caught sight of her arm. "Hold on a second," he said, reaching for her elbow.

Stopping, she glanced down, and then back up at him. "It's only a bruise."

"You should have put ice on it."

"I'll rig up something," she said, pulling at his hold on her as she tried to leave.

"Ten to twenty minutes, three to four times a day, for the first two days," he told her. "It'll not only help with the swelling, but the pain, too." And then he let her go.

He watched her leave a slightly larger crack than before in the door between their rooms, and reached for his wine.

He might not be able to coexist full-time in the same space—the same life—as the woman, but God, he wanted her. Physically.

In his bed. That night.

Why in the hell had he kissed her?

Talk about dumbass choices…

Up until the point where his lips had touched hers, he'd been pretty good at convincing himself that the occasional bouts of intense desire he'd been feeling for her on tour had been the result of muscle memory due to their proximity.

That brief, electrifying touch of her lips against his had shot that theory straight to hell.

Which meant, he not only had to use every ounce of his focus to keep her alive and well, but he was going to do have to do it with a hard-on.

* * *

He'd kissed her. What had that been about?

Stella threw the question aside, focusing on her computer instead as it came into view. Making a beeline for it. She had critical time to make up for. Hated that her socials had been quiet during crucial gathering stages. And holding ones, too. Her followers were always active immediately after and the night before, every rally.

The more they posted, the more their message got out into friends' feeds. Many of those who were local to Charmaine would see their posts. Statistically, and historically, some of those would join them at the rally. And some of those would become advocates.

Her computer had gone to sleep. She pushed the on button with an urgent finger.

He'd kissed her. Why the hell had he done that? Thane was the farthest thing from an impulsive man she'd ever known. It was part of the reason she'd fallen in love with him to begin with.

His stability had filled major gaps inside her.

Had she ever told him that?

Her screen flashed on and she scrolled and clicked to log in to the first of her six current social media platforms. She'd recorded the day's video before dinner and got that uploaded immediately. Clicking to promote the video for the most views for a one-day period. But didn't limit the area. The more clicks, the more advocates they could gain. Oceans existed all over the world. Not just in Florida.

Or the States.

His lips…he'd actually kissed her…had been like coming home. To the best place she'd ever been. Her happiest place. Where nothing but physical hunger, anticipation and sensory overload of ecstasy existed.

The beep of confirmation of her video uploading to the second site sounded. She typed a post to go with it. Hit Post. And then, on the same site, uploaded the video as a short.

She'd amassed over a thousand notifications on the platform, just since she'd been on earlier. Would have to get back to them after she finished her posts. Her interaction mattered. Her presence on all her platforms mattered more.

Had the kiss done anything for him? Had he felt *it*? Even a little bit? He'd ended it so abruptly. But she'd felt the pressure already burgeoning against her pelvis during the brief moment he'd pressed his body to hers.

Unless…had she done the pushing? She'd wanted to. Expected to. But…it could have been his hip. Or his jacket bunching up in the way.

It had all happened so fast, she might have imagined…

The next site loaded, and she clicked to log in. Glanced at notifications, thrilled to see almost two thousand of them, and quickly typed. Uploading photos Amelia had sent of Stella from the rally to go with the post.

She scrolled through private messages sent to her via the platform. Recognized a lot of the names. Some of the faces.

Including the kid who'd expressed concern for her welfare—at least that was how she'd taken his questions—at the little impromptu gathering she'd hosted in the hotel the previous week. The kid with the freckles and a nose that dominated his face. Stopping to respond to him, assuring him she was fine and would be out the next day as planned, she added a sentence about hoping she'd see him there, and hit Send.

Making a note to herself to tell Thane the young man,

Shawn was his name, was still "on tour" with her. While social media had a much larger reach than rallies, the in-person events touched people more deeply. Drew in the faithful. She celebrated every single time she saw someone from a rally become a follower.

Thane. The kiss. She wanted him to do it again.

No. No, she didn't. They didn't work as a couple. No way she could face going through the breakup again. The first time had stolen her joy for months.

She still didn't have it all back. Probably never would. She couldn't afford to lose any more.

And hurting him again would take it all. Maybe permanently the second time through.

Next platform. Post. And…before she could click away from it to view her notifications, there was already a comment.

Smart bitches take the hint.

She clicked immediately for a screenshot, then deleted the comment. And blocked the sender. Then, from the screenshot, grabbed the profile information and searched it.

The name was there. No profile photo. No followers.

Just someone wanting to harass her.

It wasn't the first time. Wouldn't be the last. Or even the last that week. Or that night. Came with the territory. Advocating always brought opposers. Always. Most particularly when she was on tour. Which was why she had to stay focused on what mattered most.

And forget about kissing the man who, with good reason, had divorced her.

Chapter 12

Thane sat straight up in bed. After lying there for nearly an hour, he knew why he hadn't been able to sleep. Grabbing the shirt that went with the silk pajama bottoms that Stella had bought him for Christmas one year—the pair that remained his favorite no matter how faded they'd grown—he slid his arms into the sleeves, and had a middle button closure completed by the time he tapped lightly on Stella's door. Hearing nothing from her, he ducked his head inside.

She was lying in the fetal position, her head toward the window, not the door, covered up to her ears with the sheet. Based on the even movement up and down of the shape in the bed, and the fact that she hadn't flopped over demanding to know what in the hell he was doing in her room, he retreated into his own room long enough to finish buttoning up, and then grab his phone.

He rapped louder the second time, calling "Stella?" in as nonthreatening a tone as he could get out with his deep voice.

"Wha-what!" she half gasped, springing up in bed. Exposed her top half to him. Covered in a short-sleeved cotton shirt. No bra. He knew her. Was male. Noted. And moved immediately past the fact that he didn't recognize her sleep shirt.

"I'm sorry, Stel, but I need a photo of your arm. It's already been too long, but there's still a chance we can get a good enough read. By morning it'll be too late." He needed to snap and go.

Snap and go. That was it. The tousled hair, and almost welcoming glow in her eyes—welcome, he was sure, because he'd just scared the wits out of a woman who was being terrorized and she'd realized he wasn't a threat.

Not to her life anyway.

To her well-being, if he offered sex and she accepted, was another story. One he couldn't write.

"I've been lying in bed trying to figure out what was eating at me, and it finally landed," he said, still standing in the fully opened doorway, as she reached for and flipped on the lamp on her nightstand.

Landed because he'd finally cleared his mind enough to get there. "The tube that was left on the bench today, it was only two inches in diameter. Had the burned fuse. The paint stain. But…your initial bruising, the circle inside the bigger circle formed from the actual impact. It was larger than two inches. I need a photo to send to forensics. Doug's working with Ben's FBI forensics friend, and the lab's open all night."

"I get needing the photo now, before the bruise settles more and it's harder to distinguish point of impact," Stella was saying as she pushed her sleeve up over her shoulder. "But why call Ben's friend tonight?"

Reminding himself he was on duty, he stepped up to his ex-wife's bed. Got the photo. And then several more, from different angles, before quickly stepping back to the doorway. Then answered her with, "I have to know by morning. In case we need to prepare for more than just smoke bombs and paint balls."

She frowned, and he knew his quickest way out of there was to just tell her what he was thinking. Whether she blew him off as overcautious or not. She wanted him there. Wanted what he had to give. And his overactive mind was it. "The police are working on the theory that the paint ball shooter got spooked, ditching his weapon on the bench as he slipped away, so he wouldn't be caught with evidence on him. But what if that plumbing pipe, while clearly used to shoot a red paint ball, had been deliberately left to throw them off course?"

Her sharpened gaze homed in on him. "What are you saying?" She asked as if she had an idea. Was hoping she wouldn't get confirmation of it.

"What if there'd been an actual gun in the crowd that had shot it off?" he hated to say the words aloud. To give them that much stature. But also because he did not want to be in any way responsible for the sudden shock of fear that crossed her face.

"You're thinking that someone there who'd had clearance to carry a weapon and, therefore, hadn't been searched, was the shooter?"

Yep. He'd known she'd get there quickly. Which was why, if he'd had any other way to gather the evidence he'd needed, he'd have waited until morning to talk to her about it.

If there'd been need.

"It's just a theory, Stel. Hopefully, these photos will prove that the pipe in evidence was the one used, as everyone, including me assumed. It's just, when I saw your bruise…the pipe used…the fuse…there's no way that could have done anything more than stain your sleeve.

And I sent over a photo of that. But that bruise…not only is it wider in circumference, but it explains why you were in such excruciating pain when it first hit…"

Rather than talking her down, he was talking himself—and probably her—up further. He should have seen it sooner. Would have if he hadn't been distracted by his desire to bed the woman.

She nodded. Visibly swallowed. And said, "You need to get those photos sent. We need to know, before we head to the site tomorrow, that we can trust the security that will be there." Pulling her pillow up behind her, she looked as though she was preparing to sit up until she knew, one way or the other.

"Even if the ball that hit you wasn't shot from the pipe, it doesn't mean for sure that someone in the crowd shot it. They're looking into the possibility of some kind of drone. And other things, too, I'm sure."

"Okay." She met his gaze clearly.

He gave her an awkward half smile. Wanted to stay with her. Just until she fell asleep. But knew he couldn't. "Can I just grab the jacket now?" he asked, thinking that while he was up, he'd arrange for a courier to get the jacket to the forensic lab in Georgia. As evidence, it was tainted in terms of handling, but all they needed at that point was a match on the paint.

"It's on the floor, under the luggage rack, inside the closet door."

Where she always kept her dirty clothes while staying in hotel rooms. He went straight to it. Grabbed it up and was back at the door.

"If you need anything, just call out," he told her softly. Hating how vulnerable she looked.

Stella's gaze left him and turned toward the remote

control she grabbed off the nightstand. "I'm just going to stream something light for a bit," she said. "I'll be asleep in no time."

He doubted that, but knew that if her will had its way, she would be. She believed that she could make it happen.

Leaving her fear to duke it out with her determination, Thane headed through the door.

"Let me know if it's up too loud. Keeping you awake," Stella's voice sounded behind him.

Calling out a completely different message than the words implied. She was reaching out to him, benignly, but trying. There was no other explanation for her comment. Because she knew damned well that once he relaxed enough to slumber, her late-night television sleep aid was not going to bother him a bit.

It never had.

Stella woke up the next morning with the television still on. But she'd slept all night. Felt rested, and ready to take on the day. Eager to get to it.

SML had given them an ultimatum, and Thane had opted to stay. The knowledge gave birth to a private little smile inside her.

One born of warmth, not victory. It was her own private little budding ember, and she cradled it within her as she showered and prepared herself physically for the day's rally. Extra makeup so she didn't look washed-out onstage. Her favorite blue suit. The formfitting pants and short jacket, paired with an off-white cami, put confidence in her step. And she added more spray to her tousled hair, for a little extra sassiness.

A text on her phone when she came out of the bathroom told her to meet Thane in his room for breakfast.

While she'd planned on their usual routine of consuming the small meal alone at their respective desks, to give her as much time as possible with her socials, that tiny newly birthed smile inside her seemed to settle in a little more.

Preventing any defensive need to assert her independence by pointing out that she should have been asked, not commanded. Truth was, she didn't want to be wholly independent right then. Not with all the negativity coming at them. Her.

She appreciated the protection protocols that Thane was providing. And just felt better having him close. Because of Kara's recent trauma. She understood her inner workings. Had them under control. And wasn't going to silence them just as she didn't allow anyone to take away her right to speak out. If she did, life would end up biting her in the ass.

With ten minutes to herself before she was due to report, she sat down at her computer for a quick pass through her socials, was pumped up as usual by the huge amounts of support—made known to her in that quick check simply by the numbers of comments and new followers. She pasted the posts she'd written the night before, promoting the day's rally, hit Send, and made it to breakfast with a full minute to spare.

Her oatmeal and fruit—her standard breakfast every day—was already on the small table by the window. A dish on a plate with separate small pouring cups of milk and brown sugar, a separate bowl of fresh cut fruit, a spoon, and a glass of diet soda all sat there, next to another larger plate with a metal warmer over the top.

They made a pretty picture. Complementing each other in their differences.

Coinciding in the intimate space as though they belonged together. Her single utensil, the spoon, next to Thane's more varied display of knife and fork with the spoon.

Kind of like them, the thought struck. Her, with her one-dimensional life, him being three-dimensional sharing the same space.

Just for the moment, though. The one meal. Or other select meals to come. Not as a way of life.

He sat down just after she did. Lifted the lid off his traditional bacon, eggs, and toast, and before she'd even poured her milk onto her cereal said, "We need to talk about your social media platforms."

Stomach tensing, she continued with the milk cup, positioning it over the middle of the bowl, tipping it and watching as the milk poured out. Drowning the sense of goodwill and optimism she'd awoken with that morning.

He wasn't going to take her socials from her.

That would be a deal-breaker.

And before breakfast.

"Doug has someone at the station in North Haven watching them," he told her. She sprinkled a hefty dose of sugar in the milk she'd dispensed. Something was telling her she was going to need all the sweetening she could get. "Has had since the shooting."

She took a bite of the freshly made hot cereal. Felt it slide down, leaving a path of warmth in its wake. And figured that someone watching her channels made sense. She should have already assumed that it was an ongoing part of her protection. Perpetrators were known to express themselves in the ether.

Thane had his fork in hand, but had yet to take his first bite. "There was a defamatory post last evening. But was gone within seconds. Before we could obtain profile information."

"There were several of them last night." She nodded. Refusing to allow the posters to mar her enjoyment of what was turning out to be some great oatmeal. Not only the flavor, but the texture, was near perfect. "There are always going to be haters and accounts like mine draw them on a regular basis. That's why I monitor my sites on my phone throughout the day. I delete and move on."

If that was all he was worried about, he should get to eating before his food got cold. She'd tested the fruit, too. Pieces of a couple of different melons mixed with cut-up strawberries. Juicy. Flavorful. Just what she'd needed.

"You've been getting hate messages every day?"

She nodded. Then clarified. "Not just on this tour, Thane. They're just part of the job. You know, the trash you have to take out at the end of the shift."

"How many of these do you get in a day?"

She'd never counted. Didn't want to know. Shrugging, she guessed, "Anywhere from twenty to a couple of hundred." Depending on the day. The cause. Maybe even the weather, if it was keeping people indoors.

"We need you to not delete them, Stella," Thane said, his tone firm. With a hint of a warning that she knew he couldn't deliver on. The threat of him ending her stint on the tour no longer held.

She swallowed and almost choked on the bite as she realized the actual truth of the matter. Thane's threat didn't hold weight, but the ones aiming at her with increasing menace did. And he was her protection against them.

She wanted those working on her behalf to be able to keep her safe. But she had to work. "They're counterproductive to my messaging," she told him. "I'm there to educate, not to debate. Anyone who doesn't like what I have to say is free to block me. But they aren't free to try to drown out my words."

Thane finished his egg in four bites. Picked up a piece of bacon and held it between two fingers as he looked over at her. "It's likely that whoever is funding this movement against that message, and targeting you, is either online personally, or has hired someone to monitor your sites. We need to know who those people are, to be able to back-trace profiles, study them, to know their locations. Anyone who finds it necessary to spew hate in your direction is suspect."

Right. A lump of melon caught in her throat. Eyes watering, she swallowed hard. Blinking to contain the moisture so that it didn't diminish her mascara or eye liner. She had the solution to Thane's dilemma.

"I'll give Doug's person my logins, once they get the profile URLs, they can delete the messaging." A win-win. They'd have what they wanted, and she didn't have to see any more vile comments like, *Smart bitches take the hint*.

With a nod, Thane ate his bacon.

They might just be able to make their little changed status partnership work—as Thane's client had mandated. He could quit. Wouldn't make a difference to his bottom line. He charged the small nonprofits almost a pro bono fee—just enough to allow him to be able to write off his expenses.

But he couldn't wrap his mind around walking away from Stella when she needed him. Because her current needs were ones he could meet. If she'd let him. And somewhat to his disbelief, she was letting him.

And while that realization was a mood lifter, it was

also sobering. Stella had to be truly rattled by the protest events to be showing any weakness at all. Which told him that, the shooting aside, the pranks, such as they were, were not at all a normal part of her being on tour.

He also had to acknowledge that he was, perhaps, a bit overboard in his concern. Coming off recent events—having gone through the supposed death of his sister-in-law, first with his best friend, and then, when Stella called, with her and from there, having imagined how horrible it would have been to lose Stella—made sense that he would be zealously charged. Making things bigger than they were.

He wasn't going to stop doing so. Just admitting to himself that he'd been responsible for the text his employer had sent him the night before. *If it comes to you or her, we have to go with her. Work this out.*

The first professional slap of his career. Kind of humorous, in a dark sort of way, that Stella had been involved. The woman had been keeping him off his mark the whole time he'd known her. And held the distinction of being the only person he'd ever known who could truly rattle him.

Which drew him to her like a man in some kind of a trance and made it impossible for him to live with her, too.

As fate would have it, the Charmaine rally went off like clockwork. Not even a technical glitch with an echo on a mic. The sound check was perfect the first time. The crowd was their largest one yet—Stella's self-set goal for each new rally on tour. Thane was starting to recognize more and more of the rapt faces in the crowd.

With a new concern, too. Could their attacker be someone who was too enraptured of her? Someone who was perhaps jealous of attention she gave to others? Stella made herself available to anyone who was interested in her causes. They were her life. And if someone had taken her attention personally, feeling a special connection, believing there was more there than Stella had ever intended, only to have her bestow the same attention on others... jealousy was a motive for a whole lot of violent episodes. He wasn't sure what, of their meager evidence from the attacks on tour, would point to the theory, but it was something he mentioned to Doug in their afternoon briefing.

A possibility Doug had taken seriously and was investigating.

With Saturday's rally in the bag, and another week behind them, Thane had opted to stay at the hotel in Charmaine for their one day off as Monday's rally was on the opposite end of the same metropolis.

And because Stella had been so enamored with the view outside their rooms.

Due to their schedule, he couldn't get her back to the cottage on the beach, but he could at least keep the ocean in sight. It seemed to fill her up, to calm her, like old sitcoms running softly on the television as white noise did at night.

James and Amelia had made it clear to both Stella and Thane, in a text thread before the rally that morning, that while Stella was the activist they wanted, Thane was in charge of all details pertaining to her partnership with them. SML needed them both. Valued them both. And the executive director and promotions director were thankful Stella and Thane had been able to come to an agreement that worked for both of them.

He didn't think of it so much as an agreement, as he did a mutual inability to walk away from the situation.

One which was going to have him and his ex-wife in close quarters over the next twenty-four hours. Until they had more answers, some way to tie in the various incidents that had been occurring, Thane was going with Doug's "better safe than sorry" approach and curtailing any trips outside their hotel rooms until they checked out on Monday.

Without more of a clear threat, they weren't being granted extra security anywhere but at the rallies. And Thane, while an impressive shot, was a respected lawyer at the top of his field, not a trained bodyguard.

He would be placing all orders for anything they needed or wanted, and everything would be delivered to his room.

The one concession he made was in conjunction with the hotel. He and Stella had been granted, at a cost, exclusive use of the fitness center during specified times during the day. As the center was in a somewhat remote location, and not in use much except for early mornings, the deal hadn't been a tough one to broker. And she had to get her bike-riding in.

While he stood behind the locked workout facility door, peering out the blinds he closed over the windows, Stella rode for over an hour late that afternoon. And was so calm, so peaceful, as they took the elevator back up to their rooms that Thane reframed the tedious hour he'd spent staring at empty hall space when he could have been on his computer, going through photos of crowds, following up with internet searches, looking for Stella's hater. Or haters. His time spent had been valuable in and of itself.

Keeping his gaze on the lighted floor numbers above the elevator doors—and off from Stella's mouthwatering curves, delineated so expertly by her workout attire—he was feeling awkwardly overdressed in his suit coat and tie, when she said, "Thank you, Thane. I know you've got better things to do than stand guard over me as I exercise. If you'd rather, I'm willing to hire a bodyguard to follow me down there and back. I can afford it. And it's my unwillingness to leave the tour that's put you in this position."

"If I felt that I could be of better use elsewhere, I'd go," he told her, uncomfortable with the suddenly nonsexual rush of emotion her words had lighted within him.

Nothing to do with the offer of a bodyguard hire. But with the rest of it. Her consideration of him, trying to meld their opposite needs.

Mostly because it wasn't anything new. Stella had always done her best to be fair, to pay attention to his needs as well as her own. She'd just never been so…kind about it.

Or maybe he'd just been too defensive—needing to always keep his guard up because he'd known that, ultimately, her need to speak out would be her deciding factor in every situation—to see the sensitivity that also lived inside of his ex-wife.

"I…um…wasn't asking you to go," she said then, from right beside him. He felt her gaze on him. Didn't allow himself to meet it. Not with their quarters so close. Her dressed like that. And being so…reasonable.

He bowed his head. Then glanced back up at the numbers. Only one more floor to go. "I know, Stel. I'm just… used to fighting with you."

He turned to look at her then. His gaze open. His heart mostly still encased in the walls the years of their marriage had slowly built around it. At least he hoped it was. Was trying to ensure that it was.

Her blue eyes held an understanding that he didn't recognize. And a sense of acknowledgment, too.

"It's kind of weird, us getting along again, huh?" she asked as the elevator stopped at their floor.

Waiting for the doors to open, he gave her one last long look, and then, with an arm held against the opened door, keeping it from closing on her, he stepped out beside her, and swallowing back a string of words attached to deeper connective emotions that didn't belong to them anymore, said, "It's nice," and unlocked the door to his room.

Chapter 13

Stella didn't glance back at Thane as she preceded him inside the unlocked door. She made a purposeful, straight shot to her own space, closing the door to within an inch behind her. It wasn't fair to him, her needing him like she did.

Not when she couldn't give the man what he needed. The traditional marriage and home. Mom, Dad, and the kids. Not only did she have no internal concept of how to make that happen, emotionally, within her, she wasn't going to risk screwing it up.

No way could she bring a human into the world knowing the risk to that vulnerable soul if she messed up as a mother. As she had as a wife. Always saying what she thought. Speaking her mind honestly and openly.

Hurting Thane with her words.

And her inability to allow herself to be as vulnerable to him as he'd allowed himself to become with her. Thane hadn't known what it felt like to be abandoned, emotionally, until she'd come along. Yay, her. Great lesson she'd taught.

Which was why she stuck to causes. Predetermined rhetoric into which she could pour her heart and soul. Her passions.

And offstage, she was meant to be the friend. The auntie. The one who was there and then gone. And there and then gone.

But one you could always rely upon to come back. No matter what.

Uncomfortable with the emotions trying to boil up inside her, Stella went straight to her computer, workout clothes and all. Her emotional outlet, what kept her healthy and strong on the inside, was speaking out to help those she could help.

She had her failings, but she was also putting her talents, her gifts to work and by doing so, helping to make the world a better place.

The screen booted up, and Stella tapped her tennis shoe heel against the carpet as she signed in and waited for connectivity. Thinking over the day's work. They'd had such a great gathering. Amelia and her associates had been surrounded in crowds wanting more information afterward. Signing clipboards to be added to email contact lists.

And...she was on. Clicked the first of her six platforms, ready to get an hour of good work in before dinner. Felt her heart drop. And stared.

Wrong username or password.

They were preprogrammed. She hadn't typed anything. Just clicked. And she'd been on that morning. Using her own hotspot internet. Never a hotel's.

Figuring the platform was in the middle of an update, or experiencing a glitch, she clicked to the next. And the next. Finding the same at every single one.

Heart beating, her blood thrumming so hard she felt

like she could feel it in her veins, she turned off her computer. Paced while it rebooted. Her chest tight, anxiety fluttering in her stomach, Stella went to her programs after the reboot, rather than clicking icons on her front screen. Scrolling through the list, she opened the first of her social platforms that she came to.

And couldn't get on.

"What the... Thane!" She stood, ran for the door between their rooms, and plowed into her ex-husband as he rushed in. Barely aware of his hands on her shoulders, steadying her, she said, "I can't get onto any of my social media platforms! Doug's people must have done something. I can't get on, Thane. Millions of followers, and right after a rally when they're going to be waiting for me, and I can't get on. They'll be expecting my post-rally video, and I have no way to even let them know it'll be late!"

"Hold on, Stel, I'm sure it's just a momentary glitch. Did you reboot?"

Did she *reboot*? "Of course I did!" She wasn't lacking in know-how. And had spoken harshly. "I'm sorry, but I never should have turned over the login information." She was whining and pacing while Thane sat down at her computer. And continued with, "I'm always so careful, handling everything myself for just this reason... Oh my God. Oh my God." She had to keep talking. It was the only way to combat the rush of panicky emotions attacking her on the inside. To prevent them from taking control.

Talking kept her brain active. And when it came to being overwhelmed by uncontrollable emotions, the antidote was mind over matter.

"I signed in this morning, just fine," she said. Growing more agitated inside as she saw his attempts to sign her in meeting with the same failure screens she'd received. "The only thing that makes sense is Doug's people. You need to call Doug, Thane. They have to undo whatever they did..."

She was wringing her hands, staring at the computer over his shoulder. And continued to stare even as he stood. She couldn't lose her socials. "Ten years' worth of platform building!" She threw up her hands, then took two steps to the side, and was right back where she'd been another two steps later.

Thane, with his phone to his ear, was heading through the door into his room, and she followed right behind him. So closely that when he paused, she ran into his back.

He turned, looking at her, as Doug picked up, and Thane started talking. Explaining the situation. She could hear the slight rumble of a masculine voice on the other end of the line, but couldn't make out words.

She needed words. And immediate action.

Millions of followers. More than a decade of pretty much daily reliable presence and interaction.

The crowd that day! All the new faces and names being added to those clipboards. They'd all been handed a card containing her socials as well as SML's.

Ohhhh. She couldn't believe it. Couldn't believe it was happening. Millions of followers, and she was helpless?

No.

Shaking her head, she went back to her computer. Brought up the first platform. Created a new account. And searched for hers. Like anyone else looking to find her, follow her, might do.

And...thank God! There she was! Knee bobbing, heart pumping, she took an easier breath when the familiarity of her profile first flashed on her screen. Until she saw the post pinned at the top. One she didn't recognize at all. Telling all her followers that her father had died, and she was selling his furniture. Twenty-five photos of high-end home furnishings followed with a note to DM her if they were interested.

The post had been live for over an hour. There were more than three thousand comments.

Shaking from the inside out, so hard she could barely get her mouse to the comment icon, to click to respond, she hurriedly, and with too many hits on the delete keys, got a message out to her followers that the post wasn't from her.

And knew it wasn't enough. Not even close. Three thousand comments. Who was going to read them all to find hers?

Feeling helpless, violated, she blinked back tears, was trying to figure out how to report to the platform, when Thane appeared in her room, coming toward her.

"The two techies Doug assigned to monitor your platforms discovered that takeover an hour ago. They've been working to figure out what happened, and to have your platforms restored ever since. Doug didn't realize how often you're on them, or how critical that you know immediately there was an issue. Like me, he's not on social media at all. And based on the skill levels of the people helping him, he'd expected things to be cleared up within a few minutes."

Finding it difficult to hold on to the tears that were threatening, Stella looked up at him and asked, "What did they do? They have to undo whatever it was."

Physically turning the chair on which she sat away from the computer, he then dropped down on the bed, facing her. "It wasn't them, Stel. They were actually on two of the platforms when it happened, one right after the other. They saw the posts appear about the furniture sale." His expression as serious as she'd ever seen it, he glanced at the post on her screen, and then, taking her hands in his said, "You were hacked, by someone who had your email and passwords. They went in and changed your email to theirs, changed your password, and took over your accounts."

Stella's entire being dropped. Her head. Her shoulders. Her heart. What was she going to do? She had to do something.

Shine light on the situation. She had to speak out against the atrocity.

With no audience to hear her. None. At all. They were gone. All of them. Since high school, she'd had her social media outlet. Her voice. Long before she'd established her current professional platforms.

Gone. Millions of followers.

Dread filled her. Staring at Thane, leaving her hands encased in his, she felt lost. Frightened. Powerless.

Except that, "My father's alive and well." That was the fact. The truth. Unless... Mouth dropping open she stared at Thane. "Isn't he?"

With long, slow nods, Thane killed off that fear before it had a chance to take root. "Doug already verified that. Your dad would like to hear from you, by the way. He didn't know you were on tour again."

She hadn't wanted to hear his doom and gloom with her being on the road so soon after they'd all thought they'd lost Kara. So soon after they almost *had* lost her. If not for Ben, she'd have been...

No. It hadn't gone that way and she couldn't let her

mind do so, either. Ben had been there. Thank God. End of story.

"All six platforms have already been contacted, Stel," Thane said. "They're working with law enforcement to get your platforms returned to you."

His calm slid inside her. In small doses, but there. Until it was done, it wasn't done. But she could trust Thane to be on top of it. And to sue the ass off of whoever tried to rob her of her voice.

But his expression was so grave. With returning calm, came clearer thoughts. And looking Thane in the eye, she asked, "You all think this was another purposeful attack, don't you? That's why we were left alone at the rally today…"

"We'd be remiss not to take that angle," he told her. "It's just too much of a coincidence, don't you think? That all six of your platforms would be stolen, right now? In the midst of all the other couched violence being thrown at you?"

She didn't want to think like that. "It could just be some computer nerd who likes lower gas prices more than whales, you know one of the vituperative naysayers whose negative comments I delete every single day. Maybe by deleting him, I made him feel powerless and so he retaliated." Made perfect sense to her.

"Yeah, but you've been at this for ten years, and it's never happened before."

She couldn't argue the timing of another's mental or emotional breakdown and lashing out.

"Doug called his FBI contact and they have a team of investigators following up on the profile identities of all the negative comments that appeared today. And have requested a log of your deleted comments from the past two weeks."

"Does that exist?"

Thane shrugged, looking tired suddenly. "It's supposed to." Didn't mean it hadn't been permanently wiped out by one with the capabilities to do so.

And Stella had to admit, "It looks like Big Money really is behind this attempt to silence me, huh? Someone has pretty deep pockets if they're really paying off locals to enact all these misdemeanors against me." Other than the shooting. Duane Riker had had his first court hearing. Was still in jail and facing several criminal charges.

But hadn't ever swayed from his story, that he'd been acting of his own accord, and hadn't meant to shoot her. Only to scare her. She'd just moved her arm right when he'd pulled the trigger. Stella didn't waste mental and emotional energy dwelling on the matter. If she was called to testify in court, she'd be there. Otherwise, her arm had mostly healed, and she'd moved on.

To a void of nothingness.

Facing the fact that someone had hit her where she hurt far more than just physically. Showing her how vulnerable she was?

Except that she wouldn't be anyone's victim. "Once I get the accounts back, what do I do to prevent this from happening again?" she asked Thane, as though she felt a whole lot better than the trembling and clutching of muscles inside of her would have her believe.

Thanks to Thane, and his reaching out, she had highly skilled agents out there getting her accounts switched back under her control. She just had to sit tight for a few.

And plan for the future.

"I have no idea," Thane told her, giving her hands a squeeze before letting them go and standing. "But I'm sure Doug's people will be able to point you to someone who can answer that question. I'll be sure and pose it once we get the all clear. In the meantime, Italian for dinner?"

Along with Asian salad, one of her comfort foods. "Yes, please."

"Fettucine or eggplant Parmesan?" His memory had been one of the things that Stella had first admired about the man. At the moment, having just been erased from the identity she'd spent so long building, being with someone who knew her made her feel more alive. More valid. And she stood, too. No point in sitting there crying, or staring at the spilled milk she was incapable of cleaning up. "In your room?" she asked, following him to the door.

"Sure."

"You mind if I sit and enjoy the view now, over a glass of wine?" With her voice erased, her calming abilities weren't keeping up. They needed a boost while she waited to hear that someone really was able to reconnect her to profiles.

She stopped her forward movement to said destination abruptly as Thane turned in the doorway between their rooms. "You're quite welcome to join me in the glass of wine I was about to pour," he said. "But not in those clothes." His pointed glance toward her breasts, exposed midsection, and thighs in their skintight leggings, made her tingle.

In a completely inappropriate and alarmingly arousing way.

"On it," she said, and with a quick spin, got herself out of his sight.

* * *

The first time Thane had ever seen Stella rattled to her core had been the month before, when they'd thought Kara had been killed during the bombing of a house she'd been hiding out in. And he'd just seen it a second time.

Two decades of knowing the woman, most of those years loving and living with her, and he'd never seen her teetering on the edge of her composure—until recently.

Shaken, more than just a little uneasy, he opened a bottle of wine, poured two glasses, read a text from Doug, and paced.

Kara's supposed death, he got completely. He'd always known that Stella adored her baby sister. Or, at the very least, had set herself up as Kara's protector. And in the current situation, her extreme level of distress made sense as well. Stella's ability to shout the truth was the one thing that she needed, personally, more than anything else.

And where did that leave him?

Not presently, but in the past. She'd barely blinked when he'd told her he felt like their marriage had to end. She damned sure hadn't fought for them. Not even with an *Are you sure?* Nope, she'd nodded. Told him to write it up however he wanted and she'd sign the papers. And then had locked herself in her office.

He didn't know that because he'd tried to follow her, to talk things out. He knew because he'd heard the lock click against the doorjamb.

He'd had no intention of following her. He'd gone straight to his own office and called his lawyer. The whole thing had been over in a matter of weeks.

And he'd just had confirmation that his choice had been the right one. Stella relied on him, as a friend, probably, as a lawyer who knew his stuff better than anyone, sure. But he'd never had a place deep enough inside her tough shell to make even a blip on her equilibrium when he walked out.

Yet there he stood, firmly, determined to get her back to North Haven safely. Without a single doubt that it was the right thing to do.

Recognizing the facts, Thane didn't try to argue himself out of them. They were truth. Acceptance had a bit of a bitter taste, and yet it freed him, too. Allowed him to let go of the past and concentrate on the present.

A present in which, when Stella was at her lowest the previous month, he was the one she'd called. He'd known about Kara's troubles, of course, through Ben. But hadn't reached out to her. She'd contacted him.

And he'd dropped everything and run to her.

Just as he was currently doing. Putting lucrative work aside so he could ensure that Stella made it home safely.

He cared about her.

And in her own way, she cared about him, too. Not as much as her sisters, or her work, but he'd gamble his career that he was third on the list.

Not enough to sustain a marriage.

But enough.

He heard her short rap on the door and when he swung around to greet her, almost burst out laughing. In sweatpants, and a matching jacket zipped up to her chin, her message couldn't have been any more clear.

And she hadn't even opened her mouth. Let alone given him a spiel of what was obviously on her mind.

No more intimation of physical anything between them. His once hot lover had become the virgin incarnate.

For a second there he wondered if she was more worried about him, or herself, but one glance at the "deer in the headlights" look in those blue eyes and he said, "Nothing yet on the socials."

Her glance rested on the wineglasses he'd filled and without a word she made a beeline for the chair she'd occupied the night before. And the glass.

He had other news. Gave her a few minutes to sip. And ocean gaze. Then joined her.

"The bruise on your arm was not made by the rudimentary paint gun that was left on the bench. They're back to square one there."

Doug's text had been blunt. Thane tempered his words as he continued with, "We have to accept that you, in particular, are being targeted, Stella."

She nodded. "Because I'm the activist in charge," she said, not moving her gaze from outward, toward the ocean. "Hire another activist, the attacks will be on them."

He couldn't deny the logic, the possibility in her words. Nor did they, in any way, help his situation.

"Still nothing on who tampered with the rotted stage board," he told her. "And Riker—" the shooter "—isn't talking, beyond his original statements." Which in itself made him suspect. His rhetoric not changing at all, not a single added detail that might have come back to him, led Thane, and others, to believe that the spiel was rehearsed. "The man's willing to go to jail rather than turn on who hired him."

He'd been watching Stella the entire time he spoke. On that last sentence, her head snapped in his direction. "You sound certain that someone did."

He nodded slowly. Took a sip of his wine, and said, "They found a large deposit in an account in his name in the Cayman Islands. He'd written it down on a notepad in his office. Had ripped the sheet off the pad, but the pen left impressions that the lab was able to pick up. He's denying knowing what was there, claiming that someone else had to have written it."

"That sounds bogus." She'd turned back to the ocean view with a disgusted snort.

"And yet, he doesn't budge from the words. Looks interrogators straight in the eye as he repeats them."

He was purposely not sugarcoating. Had no inkling if she was getting the message. And while he hated hitting her when she was down, he only had twenty-four hours before she was going to march herself onstage again and put whatever came next into action.

Because he was damned sure, as were others, that whoever was behind the attacks was only getting started. They were playing with Stella. Hacking her platforms had been the final piece of evidence that had convinced every one of the men and women working on the series of crimes that were following in Stella's wake.

And whoever was out there after her was going to quit playing at some point.

The impromptu team Doug had pulled together would all bet their lives on that one.

Chapter 14

Stella didn't want to hear Thane's doom and gloom. Didn't need it. She had enough of her own that threatened to overwhelm her. Was fighting her way out even as he seemed intent on shoving her back in deeper than before.

In her most rational moments, she was thankful for his honesty.

But without her socials, and a day off looming in front of her, she didn't have to be rational. Had nothing to focus on to keep her head from taking the dark trips into fear she'd been living with since she was ten years old.

With any luck, the wine would make her sleepy, before it depressed her further, and she could escape into oblivion long enough for Doug's people to get her socials back under her control. And then she'd have a load of work to do.

Undoing whatever in the hell "they" were doing to her. And blasting her own message all over her platforms so that at least one of them showed up in every follower's feed at some point.

Undoing what they were doing...

The words stuck in her head. On repeat mode. What in the hell were they doing?

She couldn't do anything about it. Couldn't stop them.

They were going to do whatever they wanted. Could be sending direct messages to every one of her millions of followers. Lose her the credibility she'd spent a lifetime building.

If they...

"Stel?" Thane's voice broke into the panicked hell her world was becoming.

Shaking the smog from her head, she turned to him, "Yeah?"

He held up his phone. "I just got a text. Dinner's on its way up."

Right. Italian. She'd forgotten. Wasn't sure how much of it she was going to be able to eat, no matter how good it was.

They wanted her to quit. To give up. All of them. The bad guys. And the good ones, too. Other than SML. And her followers.

Her family, most of all, wanted her to give up and go home.

"I can't do it," she said to Thane as he stood, getting ready to head to the door when the knock sounded. "I can't let evil chase me off, to silence a valid message of harm that needs to be stopped. I'm not advocating for no more shipping or mining from the ocean floor. But there are better, safer ways to go about it..."

Setting his wineglass down, Thane squatted on his haunches in front of her.

Planning to beg to try to get her to see reason? His version of it?

She had to look at him. The man was her rock.

And when she met his gaze, he said, "I know, Stel. I'm not asking you to quit. Even if SML decided they were out,

I wouldn't encourage you to be quiet. I just need you to let me help you do what you have to do as safely as possible."

Her eyes teared up, right there in front of him. She nodded. Wanted to smile, to thank him.

Couldn't get words past the constriction in her throat.

And was saved by the knock on the door.

"Get your things together, we're leaving." Thane barked the words as he came back from the door with a bag of delicious-smelling food in his hand. "Now, Stella, or you leave them behind. And turn off your phone."

Jumping up so fast she spilled her wine, Stella bent to wipe up the mess and, already throwing his suits in a pile in his suitcase, he said, "Leave it. Go."

She ran more than walked to her room, tapping on her phone as she went, and he listened intently as she moved about. Shutting down his own phone and moving his gun to his belt, he grabbed the burner phone Doug had had delivered to him, just in case, and sent a brusque text to the detective, then gathered the rest of his things and threw them, literally, into the case he generally packed with precision.

Getting Stella out safely was the only thing on his mind. Which meant waiting critical minutes before exiting the room.

To that end, he cleared out his bathroom with a sweep of the counter into what was meant to be a laundry bag he'd pulled from a hanger in the closet.

And had a text back by the time Stella stood in the doorway, her suitcase roller handle clutched in her fingers, and her satchels over her shoulder and resting on her back.

He'd just zipped up. Didn't take a last glance around.

If he left something he'd replace it. He had his computer, which contained everything important to him.

And even then, none of it was nearly as important as Stella was.

"We're going down the stairs," he told her. "A plainclothes detective in an unmarked police car is going to be waiting at the door for us."

Stella went ahead of him, as he directed, but didn't slow them down a bit. The woman raced as though she was riding her bike. And didn't ask a single question.

"The detective was in the vicinity." he told her, because he'd need more if it was him blindly following such over-the-top orders. "Doug called his contact at the Charmaine Police Department and was immediately put through to Lisa Harris, the detective picking us up."

Stella didn't miss a beat in her flight down the stairs. Or look back at him. She was one person you could trust with a mission. Always had been.

They made it to the darkness falling outside without mishap. Were in the car and speeding away with a brief showing of credentials. And silently rode to a destination Doug texted to him.

A private bed-and-breakfast cottage owned by someone in the department. It wasn't on the ocean, only had one bedroom, and one bath, but it was in a gated community with a ten-foot-high brick wall lining the home's yard and security cameras showing both sides of it. Doug was adding the cameras to the watch list being monitored by the team who'd been watching Stella's socials. Probably on Thane's dime. About which he didn't give even half a whit.

Other than thanking Lisa for her help, Stella hadn't spoken since he'd stood up at the knock on his hotel room door. And that was scaring the shit out of him. The woman had lungs that could carry and a need to exercise them every chance she got.

Especially when it came to her life and what was happening around her.

Inside the elegant little cottage, she was still quiet while she had a look around. Until she came to a halt, standing in front of the gas fireplace he'd turned on—more to feel like a welcome than to get the night's chill out of the room—and asked, "Why would someone have such a small place if they can afford elegance like this?"

Not at all the questions that would have been pouring from his mouth. Nor anything like the spewing he'd expected from her.

Eyes narrowed, watching her, he said, "It's a golf resort with two PGA courses, hence the high walls. And the owner is a divorced male, high up in the department, and also an avid golfer, who likes to hide out in peace on his days off. There's a built-in lap pool and spa out back."

Sitting on the couch, Stella continued to watch the fire as she said, "I'll sleep here."

While he was relieved at a sign of her backbone, he wasn't done calling the shots. "Then you'll be sharing it with me."

The windows on the back of the property all had bars on them, in the event of wildly high-flying golf balls, and the bedroom faced the back.

The front windows were not barred, and there were two big ones—wired with security, but still breachable—in the large open-floor-plan living space, kitchen, and eating area.

If she got up and went to bed, without another word, he'd let her go. And sit up and worry about her, too. He thought he'd known every one of Stella's moods, mindsets, and frames of mind. He was witnessing a facet of her that was unfamiliar to him.

Which made him uneasy in ways he couldn't logically explain to himself.

"It looks like it pulls out," she said, then, standing to prove herself correct. Igniting all kinds of warning signs inside him.

"Stella, what's going on here?"

Lips pursed, she looked over at him. "Honestly? I don't know, Thane. And that's the problem, isn't it?" The snap in her tone eased him some. Told him she was fighting, at least.

And he chose to take her words at face value, concerning their current situation, though he knew they alluded to more than that. He just wasn't sure how far in she'd gone to search for answers she wasn't finding.

"I ordered dinner from an app I use at home. The one I always use. The person who showed up at my door with our order was a rideshare driver."

She didn't squelch over his mammoth departure plan, involving important people in local law enforcement, over such a small detail. Didn't rail against him for making mountains out of molehills—not that she ever had.

He'd just had a few minutes of doubt on the ride to the cottage. Was he losing sight of reality when it came to the threats against Stella? Because…it was her?

"I left the bag of food with Lisa," he had to say then. Meaning they had no dinner. Though they'd been told to help themselves to whatever was in the kitchen. "There's a lab here that's going to analyze it tonight."

"Because a rideshare person delivered our dinner." A statement. Not a question. And yet, with no sense of judgment, either. No *opinion*. And that was bothering the hell out of him.

"A call was made from the police department to the restaurant I ordered from. They have proof that they released the food to the driver from the app I used." He'd received that text in the car.

Still didn't mean anything. Could be that the app driver had car trouble and didn't want to lose his job, so called a rideshare to deliver the order while he waited with his car. He'd already come up with the most plausible explanation.

One that fit far better than some paranoid idea of their food having been tampered with. With the added sting of showing Stella that they knew where she was.

Well, let them try and find her that night...

"No computer time here, Stel." The words came of their own accord. Then Thane pulled out the burner to text Doug. Asking for the team to see if they could find evidence that someone was somehow following the location of Stella's computer. Or pinging her phone.

For all he knew, the detective had already done so. Was Thane thinking he was smarter than the ace detectives working with him, too?

Surely, he hadn't gone off the rails to that extent.

Nor could he ignore the things that were occurring to him out of nowhere. He'd learned to trust his mind at a very young age, and it rarely led him wrong.

"Right now, being on the computer is probably not a good idea for my mental health," she muttered and made her way to the kitchen. "Dammit. No wine!" She half yelled. Half whined.

Grabbing his satchel, unzipping and pulling out the unopened bottle that had still been in his hotel room, he brought it out to her. "It's warm. But it's here."

He handed it to her. Watched her scrounge for an opener, pulling out two drawers at a time to do so, and then, spying the corkscrew hanging on the refrigerator, he grabbed it, took the bottle from Stella, and paused to look at her.

She was trembling. He'd felt the tremor in her hand.

"Wine, Wilson," she said, last-naming him in a warning tone that didn't quite hold muster.

She was driving herself crazy with not knowing. And with their list of needed answers growing, seemingly by the hour, he didn't see any clear way to help. Except, "Why don't you look and see what we can put together for dinner? We've been given carte blanche."

With her brow raised and a bit of an "oops" expression on her mouth, she said, "I was going to steal the wine and leave a hundred bucks for it," she said. "I had no idea we were free to…"

She glanced down at the two drawers still opened in front of her. Carefully closed them. And started searching slowly, gently, through the refrigerator, freezer, and cupboards.

And in that moment, Thane was swamped with a distinctly warm boatload of admiration for the woman.

Thane was how she was going to get through the night. That and an internal and very determined mental insistence that by morning she'd have her social properties back.

Until then, because she'd been so totally silenced, she was actually kind of okay with the time off. Ten years of daily tending to her platforms had become habit. As much a part of her day as showering, eating, and sleeping.

Or raising a child that depended on you for every physical need, and later, emotional guidance. You didn't get to take time off. Another innocent, vulnerable life depended on you to be there, or have someone in your stead, at your command, following your edicts, if you absolutely had to be away.

She couldn't ever remember her mother away from her during the first ten years of her life. Not one time had she had an overnight babysitter—not even Melanie—until the week her mother had run away to the beach and thrown them all away.

Forgotten them as if they were trash. She hadn't even called to check in.

Stella had waited. Every night. Certain that she would.

To hear how their days were going. How she'd done on the math test her mother had helped her study for. How her first ever debate had gone.

Sitting on the couch in front of a fire that wasn't putting out enough heat to warm her, with a stomach full of the rice and veggie bowls she'd made for dinner—with canned vegetables, but they'd done okay—she ached with a need to reach out to her followers. To be there for them.

Hated the idea of leaving even one of them wondering why she'd deserted them right in the middle of a tour.

Going beyond that—to what the abuser was doing with her platforms, how they could be manipulating her followers' minds, playing with their hearts or stealing from their wallets—brought back another bout of panic. Trembling.

Lifting her wineglass calmly to her mouth, she took another small sip. Had promised herself that she'd drink slowly. And was adamant about keeping her word.

She had to have at least one thing she could trust.

She was it.

"All cleaned up," Thane said, appearing right at that

exact moment from around the corner where he'd been doing the dishes. His insistence, not hers.

She watched him approach, trust still on her mind.

"What?" he asked her, standing there, assessing her.

Wondering if she was going to hold to her assertion that she was sleeping on the couch?

She was.

And was wondering if he was going to hold to his.

"I can't be shut up in a little bedroom tonight, Thane. No television. Not even my phone…" Her voice started to rise as she contemplated the darkness, the panic rising with her having none of her usual panaceas at hand. She *always* had her cell phone. Could stream from there.

"I know." He pulled out his burner phone, set it on the table, before dropping down to the corner of the couch farthest from her. Seemingly just fine with the idea of sharing a bed with her.

And why not? They'd done so for twenty years, give or take. Between becoming lovers in college and staying over, and then the years of their marriage. It was at least close to two decades.

She knew he breathed heavily when he slept. He knew she didn't.

And if either of them got in bed and turned their backs, it meant no sex. The signals had been set long ago. They knew what to do.

No need to talk about any of it.

Thane grabbed the remote. The cottage's owner seemed to have subscribed to every sports streaming service available, and a couple of major network-owned services as well. They talked about different shows as Thane scrolled. Hadn't landed on one yet when the burner buzzed against the coffee table.

Stella stared. Praying her accounts were back up. And that the hotel food delivery was about to be explained as harmless so that she could get online and get to work.

It was too hard, sitting there with the husband she'd never wanted to divorce, with him being so nice to her, and not craving what she knew he wanted. And would wholly regret. All of her coping mechanisms had been stripped away and there she was, with only Thane to focus on.

Talk about a cruel twist of fate.

Thane had walked over to the front window as he'd answered the phone. Was looking out front—because he'd been warned someone was out there?—but was saying very little. An occasional, "Right." Then, "You're sure."

Tension crawled through Stella's stomach, churning through the dinner she'd consumed, tying her muscles into knots around it.

It could be good news. Thane was in his head. Working. Taking in detail. He'd be looking for mistakes, loopholes. Making certain, in his mind, that nothing had been missed.

Before he'd smile or celebrate.

Or give her any indication that she had cause to do so.

"Damn." His tone gave nothing away.

But she knew, once he told her everything was fine, she trusted that it was. He wouldn't leave stones unturned.

Something she'd always loved about him. If one was to speak the truth, they had to know that what they'd been told, read, or seen was accurate. She'd always been able to count on Thane to straighten out her information if she had it wrong. Saw it in a skewed version. Or was trusting someone's information who'd been lying to her.

She wasn't and never had been a know-it-all. She just

had to communicate what she knew when doing so could help others.

And the millions of creatures in the sea…they had no voice at all. It was like she could physically feel them, their panic when their instinctive way to communicate was cut off. When they didn't know how to find food sources or family because of interruptions and intrusions in their home.

It was her at ten all over again.

"Yeah. I will." Thane's tone sounded final. And not at all uplifting or positive. Heart pounding, Stella watched him drop the hand holding the phone and put the burner into his pocket.

Staring, she saw him turn, and knew as soon as she got her first glimpse of his tight features that she didn't want to hear whatever he had to say.

Having just been thinking of her ten-year-old self, she suddenly wanted to plug her ears and start humming. A happy tune. Something her mother had sung to her.

Except that none came immediately to mind. She'd wiped as much of that away as she could.

She was no longer a child. And it was time to face the music, not hide behind it.

No matter how out of tune it might turn out to be.

Chapter 15

Thane's gut filled with dread even as anger coursed through him. How dare anyone think they had the right to target an innocent person with a good heart doing a job she excelled at and was well paid for, a person who always had the best goal of all. To help those who couldn't speak for themselves.

"There was campylobacter found in both meals," he started in even before he reached the couch. Stella was on the edge of her ability to find any calm at all. She'd need it all at once. As succinctly as possible. Over and done.

"It's the most common cause of food poisoning and there was enough of it to have you down for more than twenty-four hours."

Stella's expression softened. "Food poisoning? I mean, you couldn't have known the restaurant you picked had an issue, but I do love that radar of yours. It wasn't about the driver, like you thought…it was the restaurant itself!" She was smiling up at him like he was some kind of god. Or king of the world.

He couldn't let himself take in the instant shot of pleasure that look tried to shoot through him. "It wasn't the restaurant, Stel. The bacteria wasn't in the food, it was on top of it. Only in the sauce. Samples of the sauce from the restaurant were tested, and while the place was shut down out of an abundance of caution and further testing is being done, every indication is that the food was tampered with *after* it left the restaurant."

She was shaking her head. He saw the protest building within her.

"No," he cut it off. "The food service worker who'd put the food in their respective containers gave her fingerprints. They were found on the container. But another set was there as well. On the top and bottom, right where the foam latch slid together."

She took a breath. He shook his head. "The prints match the driver who showed up at our door. He claims he was paid a thousand dollars to sprinkle some hot sauce on two meals, as a prank, and to deliver them to my room."

"And you believe him?" Stella asked then, her chin, cheeks, and forehead creased with tension.

"Based on what her lab technicians have shown her, and the interviews she's done, Lisa Harris does," he said. Though Stella hadn't spoken in the car when the detective had driven them to the small little house, she'd seemed to trust that the detective was going to keep them safe. She'd ridden calmly. Without fidgeting or keeping her eyes peeled at every turn, every car that had passed.

As he sat back down on the far corner of the couch, he continued doling out information he'd much rather have kept to himself. "The delivery driver from the restaurant had a flat tire halfway between there and the hotel. The rideshare driver who delivered the food had been following him, expecting to waylay him at the hotel, but, instead, he offered to deliver the food so it didn't get cold."

With a disdaining twist of her nose, Stella said, "I'd

be checking into the rideshare guy more thoroughly if it were me. I'll bet he slit that tire, causing the flat."

Thane almost grinned at her. Would have if the case they were discussing wasn't wrapped around her. And if there wasn't much worse to come. "Already done. According to him, the flat tire idea was his—and it might have been. He was earning a pretty good clip for a few minutes' work. He'd want to make certain he got ahold of that food. Beyond that, he swears he has no idea who hired him. He got a message on some app he uses where whatever pops up disappears shortly afterward. He'd been told the money would be left in a cereal box in a dumpster a block over from the hotel."

Stella's head dropped back to the couch. She rolled it sideways to look at him as she said, "Let me guess. The money was there, with no prints on either it or the cereal box."

Thane nodded.

Blinking, her head still laid back, but facing him, Stella said, "Those apps where things disappear, I heard that the messages could still be traced."

"They're working on that, getting the warrants. But it will most likely lead to a burner phone."

Lifting her head, Stella's eyes narrowed as she studied him.

"What else?"

He started to shake his head.

"I know you, Thane Jeffrey Wilson. There's more. Surely, with us here, all that's going on, you aren't going to try to hide information from me."

He took a deep breath. Tried to pretend that Stella was just a contractor working for his client. "I was thinking about trying. Wasn't sure I'd follow through. Or get away with it if I did," he told her. More to borrow them both time than anything else.

Lips pursed, she moved them just long enough to say, "So?" as her gaze continued to bore into him.

"The cereal box was Toasted Mini Squares."

Stella's mouth dropped open, her face turned white as he named the only boxed cereal she'd eat. If it was a no oatmeal morning, it was the Mini Squares. "Hh...hhh..."

Assuming she was trying to ask him how someone would know that, Thane quickly rattled off the answer that Doug had relayed, a conclusion Thane had arrived at on his own as soon as Doug had said the name.

"It has to be from on the tour, Stel. Whoever this person, or persons, are, they're on this tour. Watching you every minute." And he gave her the rest. "From what the lab technician relayed, the amount of bacteria on the food tonight could have put you in the hospital. It most definitely would have put you in gastric distress."

But that wasn't the worst message the most recent attempted attack had delivered as far as Thane and Doug were concerned. "They've upped their game, Stel. They're making it intimately personal, letting us know they're watching what you eat. And they're making it physically dangerous, too. Not just uncomfortable. The shooting aside."

She nodded. Pursed her chin. And said the one thing that Thane had known she'd say. And that he'd dreaded hearing.

"They aren't going to shut me up."

Stella knew, as soon as Thane had started talking about food and rideshare drivers that her socials were not yet returned to her control. He'd have led with the news.

And she had to know how bad it was. If she didn't have them back by morning, she'd have to go somewhere she could get online and start new accounts. The idea was overwhelming. But if she could access her old accounts as a user, she could start friending and following her old followers from there. One at a time—for millions—on several platforms, was daunting as hell.

It wasn't impossible. She'd hire someone, pay them to go back and forth between the accounts, to message people, even, to let them know she had new platforms.

She'd give them a catchy name—Stella Who Won't Be Silenced—or some such thing. The same name on every platform...

"No word on your platforms, yet," Thane finally said. He'd followed where her mind had gone. A nice thing about having someone know you so well.

And a curse, too, when you can't give them what they need and they know it and leave you.

"Do we know, at least, that they're still trying?"

"We do. An FBI tech expert is involved since we're talking multistate theft—and because we have convincing reason to believe that the thefts are part of a larger, serial attacker out to get you."

His words made her feel a little better, surprisingly. Not great, but she'd been about out of hope and he'd just given her a smidgen of it.

"We should get some rest," Thane said, meeting her gaze. "It's getting late, and we don't know if we'll be on the move again by morning."

Stella didn't like the sound of that. She'd thought they were set until Monday's rally. Other than if she had to travel for computer usage. Brows raised, she stared at him.

"Doug and a few of the others are following some leads

as to the identity of the boss calling the shots where you're concerned. That cereal box...in the first place..."

"I've had oatmeal and fruit every breakfast I've eaten since we've been on tour," Stella interjected. The thought had hit earlier. She hadn't wanted to dwell on it.

"But you bought a box the day after we finished the first rally. To refill the plastic bag of it you keep in your bag."

Right. In case she started to feel anxious. It was one of her quick and immediate go-tos. Comfort food on the go.

"And you grabbed a couple of single-sized servings from two different hotels we stayed at."

She had. They were both still in her satchel.

"Teams are spending the night looking at footage of all three locations, including traffic cameras in the surrounding areas, hoping to find the same person in all three places."

"I can already tell you there'll be a lot of them. You know that, too. Those who follow me regularly, in person, on tour."

"I took photos of the meeting you held after you were first hurt. Someone in Doug's office already has identities on every person there. And has been checking them out, one by one. Assuming they all come back clean, they can eliminate all of them from rally crowds, so that's a start. They're also looking at traffic cameras around the areas of the money drops. If they get a match from someone by the dumpster, or—"

"You really think Big Money would make his own drop?" she asked, because the more he talked, the more uptight she was growing. No way was sleep coming anytime soon.

"No. But they'd be remiss not to see if anyone they

could identify from a rally also made any of the drops. Gives them more players to interrogate in the hopes of getting someone to roll on the boss."

She nodded. Just wanted it all to go away. To be allowed to do her job and maybe have a minute or two to mourn her broken marriage all over again since she was being reminded minute by minute of all that she'd lost.

Looking at Thane, not blaming him, but wishing things were different, she said, "I don't really get any of this. Making it so personal. They have to know that if I quit, SML is just going to hire someone else to do exactly what I'm doing. Even if the next person isn't as well-known, the word will still infiltrate a lot of the right people." She was on a roll and just kept spilling. "Beyond that, taking me out would be news. I'd be perceived as a victim of sorts, too, which would inevitably gain SML exposure. Maybe as much as having me on tour is doing."

She stopped. Stared at Thane. And said, "You all think that someone at SML is behind this, don't you? At a thousand dollars a pop to hire people off the street, they're out, what, ten thousand, to potentially make ten times that if the sabotage of me, while fighting for their cause, goes viral."

She knew the second Thane's gaze softened that she'd hit on a concern. But not the biggest one.

"What?" she asked him.

"Torrence Spelling is from Florida, Stel." Stella's entire being froze. Inside to out. That name. The man her mother had testified against. The one who'd killed his own little brother—and Kara's father.

The way Thane was looking at her, the sorrow in his gaze, the softness of his voice when he'd spoken told her that he hadn't been planning on dropping the name within her hearing range.

But she'd pushed. Said what she was thinking. Needing to be heard. And to make certain that she had true facts. That they made sense.

She almost wished she hadn't.

And that Thane hadn't engaged with her when he'd seen her going down that road.

Except that she knew both would be the absolute wrong road to take. No burying her head in the sand. No silence just because the truth was horrid.

"You said Spelling had been transferred to a federal prison in Montana."

"He was. But no one knew about Grossman until he tried to kill Kara. There might be others…"

She shook her head. Didn't want to hear that. "You telling me that now that Grossman found us, because Kara was looking up details of Mom's disappearance on the internet, that all three of us are in danger? And may need to go into witness protection?" She was being dramatic. Please, let it be that.

She couldn't possibly be forced into a lifetime of silent lies. Could she?

And she'd thought losing her online life had been the tragedy.

"No one's saying yet that there *is* someone, Stel. Only that they're checking every angle. They'd be remiss not to do so."

His words held truth. She took a deep breath. Looking for hope. Trying to thread some positivity into her thoughts with a reminder that she was dealing with Thane. The one who didn't leave a single stone unturned.

She stood when he mentioned again that they needed

rest. Followed his edict that she take the bathroom first and get ready for bed, while he pulled the mattress out from the couch and got bedding on it. Though she knew she should stay and help, Stella took the out, allowing that he possibly needed some immediate space between them, as she did, and, after brushing her teeth, she pulled her sweats back on with a T-shirt to sleep in. She thought about leaving her bra top on, too, but the fact that she was already going to be struggling to sleep had her change her mind on that one.

She passed him on the way from the bathroom to the living room. She already had herself on the back wall side of the couch, on the edge of the mattress, under the covers, with her back turned toward the rest of the bed by the time Thane came back out, turning off lights.

He left one dim glow shining from above the stove in the kitchen. And had left the remote on the arm of the couch of the side she'd chosen. She'd be fine.

Was thirty-nine-year's old for God's sake. Not thirteen.

She felt as well as heard the thinnish mattress dip into the springs that supported it as he slid in beside her. Forced herself to lie completely still. Listening for the louder breathing that would tell her Thane was fully asleep.

Five minutes passed. Then ten.

Had he done something to curtail his snoring? Turning only enough to get a glimpse at his back—thinking she'd be able to tell by his even breathing that he was out and then be able to at least try to get comfortable—Stella was shocked into complete stillness again as she saw Thane facing her, watching her.

Waiting for her to get to sleep? Knowing that she'd been lying stiffly, far too tense to sleep?

He was facing her. In the bed. Wide-awake. Facing her.

And there was absolutely no way Stella could be quiet about that.

Opening her mouth, she was still scrambling for words to express what had to be spoken. And ended up with only two. Uttered softly, but with every ounce of feeling inside her.

"Hold me?"

She'd had her back turned. A silent communication from the latter years of their marriage. Back turned, don't touch.

The message had been clear. Freeing Thane to keep an eye on his ex-wife, just because it calmed him to do so. While he lay there trying to figure out what they were all missing. What piece of logic would pull together all of the menacing incidents that had been befalling Stella since the beginning of the tour?

Until she'd turned.

Hold me?

His arms reached out before he'd switched gears enough to weigh the consequences of what he was doing. In the back of his mind, a voice was trying to get through.

Thane couldn't hear it for the pounding of blood through his veins. Stella's body against him, her arms sliding solid around him, were all that was clear. She held on so tight.

His reaction was a foregone conclusion. A lifetime of learning each other, instincts that were well honed...and a need that had gone unsatiated for far too long...took control.

When her face lifted to his, her mouth slightly open, he leaned into her, covering her lips with his own. Tonguing her happened as it always had. Instantly. Hungrily. A duel and a dance.

As their bodies moved together, melding, fitting as they always had, from the very first time. Thane pressed his rigid, aching groin against her pelvis, right where he knew she'd want the pressure most. His hands slid up her bare back under her shirt, to cover her breasts, his fingers finding her nipples, teasing them into instant hardness.

"Oh, God, Thane, I've missed this." She breathed the words into his mouth and then slid lower, nibbling his neck. Reaching the neckline of the T-shirt he'd pulled on to sleep in. "Off," she said, and reached for the bottom hem as he lifted enough for her to pull the garment up and over his head.

"Your turn," he said then, pulling at the hem of her shirt and nearly came when her shapely breasts appeared, completely naked, in front of him. His lips dove for the one closest to him, and he pushed her back against that bed as he took his time reacquainting himself with her taste, her smell, the softness of her.

Writhing and moaning—egging on his manly fire—she reached down inside his pajama pants for his main muscle and grabbed hold. Squeezing gently. Stroking. And then dipped her hand in farther, too. Cupping him.

"Mmm, yeah. Right there," he moaned. His hands sliding down her sides and over to dip under the elastic of her sweats to find her feminine bounty wet and ready for him.

As they explored and groaned with pleasure, their pants came off, slowly, sensually and Thane was in heaven every second of the way.

His fingers found her most tender place, played until her hips bucked against him and her legs opened wide. Breathing hard, Thane climbed on top of her and slid home with one thrust. Holding himself still when he was in as deep as he could go. She took all of him. To the hilt. A perfect union. Every time.

Stella moved first, pushing up against him, and pulling back into the thin mattress, as Thane took over, riding her slowly at first. Saying hello. Savoring the familiar ecstasy.

Until Stella's desperate sounding "More, Thane," sent him into full throttle and he moved in and out of her, with her, driving them both to the brink of mindless pleasure.

Her soft inner flesh convulsed around him, and Thane shoved in one last time, as deep as he could go, as wave after wave of release coursed through him.

He came down slowly, pulling out, but not away, and when Stella snuggled up against him, his arms closed around her, holding her so close he could feel her heartbeat.

And thanked God that she was alive.

Promising himself that he'd keep her that way.

Chapter 16

Thane was already up and showered when Stella woke up Sunday morning. She caught a glimpse of him sitting at the table, looking at his burner phone, and quickly closed her eyes again. She'd fallen asleep in his arms. At some point in the night, she'd felt him slide away, and get up. And was pretty sure she'd heard the toilet flush and then felt him climbing back in beside her.

Or she might have dreamed the incident. With twenty years of history between them, she knew his routines as well as she did her own.

Thane generally woke up shortly after sex and went in to take care of business.

Lying there feigning sleep, wanting to stretch, but not doing so since she wasn't ready for him to know that she was awake, she allowed herself a minute to bask in the pleasure of the night before. Warm, satiated, and comforted, too, for having made love with Thane again.

She took full responsibility for what had happened. She'd point-blank asked for it. And Thane had come through for her all the way.

But a new day had dawned, under the shadow of unsolved attacks, and she had to get up and fight her way through them.

It was either that or allow them to steal her life away.

First and foremost, she had to reassure her ex-husband that she wasn't making any more of what had transpired between them in bed than it was. A coupling.

Not a reunion. Or even a hope of the beginning of a second chance.

Nothing had changed where the things that had broken them up were concerned. And she wasn't going to pretend—or hope—that it had. No way either of them needed to be put through the breaking-up pain a second time.

Sliding out of bed, Stella held her clothes against her and made a beeline for the bathroom. She imagined Thane was watching her backside disappearing and breathed a sigh of relief when she closed the bathroom door behind her without any sound from him.

"Good morning" with her naked butt out there wasn't how she wanted to start the day.

Forcing herself to focus on the matters at hand, Stella showered in record time, telling herself that Thane would have good news regarding her social platforms. The rest of it, the crimes were happening on an escalating scale, but that part was completely out of her hands, and she had to trust the professionals involved to get it all resolved.

Pulling on her last pair of clean work pants and the blouse that went with them, Stella sorted her dirty clothes into two loads, and with arms filled, headed out to the little closet at the end of the kitchen. She'd discovered the night before—during her slower perusal of the kitchen—that the space not only held wire shelving for dried goods, but had a stackable washer and dryer set as well.

"If you bring me your whites, I'll put them in with mine," she said by way of greeting the new day with her ex-husband.

When he didn't respond by the time she'd dumped her lights in, she turned to see him standing at the kitchen counter, pouring a cup of coffee. Looking all manly and successful and handsome in yet another one of his full suits. Complete with knotted tie. It was the first time he'd worn brown on tour. The color of dirt. Mud. She hoped that the choice wasn't a precursor for the day ahead.

Mostly because she was wary of his odd behavior, his nonresponse to her offer to do his laundry—she took the cup of coffee he handed her.

Looked up at him when he just stood there. And, stomach clenching as he held her gaze with a serious one of his own, heard him say, "I didn't use protection last night."

Yeah, she'd briefly skimmed the news. Had chosen to let go of what she couldn't change. Sipped coffee when she figured the remark wouldn't get her on his good side.

"Middle of the month was always your fertile time, Stel, has that changed?"

Trust him to remember every little minute detail that had ever been made known to him.

It hadn't. But she was thirty-nine. Her system had to be slowing down production. And even if it wasn't, the chances weren't great. Not with her stress level. And the fact that she was on the tail end of risk. "No."

He nodded. Then said, "You aren't on any birth control."

She could be. They'd been apart well over a year. But, coffee in hand, said, "Nope."

And then, because she was who she was, she looked him in the eye and said, "I'm sorry, Thane. Seriously. I take full responsibility for what happened. Last night… I wasn't thinking about things like birth control. I just…"

His eyes softened as she said the last word, and her

brain blipped, causing her to forget for a second what she'd been about to say.

"It's okay, Stel," he filled in for her. "And you are not solely responsible. Clearly, I'm aware of your cycle and I wasn't thinking about birth control, either. And while yes, you did the initial asking, I could have said no."

Yeah. She was trying not to dwell on that part, either. Lest her traitorous far-too-sensitive half make more of his immediate acquiescence than had been party to the deed.

Instead, she dissected his response, judged it. So Thane, sticking straight with the details. The logic.

"I just needed to verify that I should be aware of possible ramifications," he said then. "I trust you'll let me know?"

"Of course." She met his gaze head-on. Tamping down any hint of a spark that the thought of having Thane's child would light inside her.

Because the news would not be good, were it to come to pass. Not only were they divorced, but Thane didn't want a child with her. And she didn't blame him. No matter how much love she had to give, she would not make a good mother. She wasn't Mel. Or Kara. She was the snarky loudmouthed sister.

With one last glance, Thane nodded, then turned, saying, "Hang on just a second, I'll get my whites."

And Stella shook her head. Sipped coffee. And figured that just about summed up her life.

Incredible sex, without any door open to anything more, followed by coffee and washing his dirty clothes.

It was her life because it was the life she'd chosen.

And when she looked at herself from the outside in, she knew that it was the life that was best for her to be living.

No matter how hard her heart cried out for more.

* * *

Stella was right. The likelihood of one of his thirty-nine-year-old swimmers finding a viable egg at the end of her cycle wasn't great.

Which was great.

The last thing he and Stella needed was a child to raise.

Except that...as he sorted his laundry, Thane dwelled on the idea. And saw a picture where they could do it. If they had to.

They'd handled divorce just fine. Living their separate lives, but there if the other needed them. No blame. Or hard feelings.

They could share parenting the same way.

Lord knew, any kid would be lucky as hell to have Stella for a mother. Because a child of her own was one thing Thane knew for sure the woman would love more than her job or anything else. Period. She knew what it was to need a mother. To lose her. And as loudly as her soul was called to help those more vulnerable than herself, she'd be all over that one.

The kid would need Thane just for bouts of emotional reality—not everyone would love deeply, fully, and unconditionally—and for lessons about fighting pain with logic.

Logic. He'd been fully focused on facts since he'd woken at four that morning. And had to have a serious talk with Stella.

Not about birth control.

Picking up his load of white clothes, he brushed by his ex-wife in the kitchen to dump them in the washer, poured in detergent from the little container Stella had left there, the one she traveled with, and started the machine.

She'd made oatmeal. Had found some dried cranberry salad topper to put on hers. Left his bowl sitting there empty by the pan on the stove and carried her own over to the small table.

"Here's what bugs me about someone from SML being involved in the incidents," she said, as though they'd been in the middle of the conversation. "They know how big this thing is being investigated. And if it comes out that someone on the inside is behind these attacks...they're done. Period. Even if they manage to salvage the organization, their donation pool will have dried up. No one will trust them. Beyond that, anyone on the inside would have known about the change in schedule. They'd have known to douse the second mic, not the first, since we'd decided not to have me open as I always do."

Glad to take his cue from her, rather than having to tell her what he'd learned that morning, Thane added some brown sugar to his bowl of freshly scooped oatmeal and joined her at the table. "The operation could have been too far along to stop without getting caught. But your points are valid. Which is why the theory isn't at the top of anyone's list. But we can't completely rule it out, either. Could be someone within the organization who's set to get a big bonus or promotion based on how much this tour earns, who is acting rogue. Carelessly so. Putting the organization's future at risk for a chance for an in-the-moment personal financial boon."

She looked at him and smiled. Not at all the reaction Thane had been expecting, due to the topic they were discussing, and the tougher it was going to get. "What?" he had to ask.

"I just like the way that you don't stop until you have final answers with proof. You keep your mind open, looking for any unforeseen possibility."

He did do that. Used to drive her up the wall. When

it pertained to her and reasons why she might want to consider compromise in her messaging rather than go all in with no other choice but the one she was advocating.

He had to focus on the case. It was his only reason for being alone with her in an isolated cottage. "Phosgene oxime can be made by using a combination of tin metal and hydrochloric acid. The trace of chemicals found on the microphone Amelia picked up don't match the mix of what's stored, or what was made, by the government. We're dealing with a homemade version." He shared one of the most recent pieces of news he'd been sent that morning.

When she just kept eating, no longer engaging with him, he knew she'd resigned herself to what was coming. Knew, too, that, though it was hard for her to hear, she wanted it all. Had to have it all in order for her to trust him. And herself with her choices, too.

No secrets.

And so he ate, and related.

"Riker's still not talking, those investigating are convinced he's hiding something and have a team deep diving on the man's entire life."

Stella pushed a cranberry to the side of her bowl, and scooped oatmeal.

"There's nothing new on the rotted board. I'm guessing, once they find the source who's doling out thousand-dollar payouts, they'll find one that corresponds with that day. In the meantime, local authorities have been on the news asking anyone who's seen anyone they know with nitrogen and potassium nitrate to please contact the police."

There were another three cranberries lining the inside of Stella's bowl. He'd only seen her take two bites.

"The nineteen-year-old woman who dropped the smoke

bomb has been charged and is out on bail. Her cash was confiscated, but a trace has turned up nothing. However, when I asked about the coffee can used for the drop, guess what the brand was?"

"Morning Star," Stella said, statement, not question. She looked up at him, but there was no hint of any stars in her eyes that morning. Not anymore.

He nodded. "We have to talk about how damned creepy this is getting, Stel."

Her gaze shot to his, and his gut dropped as he saw the steely glint in her eyes. "No. We don't," she said. "That's exactly what he wants, Thane. To break me. Get me to quit. He's trying to manipulate my mind and I'm not going to let fear win. I'm just not. Because if it wins this time, what does that mean for every other time in my life when anxiety hits?" She shook her head. "No. I won't be told I can't speak."

He'd pushed too far. Again. And in doing so, could be throwing her right into the attacker's path. Working in his favor.

Getting back on the task he'd set himself—giving her the facts without his personal commentary—he let her impassioned speech go unanswered and said, "They've narrowed down the size of the barrel of the paintball gun..."

"Let me guess," Stella interrupted, a sign to him that he'd agitated her deeply. "Common make and model, could be bought in a gazillion places, no way to narrow it down..."

She was struggling, at battle within herself, and he couldn't help her. Never had been able to. Maybe he wasn't meant to do so. Could be nobody was. Everyone was born to a life. With talents and with challenges, too.

He wasn't real fond of the quirk of fate that had locked

Stella up so tight with hers. Seemed cruel and counterproductive to him to give a person such incredible ability to communicate in a way that people opened up to, but render her unable to do so in her personal life.

"There are only a few hundred of the guns in existence," he said then. For once glad to have news that was not what she'd expected. "Four have been sold in the state of Florida, that they know of. Local investigators are following up on them."

Shoving a bite of oatmeal into her mouth, Stella swallowed. Spooned another bite, as though her life depended upon it and swallowed it, too.

"Nothing further on the food poisoning. No cameras have turned up anything yet. No matches with photos of rally crowds. Of course, as was to be expected, there was no camera directly in line with the drop-off point of the cereal box."

And they were back to where he needed her to understand that what was happening was far more intricate and personal to her than opposition to SML's cause. Not that he could prove that. But he believed it. Strongly enough that Doug was taking the possibility seriously. "Something we're considering is the fact that whoever is behind this is using packaging for items that are personal to your everyday living—not only your choice of items and brands, but the actual items themselves are habitual to you. Items you use every day. That would throw you off if you didn't have them."

Stella emptied her bowl—other than the cranberries. Put her spoon down in it and gave him a very direct look. "Tell me about my socials, Thane."

He'd known he had to. Just really, really didn't want to do so. "At the moment, no one has been able to find the identity of whoever was behind the theft. It appears as though some kind of bot was programmed to take over your profiles. Nothing traces back to an actual person. Separate email addresses were used for each platform, and all of them lead nowhere. Law enforcement is working with representatives from each of the platforms, and those that aren't already back under your complete control will be shortly." He picked up his burner, tapped and scrolled, tapped again, and set it on the table, turning it around so she could read the code written there. "This is your new password. And there's a second email address on every one of them, in addition to yours, that belongs to an IT specialist with the FBI. She'll be monitoring all the activity, checking out unknown and suspicious profiles that show up for the duration of this case. I'm to ask you to please let me know if you change your passwords so that I can see that she's notified."

Stella had been sitting there, pretty much frozen, staring at his phone as he spoke. When he fell silent, she was still for another couple of seconds, and then suddenly jumped up so fast she rattled the table as her thigh banged into it.

Taking a step toward him, she bent at the waist, her hands clasped together and, with her nose only inches from his, said, "I've got my platforms back?" She squealed loudly. And then, with just as much gusto and a lot less glee said, "And you're just now telling me?"

Yep, that had gone exactly as he'd predicted.

With a sinking heart, and a feeling of rocks in his gut, Thane nodded.

There was one last thing Thane had put off telling Stella. She was standing there, staring him down, trying not to note the lack of joy in his gaze as he let her know that he'd arisen before dawn that morning, and had already arranged with Doug to have another secure rental vehicle delivered to them, complete with bulletproof glass. Her hometown detective was going all out to keep her safe.

Stella knew it was due to Kara's near death the month before. And Doug's association with Kara's husband, Ben. She owed them all.

She also knew that the last thing Thane wanted was to have her out anywhere. Including online.

He didn't demur, though, when she insisted on leaving their little house to drive across town, at the invitation of the local police station, to use their internet and get back on her socials. Lisa, who was still working on the food poisoning incident, had arranged for them to have a private conference room at the station to work.

Thane sat with her, working on his own computer, for the three hours she spent online. He made a trip down the hall to the kitchen filled with vending machines and bought them junk food to eat, with cups of coffee and cans of fruit drink.

Lisa came in and talked to both of them. Asking questions pursuant to her case. Wanting to know if either of them had noticed anyone or anything different at the rally on Saturday. Neither had.

She also let them know that Doug's team had shared all the comments from Stella's social media platform starting from Friday night and her own IT guy was looking for any possible connections, or references that might allude to, the purchase or possession of campylobacter, the bacteria that had been found on their food delivered to the hotel.

Stella liked the woman. Trusted her. And in that building, on police bandwidth, knowing that Doug's IT person was still monitoring her accounts, the negative comments Stella had to delete weren't nearly as bothersome as they might have been. There were a lot of them. More than usual, but then she had three times the number of positive comments to read through as well.

All sympathetic to her properties having been stolen, assuring her that they weren't going anywhere.

After she posted on all six apps, and then went back through each one, the response had been almost overwhelming. Much more positive than negative.

And none of the negative were as bad as *Smart bitches take the hint*. The comment from days before was still haunting her. Not only because it had been aimed directly at her, but because it had sounded like more of a warning than a criticism or put-down.

Thane was on the phone with Doug's office, confirming that they'd copied the negative comments as they were coming in, and Stella deleted. Bothered by the large amount of vitriol being spewed on her. But as they got through them all, she was still feeling much better than she had since she'd been shot.

They were winning. She had an army of trained professionals hunting down whoever was behind the attacks, an IT specialist with connections to platform representatives watching out for her properties, and Thane was there. Overseeing every aspect of her world.

While she felt guilty for the resources being spent on her behalf, for what were mostly misdemeanor crimes, she knew that the growing numbers of law enforcement involved was due to the serial nature of the events, and all the local jurisdictions in which they'd taken place.

"I'm about done here," she told Thane not long after noon that Sunday. Not really smiling at him, but feeling a smile inside as she considered all the free hours ahead they'd have to spend relaxing together.

In a house with only one bedroom.

They'd yet to talk about what had happened between them the night before. Other than the lack of contraceptive use, which wasn't going to be an issue.

She couldn't explain to herself how she knew that. She just wasn't bothered by their lapse. Nor had Thane seemed to be. Which could have a lot to do with her own lack of uneasiness.

He'd glanced up briefly as she'd spoken, then was right back on his computer, his focus intent. He read, typed, and read, leaning into the screen. Frowning.

Sitting there watching him freely, Stella allowed the burst of love that flowed through her. She didn't often have the chance to just let herself glow within that sphere. She had to be responsible to his wishes, the divorce. Which meant her feelings for him had to be contained.

But in that room, on the tour, under current circumstances, with what had happened the night before, her restraint didn't seem as necessary. They were in another universe, time out of time. And neither of them was looking for more between them than the somewhat distant friendship they'd been able to maintain. Been there, done that. They understood why marriage between them didn't work.

Didn't mean they couldn't enjoy the great sex while they were forced together for work. The night they'd spent together at Kara's wedding the year before was proof of their ability to make love and walk away without any change to their relationship. They'd left the wedding hotel and had returned to their separate lives without a blip.

And would do so again. Just as soon as the tour was done.

So what would it hurt if, in the meantime, they found pleasure in each other's arms during a rather trying work assignment?

The suddenness with which Thane snapped his computer shut made Stella jump. He glanced at her, his gaze still as intent as it had been, and she asked, "What?"

Before he could answer her, a short knock sounded on the door just before it opened, and Lisa stood there. Her gaze brushed over Stella and then landed on Thane. "Ready?" she asked, her tone solemn.

Thane, his expression grim, didn't even look at Stella as he nodded.

And her good mood was shot to hell.

Chapter 17

He knew how it was going to go. There wasn't going to be anything he could do, or say, no threatening, or even begging that was going to change the course that was upon them.

Thane had spent the past twenty minutes attempting to find one voice, other than Ben's, that would back him up. And had come up empty.

He'd been told that he was understood by all. And wouldn't be blamed if he chose to back away. The words of many to that effect were with him as he followed Lisa and Stella to the elevator and then rode up with them to the secure room with a large screen mounted to the wall, where a video conference was about to take place.

Mel and Kara were with him. He knew that without asking. Purposely hadn't checked in with them. He had to think, listen to logic, not react emotionally, as they would have him do.

No one spoke in the elevator, but Thane could feel Stella's tension encasing him. She turned to look at him once. He withstood the glance without a flinch. She didn't say anything, but he heard her questions, her mistrust of what he was walking her into.

When the night before…

Thane shut the thought down. *Irony* didn't even begin to encapsulate the situation in which he found himself. Another cruel twist of fate. And even that didn't describe his current hell.

It was the divorce all over again. On steroids.

Lisa introduced the chief of detectives, Lloyd Overman, as the only other person in the room as the three of them silently entered. Stella hadn't said a word since Lisa had come down to get them. Thane knew her silence meant she was shoring up her defenses.

Could tell by the stiffness of her shoulders, the head held high, and the tight chin pointing slightly upward, that his cause had already been lost.

And was beset with a sudden urge to grab her to him. Kiss her. Remind her that there was so much good in the world, outside of SML and all her other causes.

Because he knew, as did everyone else who'd been in on the conversations over the past half hour, that the attacks didn't stop with SML. They'd follow Stella to her next job, and the next, unless she gave in to the mental manipulation and quit.

Not only would they continue, they'd escalate in cruelty. Until she was killed.

That last thought shot through Thane's gut and into his heart as the four of them moved toward the video screen that was currently booting up. Other than the introduction of Lloyd Overman, no one had spoken.

Everyone but Stella knew what was coming.

Thane watched as Lisa stopped next to Lloyd, who, with a remote in hand, was standing in front of the screen. Stella fell in line beside her, and Thane purposely took Stella's other side. She'd need him there.

And it was up to him whether or not he opted to stay.

He wanted to believe he'd already made up his mind. That when Stella refused to back down, he'd walk out of the room, and out of her life, too. Nothing was ever going to change. Not for him. And not for her, either.

He felt her sharp intake of breath beside him as Doug's face appeared on the screen. Alone.

"Hey, Stella," the detective greeted. He sounded friendly, but somber, too.

"No niceties, Doug, please," Stella said by way of return greeting. "If it's been determined that you're the one who's going to tell me what's going on, then please get to it."

The detective seemed to be looking right at Stella as he stood in front of a blue screen and said, "The FBI has officially taken over the case."

"So why am I not speaking with them?"

"Because I'm still working it, too," the man continued without any sound of the concern he'd expressed in messaging to the group just moments before. "They're lead on the investigation. I'm in charge of you."

So to speak. Doug had been assigned to oversee Stella's moves. To provide for her safety, as he'd already been doing. He knew her, and had detailed and multitiered plans in place to keep her as safe as possible on the tour.

As possible. Those were the words that stuck in Thane's throat as he faced the probability of an impossible task before them.

"We've done intense deep digging on your shooter, Riker. Diving into every aspect of the man's life, from present back to birth."

Thane approved of Doug's approach. Just the facts. And the depth of them, which showed the seriousness of the situation, without actually telling Stella they were looking at life and death. Hers.

"Earlier today, they found a direct link between Duane Riker and Torrence Spelling."

Duane Riker. The man who'd shot her. Spelling, the man who'd killed his own brother. The one her mother had testified against.

And there it was. The information that had brought them back to the end. Theirs.

"Wha...what link?"

"When Spelling was first arrested for his brother's murder, he'd been in a holding cell for a short time. Before he was officially booked. Awaiting his attorney. Duane Riker had been brought in for criminal trespass, a crime completely unrelated to Spelling, at the same time. Records show that they shared that holding cell for a couple of hours."

Stella didn't move. Didn't hiss. Didn't break. She just stood there, face pointed at the screen. Breathing in. Breathing out.

That's all she gave Thane. Standing. Breathing.

Why he'd expected more—a look in his direction, reaching for his hand—he didn't know. Apparently, it didn't matter how well he knew her, how deep his tutelage went, he was never really going to learn.

"We believe that Spelling is orchestrating these attacks on you, Stella. The man is diabolically cruel, vindictive, and takes pleasure in manipulating others, watching them become his prey."

Doug was really laying it all out. Thane appreciated the man's efforts, even knowing that his every word was action aimed, in a small part, at covering his department's tracks. What they were about to ask of Stella...she had to know the danger she was facing.

"Do you have direct proof?" Stella's voice was strong, and didn't sound like her.

"That Spelling is your Big Money?" he asked, making the question personal to Stella. "Not yet. But we're close. I expect it yet today."

She nodded. Lips pursed, as she continued to stare at the screen. Thane, in looking at Stella, caught Lisa's gaze on the other side of her. The detective had also been watching Stella. Lisa raised her brow at Thane, as if to say that Stella was going to be in, then turned back to the screen as well.

Lisa knew, they all knew, that Thane was adamantly against the plan. Had been from the get-go.

"So what now?" Stella asked, all business. No emotion. No questions regarding Spelling's ability to communicate with Riker. Or anyone else. She wasn't diving into details.

"Now you have a choice to make," Doug said. The exact words that would lower Stella's defenses. Putting her in control.

Thane swallowed with difficulty.

"We're fairly certain that Spelling doesn't know yet that we're onto him. Which gives us a small window of time to catch him at his own game," Doug said then, his voice gaining an emotional tone as his serious gaze bore into the camera filming him.

Stella nodded. "You have a plan, then."

Doug nodded right back at her. "We want you to stay on tour, Stella. Do exactly what you're doing. Since we now know who and what we're dealing with, we have means to catch him in action. To end this once and for all."

She didn't flinch. Sink into herself. Her shoulders didn't even drop. Chin up, Stella said, "I have one question."

Thane would have had a plethora of them. Had had.

"What's that?"

"Do you believe my sisters are now in danger as well?"

"Absolutely."

"Then I'm in." With a glance at Lisa, and then at Thane, and back to Doug, she said, "Let's get to work. Tell me what you need from me now, for the rest of today as well as going forward."

And Thane's heart sank to the floor.

Stella had never been so calm. It was as though her entire life had led her to that moment. She knew her course. Maybe she was in shock.

Her mother had left her entire existence behind, had become someone else with no family, no friends, no one who knew the real her, to protect them against this man, and he had found them. She didn't feel shock. It was almost as though, subconsciously, she'd known what the attacks on her were about. Or maybe she'd spent her entire life waiting for that moment. Believing that it would come someday.

She couldn't say for sure. She just knew that she'd made the choice she'd been meant to make.

Didn't have a single doubt. No hesitation.

Until she heard Doug say, "Thane? What about you?"

Her gaze immediately shot to her ex-husband. She'd assumed…since Thane was in the briefing, standing right next to her, that he'd already made his choice to move forward.

But when his gaze met hers, and she saw the familiar beseeching there, she accepted her mistake. Thane was Thane.

And they'd hit their crossroads again. The one where he had to go one way, and she had to go another.

Thane hadn't responded, and turning back to Doug, she said, "I'm in, either way."

She loved Thane. So much. More than life, probably. But she couldn't lose the chance to free her family from the evil that infiltrated them nearly thirty years before. The situation was untenable. She hadn't asked to be put in it, any more than she'd wanted to be a ten-year-old whose mother had chosen to leave them forever.

But getting out of it, removing the threat from her sisters, who both had families, was within her power, under her control.

"I have to let you know that if you choose to leave the tour, no one will blame you," Doug said then, looking straight at her, not at Thane. But Stella felt like the words came from the man standing stiffly beside her. "We already have plans in place for that eventuality as well. We'd ask that you take a break from your job until this situation is over, and the US Marshal's service will take over your protection from there."

US Marshals. She shuddered at the mention. Hated them. The words. The men she saw in her mind's eye when she heard the title spoken. Even as she knew her feelings were childish and irrational. The words meant fear, unbearable loss, of life, of love, of choice…

"Your sisters are both already, as of an hour ago, in protective custody in safe houses with their husbands, and your nephew, Josh, is with Darin and Mel as well."

Doug had said initially, at the opening of the meeting, that they didn't yet have definitive proof that Spelling was involved. And yet they'd gone to such lengths to protect against his evils?

She glanced at Thane. Didn't want to proceed without him. When he didn't turn to meet her gaze, but rather, kept staring at the screen, she knew that she was probably going to have to leave him behind.

Not a completely horrible thought. If he came with her, he'd be in danger, too. Instead of safe like Ben and Darin… "I'm assuming Thane is going to get that same safe house protection when he leaves here today?" she demanded.

"I'm not leaving you here alone, Stella," Thane said, his tone irritable. But firm, too. "I'd like a chance to change your mind, to talk this through…"

She so badly wanted to give him that chance. But knew that they'd be wasting invaluable time just to try to work through emotions. The end result would be the same.

"I've made my decision," she told him, looking at him, feeling lost when the glance he shot back at her was one of a stranger.

"Then you've made mine, too," he said.

Her heart wanted to be happy about the announcement, but she knew that in making the choice to save her family, she'd just lost any hope of a chance that someday she and Thane would find their way back to each other again.

Thane let anger-infused adrenaline drive him through the next hour. With Doug still on video, he started shooting off orders to everyone else in the room as to what he was going to require to get his part of the job, protecting his employer's interests, done.

First and foremost, a safe house at each stop on the tour. At least one US Marshal as a full-time bodyguard, with drivers and two other bodyguards protecting him and Stella anytime she was working, which included a private police station room in whatever town they were in while she handled the social media portion of her responsibilities. The rest of the time, they'd remain in the safe house. Without internet. Period.

"And there will be none of Stella's normal choices for anything, no brand she uses to brush her teeth, do her laundry, or even—" he stopped long enough to bite off the "wipe her ass" portion of the comment and shot out "—toilet paper. We have no idea how many people are working for this guy, nor where he has eyes and ears. There will be no purchases that could even point to Stella's preferences." He glanced at her as he finished.

She was looking at Doug. Nodding.

Smart woman.

But he wasn't staying unless he knew he had her full cooperation. "And, Stella," he said, waiting for her to meet his gaze, there, in front of everyone. "You are to follow all dictates. Immediately when they're given. Period. There could be imminent danger, and a second could be the difference between life and death. You don't want to spend that second arguing."

She held his gaze steadily. It felt deep, but he wasn't going there. He glanced away as soon as he saw her nod, and heard, "Of course."

"One of the mandates is that you're going to be asked to include certain verbiage into your normal messaging." The key to the plan—and something he was adamantly against as he considered the possibility that the words that were going to go out meant to incite Spelling, could have the same effect on any number of other over-the-top zealots out there. "In every speech you need to passionately declare that you are who you are because of the mother who bore you and taught you to always stand up for what you knew was right. To never let bullies keep you from speaking out on behalf of others. And somewhere else, mention that you are just like your mother. Find ways to bring your voice, your passion, back to her." He poured it on hard, hoping that being forced to embody Tory would be Stella's stopping point. Praying that it would be.

"I understand," Stella said, then, looking straight ahead asked, "What about SML?"

And Doug spoke from the screen. "Already fully briefed and on board." The detective's glance warmed as he said, "They said that they're honored to help someone who's spent her life helping others."

It was the first Thane had heard that. But then, he hadn't been open to anything good about the plan. He had to focus on the train wreck. In the slightest possibility that they could actually prevent it.

How did you fight a power that allowed a man to sit confined and alone in a federal prison and still have reach across the country to be able to hire a plethora of people off the streets as pawns in his lethal game of chess? Most particularly when you had no idea how Spelling was sourcing the power?

"Regardless of how this plays out, SML stands to gain from the publicity," Lisa pointed out, gaining her back a small portion of Thane's regard as the detective stuck to the cold, hard truth.

"But it could also put their people in danger," Stella said, glancing first at Thane, and then around the others. "Look at what happened to Amelia."

"They're hiring extra security," Doug told her. "And everyone on the front lines will be there fully informed and on an opt-in basis. And while what you say is true, given what happened with Amelia, the entity we're after, most likely Spelling, wants you, not anyone else. Based on the profile the FBI has of whomever we're seeking, this person most likely sees Amelia's injury as a failure and will be taking extreme measures to ensure it doesn't happen again."

"Unless a bystander is hurt as a means to get to me," Stella said then, with another glance at Thane. "They had no way of knowing which meal I'd be eating Saturday night and so poisoned both."

With a sudden insight, Thane saw where she was going. As much as she wanted him with her, she was about to try to abort his involvement.

"It's critical that the players stay as much the same as possible," he quickly jumped into the conversation. "Major changes, other than protection being put in place due to the attacks, would alert Big Money that we're onto them. If this is Spelling, he's deriving pleasure and a sense of power from playing with your mind and instilling fear in you. Wrapping yourself with a protective detail will feed his avaricious need to see you suffer. And, as Doug stated, *everyone* on the front line is aware of the danger and has chosen to do his or her job accordingly."

Including him. He didn't like the plan. At all. But he was in. One hundred percent. As Stella had just inadvertently pointed out to him.

When she met his gaze, with a look that went beyond business, he stared right back.

Giving her one very clear message. Didn't matter how much she had to say on the subject, she wasn't getting rid of him.

Chapter 18

Stella had learned young the concept of mind over matter. Back at their little house for the rest of the day and night—locked inside with people back at the station monitoring the outside cameras at all times and two on-site officers hidden around the premises—she went straight to work on the next day's program. Her educational portion of the rally was being filmed for a kid's presentation at local schools, and she needed to make certain that she hit all the right notes.

Her job was to stay focused. Maintain her mindset. To keep anxiety from taking control. And beyond that, it was easy. Just be herself. Do what she'd been doing for nearly twenty years.

And follow instructions. While she'd have thought that part would pose some issues for her, it didn't at all. She was grateful beyond measure for all the effort being put into taking down the man who'd obliterated her family.

Thane had kept to himself, not saying much on the drive back to the house, nor after they'd locked themselves inside. His mind was working, she understood that. Recognized the concentrated expression on his face.

And still felt as though something had been lost between

them. A new closeness—based on better understanding—that she didn't want to lose.

After a mostly silent dinner of baked potato, salad, and bread—all of which had been picked up and brought to the police station before they'd left—she'd had enough of his distance.

It was bringing her an anxiety she could ill afford.

In a matter of hours, a new day was going to dawn, and she was going to be on the front line of a battle she wasn't sure she could win. A fight her sisters' lives depended on her winning.

She couldn't be distracted by personal inconsistencies—mixed messages—between her and Thane.

And…truth was…if she was going to die saving her family…she wanted her last night, or nights, to be spent in heaven on earth.

Coming to decisions as she finished up the dishes and changed into the sweats she'd wear to bed, she entered the living room with purpose. Saw Thane sitting on "his" side of the couch that would become their bed, scrolling on his burner phone.

Which meant communicating with others on the team of professionals working together to keep her alive and catch the entity that would have it otherwise. Texting only. The burner, if compromised, would ping to a nearby tower, not to Thane or their house.

And he'd be using a new one every day. Was on his second since they'd given up internet at their sleeping locations.

The amount of money going into the operation was astounding. Overwhelming. Ben and Thane were both covering some of the expenses. But the rest were being picked up by all the parties involved. Spelling, Big Money, whoever, had helped out there by splitting the seemingly unrelated crimes up all over the state.

And local police departments had opted to share the cases, with the FBI as lead, rather than relinquish them altogether.

So many good people…fighting for her and her family. The scope of it all was hitting her deeply as she sat down on "her" end of the couch. With nothing to do but control her thoughts.

Giving herself what she needed at the moment—being close to Thane.

She waited for him to set his phone on his thigh, and asked, "Can we talk?"

She needed to. And her communication would only work with him as the recipient.

His look was focused on her. And impersonal. "Yes."

His walls were back up. Maybe higher than ever. But she continued. "In the past… I didn't fight for our marriage…"

She was gearing up, leading into the topic on her mind, but before she got another word out, Thane interrupted. "Nope. You fought for what mattered most to you. Your right to speak. Your causes. Helping those who were unable to be heard on their own."

He wasn't wrong. And the facts weren't where she'd been headed. So she just got there. No more lead-in. "I was super close with my mom," she said. "More so than Mel, who'd always had a self-sufficient, mothering streak about her. And Kara, she'd needed the basics, but wasn't yet at a point to have an actual relationship with anyone."

Chancing a glance at Thane, she was a bit shocked to see him focused on her. Studying her. With warmth in his eyes. That one glance she allowed herself, freed up more words than she'd ever spoken aloud on the topic. "Then one day, without warning, she was just…gone. I know a lot of kids go through the grief of losing a mother. I was in counseling with some of them for a while. But with me, it wasn't just the desertion, it was the fact that she'd had a choice. She didn't die. She left. Knowing that she'd never see us again. That we'd never be able to find her."

Or shouldn't have been. Kara had gotten close. Too close. Which had unleashed hell upon her. All of them.

Because of the lies. If Kara had known the truth…

Not her current topic. She had to stay on track. Stay focused. Swallowing, she continued to stare at the blank television screen on the wall. "I was already starting puberty." She said aloud the memories that were piling up on her. "I was too young to understand that hormones were affecting my emotional view of the world, of course, but looking back…" She stopped. Swallowed again.

Felt the couch cushions shift a bit as Thane did. But he didn't come any closer, and she didn't look at him, either. "I was a kid in the process of finding out who I was, learning from the views of me my mother showed me, the strengths within she helped me see, and then… suddenly I was being forced by everyone in my world to be someone I wasn't."

She sounded pathetic. Looked over at Thane. "I'm not hoping for sympathy here," she said, her gaze as firm as her voice. "Nor feeling sorry for myself," she added. And continued to hold his gaze steadily as she said, "I'm explaining myself. Not excusing. Explaining."

When his expression softened into something she wasn't sure she'd seen before, and couldn't really define, she had to glance away again.

"I was deserted at a critical time in my life by the one person I'd trusted to love me unconditionally, and forever."

"From everything I've heard, and it's more than you'd want it to be, that love is what drove your mother to do what she did," Thane said, his voice deep. And filled with inarguable assurance.

She nodded. Swallowed. And then looked him in the eye. "You might be right about that," she told him. "Today, for the first time since she left, I saw a piece of my mother in me. Or rather, me in her." She shook her head. "My sisters' lives are at stake, Thane," she told him. "Mel's got a fifteen-year-old son who needs her. Kara's pregnant. They're mothers with innocent beings who need them, just like I needed my mother. And I've been given the chance to stop a fiend who will rob one child of his or her life, and rob the other of the mother who will see him into adulthood with a sense of love and belonging."

Tears sprang up out of nowhere, clogging her throat, interrupting her voice as she said, "I am my mother's daughter. I have to do this."

Thane's nod was a total contrast to what she'd seen at the police station when she'd uttered words similar to those last five. Instead of the proclamation eliciting anger, it brought…acceptance. And…maybe some affection, too. It seemed to lace his voice as he said, "I know."

And her job there was done.

Thane wasn't at all ready for the door Stella had thrown open. He couldn't afford the distraction. But more, he wasn't willing to…being opened up by her, with her, again. And yet, there was more he had to say, apparently as he couldn't keep his mouth closed when the words came to him.

"That's unconditional love, Stel," he told her, repeating her own words back to her. "Your mother...she'd messed up by her association with a good man who, unknown to him, had murderous family ties. And rather than being selfish and clinging to those who she loved more than anything in the world, she chose to put herself on the front line to save her daughters' lives."

He watched as tears dripped slowly from her eyes and down her face. Fighting the urge to move closer to her, to reach up and brush away her tears with his fingers, he said, "I understand why you have to do this, Stel, which is why I'm still here. We'll get it done."

It was all he could give her. All he had to give.

And even then, he had no idea how much truth would be in those words. They'd give all they had to help law enforcement end Spelling's reign of terror once and for all, but there was no guarantee they'd succeed.

Because even if they somehow caught the devil in the act of running a scheme to terrorize and eventually kill three innocent women, if they stopped him from hurting them, saved Kara's and Melanie's and Stella's lives, all they could do was put whoever was on the outside working for Spelling in prison. The fiend was already there.

Which hadn't stopped him from getting to the women, once their identities had been made known to him.

So what? Best-case scenario, they all went into witness protection? Forcing Stella to live the rest of her life as a lie?

Better than her being dead. She'd have her sisters with her. And possibly their husbands and children.

Of which he was neither.

"But you still don't agree that it's the right choice."

Stella's words reached him softly. With understanding, not recrimination.

Drawing his gaze to her. Their eyes held, and while hers demanded truth, his portrayed his lifelong promise never to lie to her.

"No, I don't."

And there they sat. On opposite sides of a fence that would forever stand between them.

It was their divorce all over again.

With one difference. This time around, the tenderness had managed to survive.

While Thane was brushing his teeth, Stella made up the bed he'd pulled out from the couch. And climbed in before he was back out in the living room. She'd never been shy about her needs and with life on the line, there was no way she was going to pretend she didn't want what she wanted. Thane had never had a problem telling her no.

But she wanted her "pretty please" loud and clear in the event that he was vacillating in the wisdom of them spending any more time copulating when they both knew that their intimate paths weren't meant to permanently gel.

She didn't care about the future. There wasn't one out there unless she successfully lured a killer into her trap and then others managed to legally kill him. It was the only way they were ever going to be free.

If her stalker was Spelling.

And if not, Big Money was going to have one hell of a lot to answer to when the FBI got ahold of them.

Thane turned out all but the dim light they'd left glowing over the stove in the kitchen as he vacated the back portion of the small house. Preventing her from reading his expression when he came out to see her in the middle of her half of the bed, directly facing his half.

He was in shadows and she held her breath, all senses on hold, as he climbed in beside her. Until she heard his soft, deep gravelly voice say, "I brought condoms," just before his mouth covered hers.

She didn't much care about the birth control, figuring the cat was already out of the bag on that one, and had likely already jumped the fence, too. What thrilled her to the core as she heard the words was that he wasn't just pulling her into him because she'd been willing.

He'd been planning to make love to her before he'd ever left the bedroom.

An hour turned into two and Stella spent them exactly as she'd most want to do. In a world where only Thane and the mutual ecstasy they built together existed. He'd seemed as eager as she was to prolong the encounter, experimenting with touch, with his tongue, prompting her to do the same, bringing them to places they'd never been before, with a crescendo the third time through that almost made her see stars.

They didn't talk much. They'd done it all earlier.

But when Thane came back from his last trip to the bathroom, and, climbing under the covers she'd straightened, to pull her up against him, she snuggled into his arms to fall asleep. Without question.

Or judgment. She dreamed, instead. Of him. Of them. Younger versions. Holding hands filled with dreams of their future.

Why her normal darkness didn't invade her mind that night as she slept, Stella didn't know, but she awoke on Monday morning with a renewed strength that she hadn't felt in years. And thought it no mistake. The night before in Thane's arms had been predestined. And had provided exactly what was needed to face the daunting task ahead.

She hadn't spoken with either of her sisters. Doug thought it best that there not be any calls into or out of their safe houses unless an agent had to report an emergency and couldn't do so by radio.

But they were both fresh in her mind as she dressed in a pair of black pants that Melanie had put a new button on for her, and another short black-and-white-tweed jacket that Kara had given her for Christmas. While she was known for tweed jackets, and a penchant for black and white, the jacket Kara had chosen had black silk ribbon over the front pockets. The added bling felt appropriate for the day ahead.

She'd scheduled posts to hit her properties that morning before she'd left the police station the day before. And felt the first kink in her armor when she couldn't get online and answer comments first thing. In an effort to have her appear in normal mode, she'd made mention of an early breakfast in the scheduled post, and she and Thane would be driven to the police station for her to answer comments before the rally later in the morning.

They'd be returning afterward, too, for her post-rally online time. And a scheduling of the next day's posts. Assuming all hell didn't break lose in between.

Thane, who'd been up, showered, and dressed before her, was all business as they ate their respective breakfasts. He spent most of the time on his phone, reading and sending texts.

Most of which, at her request, he didn't share with her. Those involved in the day were confirming details, reporting in where necessary. All important things upon which she didn't need to dwell. She had to be pumped up. Filled with energy. Able to engage a large crowd with authenticity.

She'd done so while going through her divorce, and her heart had been breaking then. She could do so again.

Would do so.

The determination was raging strongly within her as she stood side-stage, with Thane, waiting to make her entrance to a crowd of more than a thousand. His hands hung at his sides, not touching her, but his body brushed hers every time he moved. She chose to believe the action was purposeful, not much caring in the moment if it really was or not.

An instant of panic struck her just before she heard Amelia introduce her, but the roar of the crowd fueled Stella's purpose and she was her best self, smile and all as she strutted onto the stage in beat with her own words as she yelled into the mic, "Hey everyone, ready to get fired up to save marine life?"

Turning the microphone toward the crowd, she reveled in the deafening cries of "Yes" that came back at her and then she slid naturally into her true self. Drama and trauma, love for family aside, the millions of innocent sea species that were being tormented and killed tugged at her heart, along with the knowledge that she had the ability to raise enough passionate awareness in people to help save them. The mandatory mentions of Tory Mitchell spurred her on further. Ramping up her message even more.

She was on fire. Fueled by the events threatening her personal life, rather than hampered by them. Had almost doubled the numbers of curious onlookers forming on the outskirts of the crowd, and saw people gravitating toward donation buckets secured on each side of the roped-off rally area.

And she'd yet to dive into the meatiest details that were meant to open hearts and wallets. Smiling, she stood center stage, mic at her mouth, ready for the quieter moment when she asked the crowd if they wanted to know what hurt her most about the creatures who were suffering, had opened her mouth to pose the question when a body hurled at her from side-stage, grabbing her around the waist and cushioning her fall as it knocked her over.

Before she'd taken a breath, she heard unintelligible roars from the crowd and was just realizing that some of it was laughing, when she realized that the body she was lying on was Thane's.

For a second anger coursed through her. If his prank was some sort of attempt to play with Spelling's mind, then he damned well should have given her a heads-up...

The thought evaporated when she saw the desperation in his gaze turn to consternation as he looked behind her, at the stage.

It was soaked. With what looked to be more than a dozen broken balloons scattered around it.

"Water balloons," Thane said. "I'll be damned."

Chapter 19

Thane noticed the stench before he and Stella were on their feet. With adrenaline still coursing through him, he yelled at her to put her mouth in her elbow, and, doing the same himself, intended to run her off the stage. Before he could grab her, they were met by bodyguards, one of whom picked her up and ran with her, with Thane right behind them.

After finding poison in food, and a weapon of mass destruction on a mic, they weren't taking any chances with what might have been mixed with the liquid those balloons had exploded all over the stage.

The crowd was loud as people started to catch on to the fact that Thane's race to Stella and the balloons hadn't been part of some ruse they'd been acting out. A voice over the loudspeaker instructed everyone to leave the area. A hazmat team had been standing by, and its members were already suited and on the stage.

Before she'd even been set on her feet, Stella said she felt fine, as did Thane, but they were both whisked immediately into the back of an ambulance, where their vitals were checked. Neither of them had been directly exposed to even a drop of whatever had been let loose. Nor had they breathed any of it up close. And other than slightly elevated pulse rates, they both checked out fine.

Hell yes, his pulse was elevated. He'd had his earpiece in. Had heard someone say that they'd seen a glint up in the trees just behind the scope of the rally. Heard the word *bullet*, and had launched himself into its path to stop it from hitting Stella. Not even thinking about the bodyguard who'd been hired to do just that.

"You saved my life," Stella said softly, her gaze locking with his, as though, in that moment, he was her lifeline.

Had there been a gun, and had it been fired, he'd have saved her life.

As it was, he'd proven that he could.

And could possibly use the moment to get her to quit. She wouldn't be clinging to him unless she was truly scared. Vulnerable. "It was water balloons, Stel."

He'd had an opportunity. And would rather die himself than use the fact that he knew she was in a weakened state to get his own way. She trusted him.

By the time he and Stella arrived at the police station for her to get out on her platforms—a task she'd deemed more critical than ever following the latest rally disruption—they knew that the balloon residue had tested positive for only one chemical. Sulfuric acid. In liquid, not mist form. And far enough remote from them that there was no danger to their lungs. Had even one of the balloons hit Stella, however, she'd likely have suffered some pretty severe burns. And could have been blinded if hit in the face.

Officers on-site had found the rally grounds littered with a couple of dozen plastic toys. From cars to slings. All of which were balloon launchers.

That bothered Thane most of all. Whoever was behind

the attempt to rob Stella of her mental health—and was putting her physical health at risk as well—was finding unforeseen ways to get potentially life-threatening weapons past all security measures. Camera footage of the crowd was already being scoured for the shooters, and at least some of them would likely be rounded up within the next couple of hours. But Thane didn't hold out much hope that any of them would have anything new to tell them. They'd have been hired, at one thousand dollars a pop, by someone they didn't know who'd approached them on the street wearing a hoody, or something else that made them hard to identify, and afterward, had had the payoff money dropped off in some receptacle hidden in a box or can that bore a brand name of some product Stella used regularly, including on tour.

There could be a clue in that last bit. He knew every single item she'd used over the past week, and if they could pinpoint a place or time when someone might have witnessed Stella with the product—if there was one—they could have a starting point.

He was grasping at straws.

But they were the only arsenal he had.

The monster in the dark was real. He was after her. With a bunch of water balloons, he'd reminded her that she could die at any minute. And that he planned to choose the one when she did. She got the message, loud and clear.

She'd also received another, much more bone-chilling one.

Thane could die, too.

They had no time completely alone together until they arrived in Dunham, a beach town not far from Miami, and were inside the motel room they'd been driven to for the night. A space they'd both agreed to occupy together for tighter security. Stella didn't know until they'd arrived that they had two beds. The rooms on either side of them had been rented earlier in the day, with surveillance devices set up everywhere but inside their space. The door, the roof, the front, the back, the entire parking lot was under constant watch by officers on each side of them. The place had been chosen specifically for its lack of traffic. Everyone coming and going was suspect.

The monster was using young or middle-aged ordinary people who were financially vulnerable to show their power over her.

They had microwavable frozen food packed in dry ice at the police station, which they relocated to the small freezer portion of the refrigerator in their room. Salisbury steak and mashed potatoes for dinner. Some kind of rubbery egg biscuit–looking thing for breakfast. She hadn't eaten a frozen dinner since she was in high school.

Too much sodium. And who knew what other chemicals.

No risk at all when compared to what she'd be facing onstage the next day. And it wasn't her life that had her the most agitated.

They'd been in the room less than five minutes and Thane was already settled on the couch scrolling on his burner phone.

And she had a completely original and different than she'd ever done before presentation to prepare. Bullets could fire at her in the space of a single breath, anytime she was onstage, but at least the program changes would cause whomever the monster hired to have to do some thinking on their own. There wouldn't be specific go time cues predetermined by the boss. Which left more room for sloppiness. Mistakes. Exposure.

And, she hoped to God, failure.

Sitting down on the other end of the couch—the only furniture in the inexpensive room other than a desk chair pushed under a shelf built into the wall—she tried to work. Offline, of course. But her mind conjured no words at all that were appropriate for the blank page with the blinking cursor in front of her.

Her stomach just knotted tighter as she stared. And she knew what she had to do. Stella looked at her ex-husband, so focused—and vibrant—just feet away from her, and words just came shooting out of her. "I want you to go," she said. "We aren't married. Staying together isn't professional or fair. You need to go."

With his phone still face up in his hand, his serious focus turned to her. Frowning, he said, "You want me to get a different room?"

Of course she didn't.

"I can move next door, with one of the agents," he continued while she tried to unwind enough inside to make herself clearly, and forcefully, understood.

"No, Thane." Her words were harsh sounding, emitted through gritted teeth. "Go home." And when his brows rose, she further clarified with, "As in leave. Permanently." Holding his gaze steadily right then was one of the hardest things she'd done.

Chin jutting, he kept those narrowed eyes trained firmly on her. Pinning her to the upholstery. "I'm not here on your authority," he reminded her. "I've chosen to remain on as lead counsel of SML, and as such, I'm obliged to be on this tour."

"If you don't go, I will." It was the closest thing to a lie she'd uttered in a long time. She couldn't turn her back on her sisters. But to save Thane, she'd have to make it look like she would.

He shook his head then. Glanced briefly at his phone, and then turned it face down on his thigh. "No you won't, Stel. Why don't you cut the crap and tell me what's really going on?"

She'd spent her whole life living a lie and couldn't tell one to save Thane's life? Shoulders dropping, she said, "You could have died today."

With a bit of a huff, he said, "So could you have done." As though the conversation was superfluous.

"You would have died saving me," she said then. And started to throw up the words that had been stuck inside her. "I make the choices I have to make, Thane, to do what my conscience tells me is the right thing. And putting you on the line is not a choice I can live with."

Picking up his phone, he tapped, read, put it back down, and said, "Then it's a good thing it's not your choice," he told her. Then, eyes narrowing on her again, he said, "I get to make my own choices, too, Stel. Also prompted from inside. You've got an argument to make if you don't want me sharing this room with you. Or if *you* want to exit the operation and go home. But you have absolutely no power when it comes to my presence on this tour."

Stella's gaze focused then. Astutely. He'd used that word *power* purposely. Because he knew what it meant to her. She'd overstepped. As mouthy as Stella was, she couldn't abide taking away others' personal power.

"You think you know me so well," she groused, challenging him.

"I do know you well. And you can work up whatever fight you want to bring on, Stella. I've made my choice.

Now, you ready for dinner and a glass of wine, or do you want to sit there and stew a while longer first?"

She wanted to stew until he went home.

And got up to put the frozen dinners in the microwave, instead. She was strong. Determined. But wasn't lacking in sense.

Thane was not at all okay with Stella's choice to put herself directly in the line of fire. He thought the plan they were working under was drastic to the extreme. Allowing an innocent civilian woman to be the front person in a game of life and death was ludicrous.

Not only were agents playing God with Stella's life, they were opening themselves up to a plethora of lawsuits.

But operation or not, there was no way on earth he was going to walk away while an innocent woman was being hunted.

While Stella was at risk.

Her way wasn't his way, but she was one of the most admirable human beings he'd ever known. Honest. Trustworthy. Willing to go the distance. Determined. Dedicating her life to curtailing suffering anywhere she could. Refusing to be bullied. Protecting those who were. Loyal.

The list continued to populate as he stood in the bathroom, getting ready for bed. He'd grabbed a couple of condoms, just in case, but knew there was just as much chance that when he reentered the room, Stella would be in bed facing the wall. She'd been short with him all night, engrossed in her computer work. Typing, deleting, and typing some more.

She'd even refused the glass of wine he'd poured for her.

As prepared as he'd thought he'd been, Thane flooded

with relief when he saw her lying on her side, in the bed farthest from the window, facing...the room. Not the wall. Her shoulders bare.

She'd turned off all the lights, and was in darkness, other than the sliver of bathroom light shining from the nearly closed door. But he still saw the glow in her eyes as she watched him stop to strip and then approach the bed.

He slid under the sheet, his arms reaching for her, and as he felt her smaller, softer hands against his sides and back, he wanted nothing more than the oblivion they'd always been able to find together.

But instead of bringing her mouth to his, Stella caressed the side of his face with her fingers. Running them gently down his day's worth of stubble. "I'm so sorry I can't be the person you need me to be," she said, sounding close to tears.

Hearing her, he needed to soothe. To comfort. And to speak the truth. "Don't ever be sorry for who you are, Stel." Before relaying much of his list from the bathroom. And ending with, "The world needs you just as you are."

With her finger tracing his lips, she whispered, "The world needs you, too. Just as much or more." Not her. The world.

In that moment, it didn't much matter to Thane whether or not Stella could tell him how much she needed him in her life. He knew how much she wanted him right then and proceeded to give her that and so much more. As though a cocoon had wrapped them in a sphere of their own, they touched and moved without restraint. Giving everything. Asking for nothing. Wanting for nothing. There was no past. No future. No fights or failure. Just a couple of hours of breathing perfect air. Together.

* * *

Stella was floating, peaceful, just falling asleep when she heard the buzz of Thane's burner phone vibrating against the cheap pressed-wood nightstand.

Instantly tense, she let her arms fall away from him as he reached for the device. Telling herself not to borrow trouble, she lifted herself enough to lay her head on the pillow he'd pulled up behind his own. And, still in the near darkness in which they'd planned to sleep, watched as he pushed and then tapped to open up the screen.

Lying there with his warmth, she read the text right along with him. Started to feel sick. Growing colder and colder. Until there was nothing but blessed ice inside her. Freezing out any other sensation.

FBI agents in Montana to interrogate Spelling were told he isn't there. Hasn't been for a couple of weeks. A judge ruled on sealed filings after Grossman's death claiming Spelling's innocence. He'd always testified that he hadn't been in the room, nor was he the one to pull the trigger on the gun that killed his stepbrother. Grossman's fingerprints matched the murder weapon.

She read. She understood. She just couldn't accept the content as real. True.

Completely inert, she stared at the top of the wall opposite her as Thane dialed the phone. "What the hell is going on?" she heard him say. Followed by the rumble of, she was assuming, Doug's voice on the other end of the conversation.

"What about victim notification?" Thane.

More rumbles.

"That's bullshit!" Thane, again.

Rumble. Rumble.

And Thane tossed the phone to the end of the bed.

Still feeling pretty much nothing, wondering if maybe that was what death felt like, Stella said, "Spelling's been free the whole time we've been on tour."

Shoving back the covers, Thane stood. Pulled on the suit pants he'd worn that day. Ran a hand through his hair, and picked up a pillow from the bed, punching it across the room with one blow.

"There's more to this than we know," he said then, pacing back and forth across the ends of both beds, his way lit only by the low light emanating from the crack in the bathroom door. "Montana's one of the few states that doesn't have victim protection laws mandating that a victim be notified if a perpetrator is released."

She hadn't known any state had such laws. Had never had cause to know. Wondered if she could go back to being the ten-year-old whose mother had just left her. She'd rather stay her forever.

As devastating as it had been, there'd been bliss in being unaware of what she hadn't known.

With her thoughts presenting one at a time, without urgency, she watched Thane, and announced, "If his conviction was overturned, he has no victim." Followed by, "Tory's the only victim. Maybe she was notified. The rest of us were never known to the prosecution or judge."

It wasn't like any of them would have been privy had the prosecution's star witness been told that she'd sent the wrong man to jail. Stella didn't even know her mother's name. Let alone where she'd lived for the past nearly three decades. The records were sealed up tight. Forever.

That distance felt...practical...as she lay, half sitting, against the pillow Thane had pulled up, watching him use the thin, indoor-outdoor carpet to work off some aggression in the shadows.

But really, nothing had changed. Except maybe there was more of a certainty that Torrence Spelling *was* behind the attacks on her. Which, as far as her universe was concerned, changed nothing.

She'd already taken that one on.

Her sisters and their families were in safe houses. She had an army of law enforcement protecting her while she did her part to end a reign of terror before it grew into hell on earth for more than just herself and Thane.

Thane. He was warm. And she was so cold. With only hours left to rest.

"Come back to bed," she said. Tired to the bone.

At least the comment stopped his pacing. He looked at her. "Please, Thane."

They'd had confirmation that what they'd suspected was most likely true. Spelling was their man. Didn't make much difference if the man was free, pulling the strings, or somehow doing it behind bars as they'd all expected. Ropes strangled just the same, no matter who was doing the actual tightening of them. And who was mastering the plan.

"You all wanted me to draw him out," she reminded, when Thane just stood there, his face stony-looking in the grayness.

He sat at that. Bowed his head, as though he'd been beaten. That one bothered Stella. Sitting up, she moved down the bed to him, planting herself at his back, using both hands to massage his shoulders until she felt the muscles give a little.

He could pace all night. But it would serve no good purpose. They were under constant surveillance. It wasn't like Thane would be pulling his gun at someone breaching the room.

Spelling wasn't done torturing her yet. She had a few more rallies ahead of her, which meant more chances for the monster to inflict torment.

"We need to get some rest," she said softly. "Please come back to bed."

When he nodded, and stood to take off his pants, Stella opened her arms. Welcoming the hours to come.

And refusing to think beyond them.

Chapter 20

Stella had to run. To hide. While she still had the chance. He had to get her into protective custody. Witness protection.

He had to find a way. Spelling was loose. Thane could not let Stella get onstage in the morning. He didn't give a damn how many professionals were surrounding them, tending to every aspect of the rally, to every step Stella could possibly take over the next few days.

Knowing that a mob boss was in their midst chilled him to his core. The man had managed to escape prosecution for decades of heinous crimes, and would have gotten away with his younger brother's murder had it not been for a brokenhearted housewife who'd fallen in love at first sight with the younger Spelling.

Every warning alarm in his system was screaming at him.

He had to find a way to reach Stella's deepest heart. To stop her before she got herself killed for a choice her mother had made long ago.

So he gave her what she wanted. His body to cling to. Determined to find a way, by whatever means, to get her to admit that she needed him, the clinging, more than she needed the fight.

When she snuggled up to him, shuddered, and then, wrapping her arms around him, relaxed, he said, "Let's both go home." It was the final answer. After she was in protective custody until Spelling was dead.

"I can't, Thane. I just can't. He'll come after me there and maybe get to my sisters first." She sounded tired. Resigned. And still so certain...

Wrapping his arms all the way around her he held on and said, "Even if they find Spelling, if he shows up at one of your rallies, without any proof that he's behind any of this, and his one and only conviction having been overturned, they can't arrest him."

"Not yet, maybe, but as many people as are working on this, they're going to get him, Thane." For a woman who spent most of her life fighting injustices, she sounded so incredibly naive.

"And until then?"

She shook her head without lifting it off his chest. "No, this ends here. We're drawing him out. He's taken the bait. He's all in. Playing the game. We'll get him."

If only life was that clear-cut. Or worked perfectly.

"You and you sisters have to enter witness protection," he said then, as certain, as resolute as her. It had to happen. "It's the only way to keep you safe from him. Just as it's kept him away from your mother. He'd have gone after her first if he'd known where she was."

He couldn't guarantee that, but it made logical sense. And he believed the words emphatically.

"If I do that, I let a monster live freely, to kill again, whenever it suits him. To hurt other innocent people."

Thane rubbed her back slowly. Trying to focus on the softness. To find a moment where he could breathe. He was losing her all over again.

She was lying right there, naked in his arms. And slipping away.

"That's assuming that he doesn't find us," she said. "I think it's pretty clear the monster has ties that we don't know about. High up ones. How else would he have gotten away with all his crimes over the years? And a transfer to Montana? Right after we were exposed as Tory Mitchell's family? And Kara as heir to the Spelling fortune? Of all the federal prisons in the country, he's put in one of the few states without victim rights. The one crick in his seemingly impenetrable power was my mother. She came out of nowhere, blindsiding them. And gave up everything she held dear to do so. Now it's my turn to blindside *him*."

She sighed as she said the words. And Thane knew that he could come at her with logic, with fact all he wanted. He could scare her to death. But Stella was still going to fight the battle to save her family, and others, from an evil force that wouldn't stop until he was dead.

She *was* her mother's daughter.

And, for better or worse, he'd lost her.

Stella tried to tell herself that the bombshell about Spelling's release wasn't fazing her as she got ready in the bathroom with the cheaply made countertops the next morning. It wasn't like the man himself was doing his dirty work. From what she was understanding he never had done. Which was why he was free.

Thirty years ago, they'd never found the actual murder weapon used to kill Chancellor Spelling, Kara's father. Which was why Tory's testimony had been paramount to the prosecution's case. Without it, Spelling would have walked free.

If Grossman hadn't used the same weapon to try to kill Kara, Spelling would still be behind bars.

Ironic, really.

All those years Spelling thought Grossman had been his only confidant. The one person he could trust, and the man had had the means, at any time, to get Spelling out of jail. Probably a good thing, with Spelling out, that Grossman was already dead. Being killed by law enforcement in a matter of seconds was a better way to go than the torture Torrence Spelling would have put him through.

Was putting *her* through.

Thane had breakfast, such as it was, heated and ready to eat when, in black pants and a red-and-gold short jacket to match, Stella finally got up the courage to leave the bathroom. To step out to a day that could be her last.

She wasn't kidding herself about that one. She just knew she had no other choice. She'd never be able to live with herself if she allowed herself to be silenced, putting her sisters' lives at risk by doing so.

"I'm not hungry," she told Thane. True. But she also didn't want rubbery egg stuff to be her last meal.

Which meant, what? That the Salisbury steak and mashed potatoes she'd had the night before would be?

"You need to eat, Stel," Thane said. Always looking out for her. Having her back.

Bossing her around.

Not wanting to disappoint him yet again, Stella ate. Because he'd asked for something she could actually do for him. And knew, as they barely spoke during the meal, and not at all on the drive to the morning's rally—the first of two that day—that she'd lost him.

As fabulous as their silent communication had been the night before, the final talk they'd engaged in had been his last-ditch effort to save her, but "them," too. The light of day made the fact completely clear. But she'd known then, too. The night before, when she'd explained why she couldn't back down, she'd been telling him goodbye.

Not as soon as she'd feared, though. Apparently, she'd been right that Doug and the FBI knowing the man was free didn't mean the cold-blooded killer was suddenly going to show up and shoot Stella dead.

The morning rally went off without a hitch. Turned out the rubbery egg mix hadn't been her last meal. She got to have a fancy sub sandwich in the back of the unmarked police car driving them to the station for Stella to work, and then on to the afternoon event as well. From there they'd be driving to the gulf, staying somewhere in Clearson.

Had it not been for her life being at risk, she'd have enjoyed the tour immensely.

"You okay?" Thane leaned over in the back seat to ask as they pulled up behind the stage set up for the afternoon program. Crowds of people were already there, sitting on blankets, or lawn chairs. Eating. The space had been chosen because of the row of food trucks that set up daily on the beach. They'd not only reach their loyal followers, but hopefully raise the curiosity of all those just coming up for the one-of-a-kind delicacies.

She wasn't okay. She was tense as hell. Wanting to bury her face in his chest and stay there forever. He'd obviously read at least the first part of that. Hence, his question.

"I'm fine," she told him. "We're going to have a great audience." She had to focus on her job. Delivering an impassioned program to raise money for whales and dolphins. And…snails. It was the way to fight the fear. To prevent it from controlling her mind. And then owning her life.

By the time she turned on her mic and bopped across the stage, she *was* fine. With an earpiece in her ear, to alert her by the second for any possible perceived threat, an army of mostly plainclothes protectors surrounding her to almost a mile out from the venue, and Thane right there, intensely watching every move, she felt safer than she had in a while.

The crowd was her largest yet—per prediction—and was as engaged as any had ever been. The roar they let up at her cues lifted her adrenaline ever higher, and almost drowned out the voice that started talking to her via her earpiece. "If...hear...and..."

Shaking her head, putting a hand to her ear, she tried to make out whatever someone was trying to warn her about. A glance at Thane studying the crowd showed her that he wasn't immediately alarmed.

"If you can hear me, nod twice." Another sound check. Probably Thane's idea.

"Are you with me?" she cried to the crowd, and nodded twice.

"You're going to do as I say, and no one gets hurt. Don't, and people die. Keep talking."

"Do you care about the dolphins?" she cried out again. Completely off script, but with her program changing every day who would know? The switched-out rhetoric idea had been posed for her safety. It wasn't safe. It wasn't safe.

Heart pounding, afraid her mic would start shaking, she looked out at the crowd. "My mother cared about ocean life more than anyone I ever knew," she said. A version of what she'd meant to say that day, pursuant to her new mandates.

"Do you know that with the seismic air guns being

used to drill for oil and other minerals at the bottom of the ocean, whales are unable to communicate? Even mothers with their children?" Not part of the script.

No one was going to get hurt. They just wanted her to say their message. She got that. Waited to hear what it was before she decided whether or not she'd be their voice.

She'd met the agent, briefly, who was on the other end of her earpiece. Oh God, Spelling's payroll?

"Our toxic metals, chemicals released from drilling, plastics are killing microorganisms that produce oxygen for sea creatures," she said then, her voice loud, and filled with anger.

At Spelling. And the fear he was instilling in her through others.

"Do you care?" she called out. And mixed in with the screams of "Yes," and the chants of "We care" roaring through the crown, the voice at her ear was quite clear.

"You're going to walk to the edge of the stage and sit down now. Engaging your crowd even as they rush up to the stage."

"I care, too!" Stella cried out. Walked forward, and sat. "My mother taught me to care, just like she taught me to wear makeup," she said, praying that Thane would catch the inconsistency, and watching as the crowd pushed forward. Homing in on the many followers she recognized among them.

"Think of a young one unable to communicate with a mother!" Her words carried all of the passion and pent-up pain inside her, steered by equal masses of fear and determination. "That's what happens…"

Stella felt a hard tug at her feet, and a long hard scrape at her back as the mic flew out of her hand and she went down. Arms grabbed her around the stomach, bending her in half, and a body, bending over her, ran with her through the panicking crowd.

At first, she thought one of the agents had saved her. Felt her stomach flip-flop as they raced her to safety. But when she was thrown into the bottom of some kind of big wagon, and leaves and twigs came pouring down on her, she knew. Spelling had won.

Blood roared in Thane's ears. He pushed through the crowd. Only a foot behind the blockade of bodies that was hiding Stella as they moved toward the exit. Until another surge of bodies rammed into him. Hard. From the side. Knocking him off-balance. He stayed on his feet. Continued to push forward, but he'd lost distance.

He was prepared when another group came at him, managed to sideswipe their attack, but with his focus on them, he'd lost sight of Stella.

And didn't see her again.

Nor did the more than fifty agents who were on the ground, in pursuit of...they weren't sure. She'd been there, and then been lost in the crowd. If she'd screamed, no one had been able to distinguish her voice among the hundreds of screams coming from the rabid crowd she'd riled up.

A group that grew more irate as police quickly set up barricades to keep anyone from leaving the premises until their vehicle, and person, had been checked.

Thane left the large number of law enforcement to their tasks, doing his own searching. While Kara's abductions had been driven by Grossman, the man had learned everything he knew from Spelling. Had spent a lifetime carrying out Spelling's orders.

And when Kara had been abducted from a bench on the

beach, she'd been grabbed by a landscaper and dumped in a trash receptacle.

He searched them all. Started with the closest to the rally, and spreading out from there. Large or small, he went through all of them. Climbing into the larger ones to make certain there wasn't an unconscious body there.

A truck could roll up to haul a dumpster away at any moment. He knew the plan.

Just as he'd known the second Stella had mentioned her mother teaching her how to wear makeup that she'd been in trouble. He had no idea how she'd known, but she'd been talking straight to Thane with those last words.

He just hadn't gotten to her in time. She'd been sitting there, telling him she needed help, and within seconds, she'd been gone.

He'd known. Oh God, he'd known.

Thane gave no thought to the expensive suit he wore as he dove into the last dumpster on the beach within half a mile of the rally. His sleeve caught on something metal, ripped, and he threw off the coat, leaving it there. And exposing the gun he'd been wearing at his waist every day since the beginning of the tour.

He didn't give a damn about that, either.

What ripped him up was finding not even a hint of Stella. She'd leave clues if she could. No doubt there.

So was he wrong? Spelling had found another way to haul her away from those hired to protect her?

Abducting her in plain sight? How? By what means could someone…

Before he'd finished the question, he was off and running again. SML had brought in porta-potties. By the time he made it back to them, the johns had been taped off.

And already inspected.

As had every other inch of the space. Every car, every truck, every bicycle had been stopped, every person searched.

And nothing?

It made no sense.

Landscaper. Kara had been abducted by a city employee working in the park. Seeking out Brian Carlsdale, the lead FBI agent on scene, Thane charged forward.

Every employee in the city had to be interrogated. Immediately. They were going to find Stella.

Alive.

Chapter 21

I have your sister. Make a move and she's dead. Bumping along beneath a piece of plexiglass that covered the pile of brush on top of her, Stella waited for further instruction. With a bag over her head and a gun pressing into her throat, she'd been moved from one trailer to another that looked exactly the same to her. Had been modified exactly the same way. And saw only a pair of boots and the bottom of a pair of jeans when the bag was removed just as brush came down to cover her.

She'd done everything just as the earpiece had instructed. Lay completely still on top of the grated iron on which she'd been dumped, staring at what she was figuring was a foot-high side wall on the open trailer. She couldn't see through the brush above her, but knew from her earlier sight of it that it had a tarp over it, keeping it secure.

The abduction hadn't just been planned that morning. Two trailers had been modified with fake bottoms allowing someone to open the "door" to the bottom, dump her, and close her in.

Where she was going, she had no idea. Wasn't sure it even mattered.

The only way she helped her sisters was to prolong

Spelling's enjoyment long enough for someone to find him before he bored of her and moved on to torturing Kara or Melanie.

Kara would be first, Stella knew. Probably would have been from the beginning if she hadn't been out of the country. But now that she was back, and accessible to Spelling, he'd find her. Pregnant and already traumatized, she'd be like dessert with double icing to him.

But that wasn't why he wanted her dead. She was also heir to half his fortune. Which he was once again free to spend. She'd bet he'd promised a hefty sum to whomever he had in his pocket.

Stella had no idea how long they'd been driving when the trailer came to a stop, with a backward hitch that told her the engine of the vehicle pulling it had been put in Park.

Her stomach roiled with tension, heart pounded. She heard faint voices through the blood roaring through her ears. The earpiece was silent.

She had to stay alert. Focused. Whatever happened to her was going to happen. What mattered was what she did before she died.

Fear would not win. She would not be silenced in her final minutes.

She had to channel Thane. Think like he did. Pay attention to every aspect of her situation. The smell. The sight. Every detail. Including that the trailer was black and new looking, based on the lack of scratches on the side.

The grate beneath her gave her a view of the ground where they'd stopped. Cement. Smooth. Painted. Indoors?

Had they pulled into some kind of garage?

The voices had stopped. Had her abductors left her there alone? She wasn't restrained. Other than the wall of thick plastic pressing against her, making it impossible for her to turn over.

Were they planning to just leave her there to die a slow death? How long did it take to starve to death. A week? Two?

Thane wouldn't just lie there. He'd have a plan. She had to become a problem for them. Make noise? A lot of it? It's what she was good at. Her voice was a weapon that had helped raise millions over the years. How could she best use it?

Her stomach clenched tighter. Making her nauseous. If she threw up, would it leave some kind of DNA evidence on that shiny cement? Nothing that wouldn't be wiped clean with splashes of ammonia.

Another space of time passed. Long enough that Stella was lying there thinking about sex with Thane. Their times together on tour had been the best they'd ever had. Which was saying a lot. Because they were older? More mature? Knew what mattered?

Because there'd been no relationship stuff mucking up the waters? Or, maybe just due to the fact that there'd been no expectations walling them in.

As her shoulder and hip pressing against the wrought iron beneath her started to ache, she thought about the mattress beneath her naked butt, and the thrills sweeping through her as Thane moved in and out of her, stimulating her to the point of explosion.

And had a moment of clarity. She had to figure out a way to create some kind of explosion. Words that she could shout at the right moment, to stop Spelling in his tracks. Something that would have those helping him turn on him.

Because with Thane out there, unrelenting as he

searched for her and insistently drove others to do the same, she wasn't just going to lie there and die.

A city worker was missing. Male. Not a landscaper. A maintenance man. With a trailer used to haul large items also unaccounted for. Several investigators were working to find him. Thane thought the occurrence unrelated. Or at most, a move engineered to throw them off course.

Spelling's profile and history didn't fit a clue that obvious. The man didn't make those kinds of obvious messes.

A search of the cameras surrounding the area gave no indication of any such trailer. The only one seen, not at the venue, but a block over, had been the city's brand-new landscaping trailer. And the employee responsible for it, Jeremy Green, had been fully questioned and let go. His alibi had checked out. His employment record was spotless. He had no criminal history, was the father of two boys, and his wife and neighbors had nothing but good to say about him.

Police were still keeping him under surveillance, just in case. But even Thane struggled to come up with a logical theory that could point to the man as the kidnapper.

He didn't give up trying, though. Until he had something else to go on, that trailer was the only evidence that was making any sense to him.

Unless it was there, purposely, just to throw him off the scent?

Spelling was a diabolically smart, and even crueler, man. Thane's mistake would be to underestimate him. Law enforcement, FBI, detectives out the wazoo were combing through evidence, interrogating hundreds of people, following even the most minute clues.

All Thane had to do was think.

At the police station, he'd been given a small room with a desk. And was being kept informed of every aspect of the investigation as it happened. Doug had flown down and was involved as well since he'd been the lead on the Kara Latimer case. He'd brought all the case files with him. In suitcases that he'd carried on with him.

Ben, a highly regarded investigator, was protecting his pregnant wife in a different, more secluded safe house, and was online with Thane as well.

Melanie and her family had been moved up north. Even Thane didn't know where they were.

He sat there alone, staring at his computer screen, with several windows open showing footage from several different cameras around the event area. Thane stared. And it hit him. Like a rock to the head. A punch to the gut.

The dumpster where he'd ripped his coat. He'd dropped it on top of what had looked like a brand-new box of dryer sheets. The only kind Stella had ever used. The box had had no creases in it. The lid hadn't been bent back like the ones he'd always seen in their laundry cupboard and on the dryer over the years.

Chances were likely that no one would have disposed of a brand-new full box of laundry sheets. Not even someone staying on the beach and leaving early. But someone who'd picked up a cash payment and wanted to get rid of the evidence as quickly as possible…

Hardly breathing, Thane clicked through every file of camera footage until he found one that was closest to that last dumpster. He didn't have the trash receptacle itself on film but recognized a couple of buildings that had been close by.

Opening the footage full screen, he searched methodically. Looking at time stamps. Pausing every second of footage to study the entire screen.

And noticed a familiar color of green. Just a sleeve. Above a pair of gray pants that had a coffee stain on it.

The same exact stain he'd seen on the pants Father of the Year, Employee of the Year, and Husband of the Year Jeremy Green, had been wearing.

"I've got something!" he yelled. Loudly.

And banged the wall with his chair as he stood up.

Apparently, noncriminal, upstanding hardworking citizens were even susceptible to Spelling's easy, clean money allure.

He heard voices. Footsteps coming toward him.

One thousand dollars to rent his trailer for an hour. Because that trailer had been with the man when he'd been called in to the police station. And there'd been no sign of anyone having been stowed in it. Forensics was going over every inch of the thick plastic removable bottom piece installed in all the new maintenance trailers, and the brush found inside it, too.

And Thane wanted to be present the second they found a hint of female DNA.

He had no time to lose in setting his focus on figuring out whatever had to come next.

She was moving again. Or rather, the trailer in which she lay was. Stella had lost all track of time. Either they were driving in one stupendously long underground tunnel, or darkness had fallen.

Her stomach had long since given up growling for food. She wasn't the least bit hungry. Nor had she had an opportunity to use the restroom. But then she'd had nothing to drink, either.

They weren't trying to keep her comfortable, healthy, or even alive.

Words had been running through her head. Possible ways to raise the emotions of her captors in the hopes that they'd make a mistake, or, God willing, change their plans for her. What seemed like hours passed, but no one came. Her words had no ears to hear them, but her own.

She'd gotten emotionally weak for a little while. Letting fear win. Had cried a lot. And when she'd had nothing left but emptiness, a vision of Thane's face on their wedding night had come to her.

And that's when it hit her, the Thane-like theory. Her current captors were only doing a one-time assignment for someone they didn't even know. For money that would be dropped somewhere afterward. Just like all the others. She was a commodity to them, nothing else. They had nothing against her. Were just doing a job.

And now that she was in motion again, the theory blossomed. They'd been waiting for the order to deliver her.

And it had arrived.

Jeremy Green had been brought back in. His story hadn't changed. And yet, turned out, there'd been a short period of time, coinciding with Stella's abduction, when he couldn't prove where he and his trailer had been. He'd said on a job. Named the job. But no one had been there to verify the fact. He was being held for further questioning.

Doug delivered dinner to Thane personally. Had the detective not taken a seat, giving him updates on Ben's input and reports on Kara's and Melanie's continued safety, Thane would have pushed the grilled chicken breast and baked potato aside and let them get cold. Instead, as he listened to the fact that Kara had felt the baby kick for the first time and was certain it was a sign that Stella was still fighting, Thane was reminded that he had to keep up his strength, to be sharp. They were all counting on him. Not just his ex-wife, but her sisters, too. So he ate.

And then, regardless of the fact that Doug continued to sit, as though he had more to say, Thane went back to work. So far, the forensic scientist working on the trailer had found no DNA. The suspicion was that it had been doused with ammonia. But the empty dryer sheet box had been found in the dumpster right where Thane had said it would be. And while there were no fingerprints on it, implicating Green, there'd been residue indicating that whatever had been inside had gotten damp. The lab had picked up distinctive iron compounds that were used in the creation of magnetic ink. The ink used in US paper currency.

Green claimed to know nothing about any money. No one at the station believed him.

Doug left at some point. Thane was aware, just didn't stop to chronologize the events. He was crushing through case files from thirty years before again. Once they'd had the connection between Riker, the shooter, and Spelling, Thane had been studying everything he could find on the man. Getting to know him, in order to mentally become him. He'd read something in testimony—from Tory Mitchell?—about a place. It wasn't in the trial transcript. Scrolling and clicking frantically, he exited documents, opening others. Getting back to interrogation files. Prosecutor interviews with Tory.

Hours passed. Doug tipped his head in at one point. "Get some rest, man. You aren't going to be any good to her if you don't."

He didn't even glance up. "I'm not leaving her out there in darkness alone."

Doug stood a bit. Thane had already tuned him out.

At some point the other man left.

Thane kept reading. It was the only thing that kept his thoughts from Stella. Directly. She was there, every second, like needles poking his heart, his nerves.

During those moments when he stopped reading, she filled his mind, too. With her long buried, but never gone ten-year-old child's anguished cries for help.

With his own imaginings as to what kind of tortures were happening to her. *Hang on, Stella. Fight.* The words would repeat. Over and over.

And as midnight arrived, and passed, he wondered if perhaps death wouldn't be best, if it could release her from the horror of so many hours at the hands of Torrence Spelling.

Was he being selfish, willing her so strongly not to give up? To know that they were working round the clock to find her? That they'd get there?

The thought came. And shot him right back to work.

He believed she was still alive. Fighting. And he wasn't giving up on her.

The trailer came to a halt, startling Stella out of a half-dozing stupor. The trailer. She wasn't ever getting out of it. Her body ached. Everywhere.

So long without any real movement. Crunched between the grated iron beneath her and the clear plastic flooring on top. The grating was good. It was her friend. Allowing her to breathe.

Exhaust fumes weren't good. Mixed with speeding by fresh air, they weren't horrible. Relaxed her.

Stopped. Stopped!

Fully alert, she was glad to feel her heart pounding in her chest. To know that it still could. Had only one day passed since she was abducted?

Had to be, right? There'd been no light after the darkness. Unless she'd been kept in a windowless garage for…

No. She hadn't peed herself. No one could hold it for days.

Don't think about pee. Relax. But not too much. Yeah, think about pee. Something over which she had some control.

Two truck doors slammed. Had there been two the first time she'd been put in a trailer? She didn't think so. Only one.

So, two after she'd been switched?

Or…when the shiny cement appeared? *Think. THINK.*

Words. Slamming doors meant ears to hear.

"I gotta pee!" she screamed at the top of her lungs. Over and over.

And almost wet herself when the trailer jerked and a loud sound of metal scraping against metal sounded just above her head.

The same sound she'd heard both of the two times she'd been locked in the trailer.

Stiffening, bracing herself against evil, she waited. Alert to her surroundings. Every sound, every scent.

She was outside. Heard a familiar rhythm, clicking in tandem that created a buzz, a whine. Cicadas. The sound of home. She was near woods. In woods?

Words. What worked in the woods with bugs? How did she fight with an evil audience of not that many?

"I have to pee!" she screamed again. In case they needed her silent.

Small chance, that. Spelling wouldn't have her brought anywhere that she could be heard by outside sources. Unless...was Thane out there? With his army of protectors?

"I have to PEE!" Her throat hurt with the force of the call. She choked against the dryness. Thought about food. She'd read once that doing so created saliva. Closed her eyes and imagined all her favorite dishes. Came up with the pizza she'd had with Thane the other night. And Melanie's chocolate chip cookies.

"Hold on," an irritated male voice said. Young sounding.

And...did she recognize it? Had she been rescued? Spelling was done and...

Just like that, the plastic floor containing tarped brush lifted. Shivering against the burst of air that hit her, Stella straightened her legs, rolled to her butt, and pushing through the pain, tried to stand. Dizziness hit. She stumbled. Blinked. Saw trees. Darkness. Grabbed hold of a bar on the lifted floor angled above her and straightened.

She'd expected floodlights. Dozens of people rushing to her. Saw...

No one.

With a sudden sense that she was walking into a trap, Stella considered lying back down. For less than a second. She wasn't going to die lying down. She'd die standing and fighting.

Praying those weren't her only two choices, she used her hands on the side of the trailer to climb out. Jumped down to the ground, and nearly crumpled at the pain in ankles that had been kept in the same position for far too long.

Doing a 360, she looked for whoever had spoken to

her. For anyone. Saw nothing but the truck attached to the trailer. And trees.

She'd heard two doors close. "Hello?" she called.

"You said you had to pee. Get behind a tree and do it. Try to run and you and your sisters will be dead."

The voice. Did she know it?

Stella did as she was told. Mostly because she wasn't going to die with pee all over herself. And, maybe, a little bit because she hoped if she cooperated her life would be spared?

She'd just pulled her pants back up, was fumbling with the button on them, when she heard a faint rumble behind her. Turning, she saw a pair of headlights in the distance. Couldn't see beyond them.

"You done yet?" The voice sounded less than a foot away from her. On the other side of the tree.

He'd been standing there all along? She should have figured. Hadn't heard footsteps.

Pants finally fastened, she took one step and felt steel fingers close around her upper arm.

"You should have taken the hint, bitch." The words were hissed, right at her ear, as the body attached to the hand squeezing the blood out of her upper arm came up to press against her butt.

Stella's head jerked around as memory flashed. A comment on her platform. *Smart bitches take the hint.*

She'd deleted. And...

The long nose, freckles...she *did* know the voice. Her gathering at the hotel after she'd been shot. The young man who'd asked all the questions. About her being scared...

So it wasn't Spelling? It *was* Big Money?

"What do you want with me?"

"It's not me. And you're about to find out." The male voice spitting words into her ear sounded almost eager at the thought.

And Stella felt sorry for the whales who were going to die in spite of all the work she'd done.

Chapter 22

There'd been a dwelling. Some spot where Torrence Spelling would take married women, mostly a decade or more older than him, to have sex. And where Chancellor would go whenever he wanted time away from the Spelling men his mother had married herself to.

Chancellor had taken Tory Mitchell—using the name either Susan or Amanda Moore—there. Spelling had shown up.

It was also the place where Chancellor had later been killed. There'd been a gun. With a distinct personalized carving in the base of the grip. Torrence was never without it. The murder weapon that had disappeared. And then, recently reappeared, clutched in Grossman's hand when he'd died.

Tory had testified that she'd heard Torrence threaten to kill his younger brother if Chancellor didn't do something later that night. She hadn't been able to make out what that had been. It was the last time she'd seen Torrence. She'd gone home the next day, to her daughters. And a husband asking for forgiveness for his yearlong affair and looking for a second chance for their marriage.

She hadn't found out until after Kara was born that the man she'd fallen in love with that week had been murdered. Her husband had known about the affair. And knew he wasn't Kara's father, too.

After Grossman's death, Torrence's lawyer had used the evidence of the Spelling murder weapon in the other man's possession to challenge the credibility of Tory's testimony that only Torrence Spelling ever touched that gun and had had it on him the night Torrence was killed.

The judge had thrown out Tory's testimony.

And without it, there was no case against Spelling.

The reports had finally come through. Too little too late.

Spelling was out for revenge.

And there was a dwelling. One that held all the Spelling brothers' passion. As well as the scene of the crime.

How in the hell was Thane going to find it? Prove to trained investigators that his logic had merit, without proof?

And make it there in time?

If it wasn't already too late?

Torrence Spelling was surprisingly not a huge man. Average height. Muscled, but not overly so. Not an ounce overweight. Even at, what, sixty? Seventy?

Blinking sweat from her eyes, Stella watched the man sitting across from her in the small clearing. Evil in the darkness. His cushioned iron chair, had to be her only focus. She'd been told to sit on a stump of wood, turned on end, that was uneven on the bottom. Any strong move would topple her over.

She had no restraints. Just the four—that she could count—guns pointed at her from various points in the trees.

"*I* am my mother's daughter," she said. "*I'm* the one

who refuses to be silenced." He'd told her to tell him why he should leave her sisters alone.

His grin seemed diabolical. Disgusting. Horrid. Evil.

She knew his touch was. He'd greeted her with a kiss to the lips and his hand on her breast.

Wrong move on his part. Those quick acts had killed the child in her. Leaving just the mouth.

His actions had just been to torment her. Probably a precursor of what was to come. She'd run straight into any one of the bullets pointed in her direction before she'd let the man violate her.

But if she had even a minute chance to save her sisters, first...

"You knew my mother, right? As who, Susan Moore? Or was it Amanda? Some girl you blew off as not worth a second glance, because...after all...she was dumb enough to be with sniveling little Chancellor?"

With a hiss, and a spit to the ground, Torrence Spelling jumped up out of his chair, sending it flying behind him and came at her, both hands raised toward her throat.

"Torrence?" The woman's voice came from the trees behind the man. Slender, in dark pants and long-sleeved top, she had eyes only for Stella's tormentor.

"Turn around, Torrence," the voice said then, seduction and disdain filling the air in equal measures, as the woman continued her slow approach. "You're all tough with an innocent woman, but you won't face me?" The dare was unmistakable.

Who in the hell was the woman? What in God's name was she doing?

Begging a deranged murderer to kill her?

Stella didn't dare move. Bullets would fly from all directions.

"The place is surrounded, big brother," the woman said then, and Stella, shaking and feeling sick, frowned. Neither of the Spelling stepbrothers had had another sibling.

"You've got friends in high places," she continued, moving slowly toward them as though she was out for an evening stroll. Not a gunfight in the middle of the night. "You get one chance to get out of here alive. And I've agreed to go with you. Willingly. They can't stop me. My life for hers. But first, you call off your guns. All five of them."

Torrence was eerily still for too long. The woman didn't back down.

Shaking visibly Stella jumped when Spelling whistled. And then waved his arm in a circle.

She watched in disbelief as five men, including Long Nose, come forward and lay down their weapons.

"They get in the truck and go," the woman said.

With a nod from Spelling, the men wordlessly headed to the truck without even a glance at Stella. The engine roared, and the truck kicked up rock and dirt with the speed with which it departed.

"And now we leave. Alone." The woman had reached their little clearing, and Stella got her first good look at her. She was a lot older than Stella had thought. In her sixties, at least. And...the woman looked at her once. A message in her gaze.

"No!" Stella screamed. Her word shrilling through the trees around them. "No!" The single syllable sheared her throat. Again and again.

She stood so fast she had a head rush. Stumbled after them.

But they'd disappeared.

* * *

Someone had been at the dwelling recently. In the midst of years of disrepair, agents found a pillow. Blankets. A change of women's clothing. A gallon jug of store-bought water. And a toothbrush.

Leaving officers to guard the place, the rest of the agents spread out through the woods surrounding it. Thane heard the news over the radio, along with the officer in the unmarked car, sitting with him out on the main road, which had been cordoned off for the search.

He'd been ordered to stay put. No way he was doing so. His life was his to risk.

Exiting the car on a run, he heard swearing behind him, but didn't slow. He had the coordinates of the dwelling. He was the one who'd given them to Doug, who'd passed them on to the FBI.

Stella was close. He could feel it.

He was going to see her again. He had some things to tell her.

Racing through the trees in the jeans and button-down long-sleeved shirt Doug had brought him before they'd left the station forty miles away, Thane's toes cramped in the tennis shoes he'd been loaned, but he didn't slow until he saw the pine trees. Recognizing them from the topical view he'd seen during his furious search for the building, he knew those trees were the only ones of their kind in those woods. And were only about two hundred yards from the cabin.

"I have a car parked in the usual spot." He heard the female voice. Thought at first that it was Stella. But in the next second, knew it wasn't. "We have a straight shot out of here, and then you leave the state."

The male chuckle that followed the words was eerie. Almost possessed sounding. Following the sounds, Thane tried to get close enough to see whom he was dealing with.

Couldn't allow himself to wonder what they were doing there. Or why.

That laugh. Was it Spelling? He knew it was Spelling. And the fiend would know where Stella was. No way could Thane alert the agents combing the woods. He couldn't take a chance that they'd kill Spelling before the man was made to talk.

"Come on, *Tory*, is it? I like Susan better, by the way..."

Tory?

Stella's *mother*?

Swallowing hard, Thane didn't move for fear he'd fumble and give himself away.

"You don't really think I'm going to leave you behind, do you? The local hounds are on your daughters pretty tight, and you're the one I want to enjoy the most. I'll come back for your offspring later. When the heat's died down and they least expect me."

Silence followed the words. Thane began to move again. Carefully. Toe to heel so as not to make as much sound.

"You've met those who owe me," was the next thing he heard. "You know they aren't going to look my way if you happen to be found...dead...in the woods. After all, you're nothing but a *snitch*." The last word came out as a growl.

One that left little doubt as to what happened next. Grabbing his gun from his waistband, he ran full force, loudly, causing a head to rise up, look in his direction. In that split second, Thane pointed, and shot.

* * *

Stella was racing through the woods alone, frantic. Willing dawn's light to arrive. She passed a bush she thought she recognized and let out a sob. Was she running in damned circles?

She'd heard a shot. Minutes ago? Half an hour? More? She had to get to her. To tell her that she loved her. She couldn't...

"Stella?" The voice rent through her and she jerked. Not Thane. Spelling's men, back to get her. She tried to run then, and ended up landing in the middle of a chest, being caught by hands on her arms, steadying her.

She heard a "We've got her" issued into a radio. And then, in the midst of other radio rumbles, another unfamiliar voice close by, heard the one holding her say, "I'm Agent Hall with the FBI. You're safe now, Stella."

"No!" she screamed then. Couldn't stop herself. "My mother! He has my mother!"

She wouldn't let herself be guided. Throwing out her arms on both sides of her, clearing her air, getting the touch of others away from her body, she started to march, with no idea which direction to take. "Mother!" she screamed again. Aware of agents behind her calling out to her. Ignoring them, she tried to run, stumbled, and hollered, "Don't touch me!" Followed by, "Mom!"

"Stella!" She heard the guy, Hall. Ignored him. Stumbled forward some more. With tears pouring down her face, she cried out, "Mama!"

Kept herself upright, fighting with every step she took. Using her voice.

Until she heard, "Stel." Just that one word. That one voice. Halting, head tilted, Stella was certain she was hallucinating, perhaps had even died in the midst of her nightmare. She turned toward the sound.

Saw an angel take the form of the love of her life. And, arms outstretched, she gave herself up to it.

She'd lost the fight.

Thane brushed aside agents and carried Stella to the waiting ambulance himself. She was in and out, but knew who he was. Had reached out to him. He took the win.

She knew Tory, too. The woman Thane had never met climbed into the ambulance right behind Thane and took her daughter's other hand. "Mama," Stella said, looking at the older woman, and then closed her eyes.

Nothing more was said during the ride to the hospital, and once there, there was no time without others surrounding them. But Thane exchanged more than a few glances with Tory Mitchell. He read the pain in the woman's gaze, the permanent lines etched into a face looking older than its years. And saw the adoration and fear with which the woman watched her daughter. Other than those few glances exchanged with Thane, Tory wasn't taking her eyes off her middle child.

Stella had been given an IV drip in the ambulance, and had been in and out. Before Thane had even heard the first doctor's report, Kara and Ben had shown up. Kara entered the room first, hesitantly. Staring at the woman who'd stood beside Stella's bed. And then they were rushing toward each other, arms outstretched.

Thane held back with Ben as Kara and Tory held on to each other crying. For so long it was uncomfortable to watch. The women loosened their holds briefly, long enough to stare at each other, to say a word or two, mostly just expressing love, and then hug tight again.

Until the doctor returned, interrupting a family reunion that had almost never been.

Thane was almost heady with relief when he heard the doctor's report of all good. Stella had been given a little sedative to help her rest for a few hours, but with everything else checking out fine, she should be waking up soon and could leave once she was discharged. After the doctor left, at Ben's suggestion, Thane left Kara and Tory with Stella and went with Ben to get something to eat.

And spent the entire time rehashing the events of the past twenty-four hours. Hardly believing them.

Ben filled in Thane's one major blank. After Kara's attempted murder, Tory, who'd followed East Coast news ever since she'd had access to internet, saw an article about Grossman's reign of terror on her youngest daughter. She'd broken protocol to phone Melanie.

Had left a number for Mel to call in case of emergency. And when Stella had been set up as bait for Spelling, Mel had made the call. And Tory Mitchell had snuck away from the life she'd been living to head immediately to Florida.

Thane swelled with gratitude to the woman. Wanted to thank her. And was mostly filled with an urgency to get back to his ex-wife. With her family there, he didn't really have a right to be in the intimate circle, but couldn't see himself anywhere else.

Not until she was awake. Had seen him. And released him.

Then he'd go.

He was elated for Stella. Weak with thanks that she was alive. And strangely not eager to walk away and get back to the work he'd put on the back burner while he'd been on tour with her.

He was in the midst of coming down from the huge adrenaline rush, he reasoned with himself as he walked with his ex-brother-in-law back to the room where Stella was sleeping.

His current emotional and mental status was much like jet lag. Only much, much worse.

To the point that he was actually envious of his best friend as Ben walked into the room ahead of him and straight to Kara. Because he was still married. Still had that right. The youngest Mitchell sister stepped back, her arm around her husband, as Thane came in.

"Thane," Stella said, sounding a bit like her normal self. He recognized the voice. And the eyes looking at him from the bedraggled woman lying with a hospital gown covering her top half, and a sheet over the rest of her.

"I told you he was coming," Kara said gently, while Tory leaned over the bed rail, pushing dirty hair back from her daughter's face.

Thane didn't belong there. Not in that intense family moment. Even more not as a frantic and emotional Melanie appeared in the doorway. But when Kara suggested that the four of them—Tory, Kara, Ben, and Mel—go to get something to eat, even though Ben had just eaten not long before, her intent to leave Thane and Stella alone long enough for him to say goodbye to her seemed pretty obvious.

Warmth passed through him when he watched Tory reach over for a long hug with the daughter whose life she'd saved that day, and then, taking Kara's hand, headed to the hall with Ben and Mel right behind them.

"That's my mom," Stella said, her gaze on the doorway.

"I know." Thane wanted to walk up to the bed, pull

Stella into *his* arms, and hold on. To crawl into the bed with her and not let go. Ever again.

Instead, hands in the pockets of his dirty jeans, he stood there, not sure if he should take the seat Tory had left, or not.

"She said you saved her life."

He shrugged. "Right place, right time."

Stella's gaze was clear, steady and pointed as she said, "Because you figured out what Spelling was going to do. You led the FBI to the dwelling."

Thane didn't need to live that moment ever again. "And you weren't there." He told her something she already knew. He'd felt like death had hit him when he'd heard that there were signs of a woman having been in the cabin, but that it was empty.

"Your mother is the heroine here, Stel," Thane said then, taking the chair Tory Mitchell had vacated. "She knew Spelling would return to the place at some point. And was waiting to confront him." To kill him was what the woman had said to an officer on-site right after the agents had taken Spelling away to tend to the kneecap wound Thane had delivered. Seconds before the murderer had grabbed for one of their guns, resulting in the dramatic "suicide by cop" death that set them all free.

Stella reached to touch Thane's fingers, her eyes pointed that way, too. "She said she saw the headlights come up the drive when Spelling arrived, and followed them further back into the woods, which was how she'd known where to find me. She spent the past nearly three decades reliving every second of the last time she'd been there. Had been hanging on to every moment of the week she'd spent with Chancellor. And when the time came, she'd just known what to say to manipulate Torrence."

Looking up from their fingers to meet Thane's gaze, she added one last bit. "She believes it was Chancellor guiding her from above."

Thane didn't know about that. There was no logical proof that such a thing was possible. But he didn't refute the idea, either.

What he was certain of was that he wasn't going to have much time alone with her, and he'd made his own deal with death. Stella had to be spared from its clutches because Thane had some things to say to her.

"I bailed on our marriage, Stel. I promised you for better or worse, and when the writing was clearly on the wall, I left."

She nodded. Of course she would. He wasn't telling her anything she didn't already know. She'd been there. Had watched him walk away.

"And I didn't fight for it." Her words came softly, as her eyes started to glisten. "I fought for every other cause in my path, but not the one that mattered most to me."

He stared. Was that a second chance he saw in her gaze? Hope for the possibility of some kind of future together, at the very least?

His blood thrumming through his veins, he told her the rest of what he'd come to say. "I didn't walk away this time." He wasn't singing his praises. What he was trying to tell her was so much more than that. "I didn't believe in the plan. I didn't agree with using you as bait. I saw danger heading straight for you. And I stayed to fight in a battle I didn't believe in."

She nodded. Then lifted her finger to his lips. Rubbing it gently along them. And said, "You listened to your heart."

That wasn't what he had to tell her. "I did it because I

love you, Stel. More than right or wrong, more than life or death. I love you. You. The advocate. You the woman. I love *you*."

Tears filled her eyes, trickling slowing down her cheeks toward the sad smile on her lips. "I love you, too," she said then. Not telling him anything new. They were the last words she'd said to him the night he'd asked for the divorce and moved out.

And again when she'd thanked him for coming to stay with her when Kara had been thought dead.

He'd bailed on her, not vice versa.

He knew what was coming next. He didn't blame her, but didn't want to sit there and hear the words, either. "I know that I don't deserve a second chance..." he started in, and she rose straight up in the bed, leaning forward, to kiss him.

"No, Thane. Don't." She told him. And then continued with, "I'm not asking for you to marry me again. I'm the one who let you down. I know that. I was broken when I married you. And while my mother is back in my life, I can't even wrap my mind around that yet, and I have no idea what comes next with that part of me. But I realized something over the past few days. I gave up on our marriage before it had even happened. Because as much as I loved and wanted to marry you, I didn't trust anyone to stand by me unconditionally. I didn't believe in forever. And that's what you needed. To share your life with someone who not just loved you but who believed in forever enough to fight for it."

He stared at her. Trying to make sense of her words amidst the blast going on inside him.

And suddenly it hit him. The simplicity left room for error, but he didn't need to stop and analyze.

"Stella Mitchell, née Wilson, then Mitchell again, will you marry me a second time? And let me show you that forever is something you can count on? Because in this life, and any that come after, I will love you. And fight for you."

"Hold on," Stella said then, her voice as commanding as it ever had been. Sliding off the bed, exposing her nearly bare legs, she steadied herself for a second. Then, careful of the arm that still held the IV port that she'd been waiting on to be removed so she could go, pulled him up and wrapped her arms around his neck.

"I just couldn't do this lying in a hospital bed," she said. "I *will* marry you again, Thane. As soon as possible. But more than that, I promise you, from this day forward, I will fight for you, for us, for our family before any other battle I take on."

He smiled then. A feeling more than an expression. Originating from the inside out. Then shook his head and smiled some more. They'd come full circle. She was always going to be the dynamo who'd captured his attention the first time he'd seen her blasting through a bullhorn on campus.

And she was going to love him as fiercely as he'd ever wanted to be loved, too.

The logic in it was very clear to him. They'd both had some things to learn. Most importantly that their love was real, stronger than either of their weaknesses, and something that they didn't need to fight for. They just had to welcome it. Hold on to it.

Remember it.

Love was a gift.

One that had been bestowed on the two of them. For life and beyond...

Wait... Frowning, he stared at Stella. "What did you just say? Something about *our* family?" Her sisters, once he was married to her again, would be his family, too, but...there'd been something...

Smiling, her gaze shining at him with a new glow, she said, "It's too soon to know, of course, but I still haven't had my period—no surprise there with all that's happened—but according to the complete blood panel they ran, there's a slight increase in two different chemicals in my body that generally rise just after an egg is fertilized..."

She was giving him the science. The logic. Grabbing her up off her feet, he swung her around and then sat in the chair, with her on his lap.

And came down to earth for a second. Looking her in the eye, he asked, "You're sure you're okay with this?" He damned sure was. At thirty-nine, and still in love with his ex-wife, he'd pretty much given up hope of ever having children of his own.

"Never been surer of anything in my life," she told him. And kissed him. Hard.

Then stood and called for a nurse. Informed the one who appeared that she wanted her clothes back and the cannula out of her arm so she could get back to work.

She had a couple more rallies she could still do at the end of the week.

She froze as the nurse left the room, turning to Thane, and said, "That is, if you're coming with me? I'm not doing them without you."

He hadn't needed to hear the words, but they did him good, just the same.

"I suspect your mother and sisters will be there, too," he told her. "I'll get with SML and arrange for a suite large enough to accommodate us all."

Her gaze warmed, and then grew serious. "As long as you and I have our own private space, too, Thane." Her eyes filled with something he'd never seen before. "I need my time with just you. To fall asleep in your arms. To talk. Maybe to cry a little. Just until I get this believing thing down pat."

He pulled her into his arms then. Kissed her. Tenderly. Reverently.

And made a promise he knew he would keep until death. And after.

"I'm yours, Stel. Now and forever. You need me? You just call. I'll be right here. Always."

Her eyes teared up. But she was all Stella as she said, "And you can bet I'm going to be calling as loud as I have to in the next life, too, my love. Because this time, I'm not letting you go."

* * * * *

Get up to 4 Free Books!

We'll send you 2 free books from each series you try PLUS a free Mystery Gift.

Both the **Harlequin Intrigue®** and **Harlequin® Romantic Suspense** series feature compelling novels filled with heart-racing action-packed romance that will keep you on the edge of your seat.

YES! Please send me 2 FREE novels from the Harlequin Intrigue or Harlequin Romantic Suspense series and my FREE gift (gift is worth about $10 retail). After receiving them, if I don't wish to receive any more books, I can return the shipping statement marked "cancel." If I don't cancel, I will receive 6 brand-new Harlequin Intrigue Larger-Print books every month and be billed just $7.19 each in the U.S. or $7.99 each in Canada, or 4 brand-new Harlequin Romantic Suspense books every month and be billed just $6.39 each in the U.S. or $7.19 each in Canada, a savings of 20% off the cover price. It's quite a bargain! Shipping and handling is just 50¢ per book in the U.S. and $1.25 per book in Canada.* I understand that accepting the 2 free books and gift places me under no obligation to buy anything. I can always return a shipment and cancel at any time by calling the number below. The free books and gift are mine to keep no matter what I decide.

Choose one: ☐ **Harlequin Intrigue Larger-Print** (199/399 BPA G36Y) ☐ **Harlequin Romantic Suspense** (240/340 BPA G36Y) ☐ **Or Try Both!** (199/399 & 240/340 BPA G36Z)

Name (please print)

Address / Apt. #

City / State/Province / Zip/Postal Code

Email: Please check this box ☐ if you would like to receive newsletters and promotional emails from Harlequin Enterprises ULC and its affiliates. You can unsubscribe anytime.

Mail to the Harlequin Reader Service:
IN U.S.A.: P.O. Box 1341, Buffalo, NY 14240-8531
IN CANADA: P.O. Box 603, Fort Erie, Ontario L2A 5X3

Want to explore our other series or interested in ebooks? Visit www.ReaderService.com or call 1-800-873-8635.

---

*Terms and prices subject to change without notice. Prices do not include sales taxes, which will be charged (if applicable) based on your state or country of residence. Canadian residents will be charged applicable taxes. Offer not valid in Quebec. This offer is limited to one order per household. Books received may not be as shown. Not valid for current subscribers to the Harlequin Intrigue or Harlequin Romantic Suspense series. All orders subject to approval. Credit or debit balances in a customer's account(s) may be offset by any other outstanding balance owed by or to the customer. Please allow 4 to 6 weeks for delivery. Offer available while quantities last.

Your Privacy—Your information is being collected by Harlequin Enterprises ULC, operating as Harlequin Reader Service. For a complete summary of the information we collect, how we use this information and to whom it is disclosed, please visit our privacy notice located at https://corporate.harlequin.com/privacy-notice. Notice to California Residents – Under California law, you have specific rights to control and access your data. For more information on these rights and how to exercise them, visit https://corporate.harlequin.com/california-privacy. For additional information for residents of other U.S. states that provide their residents with certain rights with respect to personal data, visit https://corporate.harlequin.com/other-state-residents-privacy-rights/.